Russell Hoban was born in 1925 in Lansdale, Pennsylvania, and was an illustrator before becoming a writer. Since 1958 he has written fifty books for children. His adult novels are *The Lion of Boaz-Jachin and Jachin-Boaz*, *Kleinzeit*, *Turtle Diary* and *Riddley Walker*, all available in Picador.

Also by Russell Hoban
in Pan Books

The Lion of Boaz-Jachin and Jachin-Boaz
Kleinzeit
Turtle Diary
Riddley Walker

Russell Hoban

Pilgermann

PICADOR

published by Pan Books

First published 1983 by Jonathan Cape Ltd
This Picador edition published 1984 by Pan Books Ltd,
Cavaye Place, London SW10 9PG
© Russell Hoban 1983
ISBN 0 330 28094 5
Printed and bound in Great Britain by
Cox & Wyman Ltd, Reading

To Esmé

. . . and after the fire a still small voice.

I Kings 19: 12

Yea, the stork in the heaven
Knoweth her appointed times;
And the turtle and the swallow
    and the crane
Observe the time of their coming;
But My people know not
The ordinance of the LORD.

Jeremiah 8:7

And being questioned by the Pharisees
when comes the kingdom of God,
he answered them and said: Comes not
the kingdom of God with observation,
nor will they say: Behold, here or:
there; behold for the kingdom of God
within you is.

Luke 17:20, 21

Nay, but man doth
Transgress all bounds,
In that he looketh
Upon himself as self-sufficient.

Quran, Sura 96:6, 7

Acknowledgments

Riddley Walker left me in a place where there was further action pending and this further action was waiting for the element that would precipitate it into the time and place of its own story. It was my daughter Esmé and her husband Moti who on May 15th, 1980 took me to the ruined stronghold of Montfort in Galilee, built in the twelfth century by the knights of the Teutonic Order of Saint Mary and enlarged by them in the thirteenth century. We slept in the open in the camping site across the gorge from the ruin, and in the morning we went down the steep path to the stream at the bottom of the gorge and then climbed the winding road up to Montfort.

The look of the stars burning and flickering over Montfort, those three stars between the Virgin and the Lion with their upward swing like the curve of a scythe, the stare into the darkness, the hooded eagleness of the stronghold high over the gorge, the paling into dawn of its gathered flaunt and power precipitated Pilgermann into his time and place and me into a place I hadn't even known was there.

For help in my researches I am indebted to Michael Freed, to Alina Edmond, to Michael Negin, Deputy Clerk to the Beth Din, to Ezra Kahn of the Jews' College Library, to Robert Irwin, to James Mellaart, to S. D. Goitein, who very graciously sent me unpublished material for reference, and to the School of Oriental and African Studies Library of the University of London and its unfailingly co-operative staff.

To Mary Banks, my copy editor, I owe a special thanks; this text required many final decisions well beyond the range of copy-editing, and her fine-tuned ear, unerring eye, and reliably sound judgment made light work of it.

R.H.

1

Pilgermann here. I call myself Pilgermann, it's a convenience. What my name was when I was walking around in the shape of a man I don't know, I simply can't remember. What I am now is waves and particles, I don't need to walk around, I just go. When I want to appear I turn up as an owl. When I see myself in my mind I see myself flying silently across the face of a full moon that is wreathed in luminous clouds; heath and swamp and wood below me, silvered rooftops, sleeping chimneys glide. Pilgermann the owl. The owl has always been big in my mind. Once as a boy I was in a ruin of some kind, old fire-blackened stones and burnt and rotted timbers. Twilight it was, the dying day shivering a little and huddling itself up in its cloak. Suddenly there came flying towards me with a mouse dangling from its beak an owl, what is called a veiled owl, with a limp mouse dangling from its cryptic heart-shaped face. 'Hear, O Israel!' I cried: 'the Lord our God, the Lord is One!'

Ah! the flickering in the darkness, the passage of what is called time!

I don't know what I am now. A whispering out of the dust. Dried blood on a sword and the sword has crumbled into rust and the wind has blown the rust away but still I am, still I am of the world, still I have something to say, how could it be otherwise, nothing comes to an end, the action never stops, it only changes, the ringing of the steel is sung in the stillness of the stone.

I speak from where I am; I speak from between the pieces; I speak from where Abram heard the voice of God:

And it came to pass, that,
when the sun went down, and
there was thick darkness,
behold a smoking furnace,
and a flaming torch that
passed between these pieces.
In that day the LORD made
a covenant with Abram. . .

A covenant with God is made from between the pieces of one-self; it's the only place where a covenant can happen, no covenant is possible until one has divided the heifer, the she-goat, the ram of oneself. The turtle-dove and the young pigeon being the heart and soul one of course does not divide them. When Abram sacrificed the animals of himself as instructed by God a deep sleep fell upon him, and the dread and the great darkness from which God spoke. Then came the thick darkness after the sun went down, and in that darkness were the smoking furnace and the flaming torch that passed between the pieces. So here already was shown the main theme of the people of Abraham: the furnace and the torch; the consuming fire and the onward flame.

If you measure with what is called time it's a long way from here back to Abram's pieces. But still there is the division of the animals of us, still the thick darkness, the smoking furnace, the flaming torch. And still there are covenants to be made between the pieces, between one fire and another. I am only the waves and particles of such as I was but I have a covenant with the Lord, the terms of it are simple: everything is required of me, for ever.

2

So. From wherever and from whatever I am now in what is called the present moment my being goes back to the year 1096 in the Christian calendar which was the year 4856 in the Jewish calendar. My being goes back to a particular morning in that year, the morning of the thirty-first of July which was for Jews the Ninth of Av, Tisha b'Av, the morning of that day when Jews who have already been fasting since the evening before sit on low stools or on the floor of the synagogue and mourn the destruction of the First and Second Temples; they mourn other disasters as well, among them that day when the twelve spies returned from Canaan and Joshua and Caleb rent their clothes because the children of Israel listened only to the evil report and turned aside from the land of milk and honey.

I no longer have a mouth with which to smile wryly but I think that the waves and particles of me must be arranged in something like a wry smile as I remember that land of milk and honey from which I did not turn aside on the Eve of the Ninth of Av, that land of milk and honey from which I was returning in the freshness of the summer dawn.

I was on my way home from the house of the tax-collector. I say tax-collector, it sounds right, but in fact I'm not certain what he was; he may well have been, may still be, something else. I know that he was an official of some kind, something of authority, a man of exactions, of that certain sort of neck, not actually fat, that in a more modern time bulges over the stiff uniform collar. The smell of such a man's freshly shaven face is oppressive across the centuries. It is a law of nature that such a man will have a wife of exquisite gentility and superb figure. A woman of regal buttocks and nervous, equine grace. A face of mercy and sweet goodness. That this man should have the management of such a woman is absolutely scientific in its manifestation of that asymmetry without which there would be no motion in the universe. Yes, such a coupling imparts spin to the cosmos, it creates action, it utterly negates stasis.

Such a man as that Herr Steuerjäger or Gerichtsvollzieher or whatever, such a man as that cannot live without a Jew to be other than. If there were no Jews he would invent them, he would dress up as a Jew and flog himself. He is like that act one sees in cabaret in which a woman is half-costumed as a gorilla with whom she dances and to whose advances she ultimately yields. What was it that he did, did he impose a candle tax on Jews because they were reading too much? Or was it that he required all circumcision knives to be inspected by his brother-in-law the butchery inspector, with an exorbitant fee to be paid for the stamp of approval? Or was it simply that he started the tale that Jews kept little live toads in their phylacteries for sorcery? It doesn't matter, if it wasn't one thing it was another.

Myself, I think I may have been a tailor or a surgeon or something of that sort. Whatever I was, my services had so far never been required by that man or his household; least of all that service I longed to render upon the body of that incomparable and to me unapproachable woman. Her name is Sophia: Wisdom. There's allegory for you, the vision of naked Wisdom and the Jew lusting after her. And such nakedness! It continues in my eye, splendouring. It will always be there, an image of such power as to confer unending Now upon the mind that holds it. Always now the great dark house in the Keinjudenstrasse late at night. Always now I, the solitary late-night Jew walking where he is not wanted. In the nights of the days before Tisha b'Av I walk there. I see late at night the dark house. Suddenly in an upper window I see a triangle of dim golden light, becoming a narrow oblong of dim golden light in which bulks the dark shape of a man in a nightshirt. The man moves away and there stands revealed, farther back within the room, the woman naked with her back to the window. Her shoulders are shaking, she has her hands up to her face. How I love her!

Never again! Always and for ever again and again. In my mind I see the night sky, I see three stars burning between the Virgin and the Lion, they are like a gesture, a Jewish gesture, the hand flung up, fingers spread: Well, then! What are your intentions, will you block the road for ever?

There she is, glorious and pathetic in that dim golden light. The splendid form of her contains her name as a candle contains its wick, her name still unknown to me, when I know it it will flame for me. Gone! the great dark house all black again.

Sophia! name unknown to me! Name that will burn in my mind like a candle flame burning straight up in still air above its translucent column of white wax.

Jews are known to be clever but I did nothing clever; I simply hung about the Keinjudenstrasse day and night with no thought for anything else until that bulging-necked man climbed heavily on to his horse and rode away. I bribed no servants, I asked no one how long he would be gone, I felt honour bound to take my naked chance. I came as one who seeks a miracle; caution seemed sacrilegious.

Nightfall, and he had not come back. I hear the hooting of an owl, I hear the wind sighing, the summer wind in the trees of the garden. Outside the forbidden garden of the great dark house I wait. This is perhaps the centre of time for me, this waiting in expectation of a miracle, this waiting in a state of transcendental desire, in a state of sin made holy by its purity.

The hours pass, the first-quarter moon appears in the sky like a password, I go into the garden. There is of course a ladder there; for the Jew desirous of Wisdom there is always a ladder. The house is all dark, there is no light showing anywhere. I have no plan, I lean the ladder up against the house and I climb up.

The shutters are open, the casement is open, I feel on my face the warm breath of the dark window, there is a scent of oranges, of bitter aloes, of lions, of tawniness, there is a scent of the nakedness of the unseen woman within. Suddenly she is there, glimmering in her nakedness like a glimmering fish in the river of night. I feel as if I am falling, falling backward with a silent scream into the garden. Has she pushed away the

15

ladder? She has not pushed away the ladder, I am not falling, her two hands grip my wrists, she is pulling me into the window, she is whispering, 'Thou Jew! My Jew!'

'Thou Jew! My Jew!' The miracle has happened, no explanations are necessary. With a miracle one is immediately *thou* and the rest follows, the rest has already been going on before one arrived, the moment is prepared and ready.

The centre of time is, as I have said, the waiting. This is now off the centre, this is the motion of the everything, the action of the universe, the destined world-line of the soul, the living heart of the mystery.

There are few words between us. I say, over and over again, 'Thou beautiful, thou beautiful!' She says, 'Thou Jew! My Jew!' Only one other thing does she say, her name when I ask it: her name is Sophia. Then I say, again and again in that wondrous warm breathy darkness, her name. Sophia, Sophia, Sophia.

3

See me, the Jew fresh from the attainment of Wisdom, the Jew returning with the dawn of the Ninth of Av. See me as a bird might see me, as might that stork that slowly flaps its way over the huddled roofs and chimneys, over the narrow twisting streets of morning. What might this stork see looking down? Here the Jew comes, turning this way, turning that way, threading his homeward path and drawing closer, closer to those others hurrying towards him, turning this way, turning that way as if by careful prearrangement, these others with billhooks and pitchforks following a sow who wears a scarlet cross. The sow has her snout uplifted and is grunting loudly. 'A Jew! A Jew!' shouts the man who holds her rope, 'She smells a Jew!' Here they come running towards me, reeking of cow dung, sweat, beer, pigs, shouting, 'A Jew! A Jew!'

They hurl themselves upon me, they throw me to the cobblestones, some of them sit on my chest, some of them hold my arms and legs. My tunic is pulled up, my hose are pulled down. O God! I feel the cool air of dawn on my nakedness. O God! I know what they are going to do and I cannot move a limb to help myself.

'The covenant!' cries some lout. 'The mark of the covenant!'

'Cut it off and make a Christian of him,' says the man with the sow.

'Look at that thing,' says someone else. 'You can be sure he's had Christian women with it, filthy brute.'

'He won't have them any more,' says the man with the sow.

O God! I pray in my mind. O God! Don't let this happen! I

feel the knife on me. I think of Rabbi Hananiah ben Teradyon martyred in the Hadrianic persecutions, wrapped in the Scroll of the Law and burned at the stake. As he died he said that he saw the parchments burning but the letters of the Torah flying up out of the fire. I too now see the black letters shimmering and twisting as they rise on the heated air, soaring above the flames like birds of holy speech to the blue sky. I see the black letters writhing round the holy nakedness of Sophia going up, up, out of sight into the blue morning.

How can I be brave, strong, a real man, a hero? All I can do is not give them a screaming Jew to laugh at. 'God wills it!' they cry with stinking breath as they cut off my manhood. I vomit but I do not scream.

'Finish him off,' says someone.

'Let him live,' says another sort of voice. It is the tax-collector on his horse at the head of the town militia.

'God wills it!' shouts the man with the sow.

'This also,' says the officer of the watch, and he prods the sow with his pike. She squeals and runs off with the peasant soldiers of Christ followed by the town militia. The tax-collector, high above me on his horse that snorts and prances and paws the cobbles, looks down at me with a pale face then looks back over his shoulder. I hear voices approaching: 'Jews, Jews! Give us more Jews!'

'Pray for me,' says the tax-collector. 'This way!' he shouts to the approaching peasants. With a scraping of hooves horse and rider plunge away, leading the peasants away from where I am, leading them towards the town gate.

Pray for him! Did he actually say that, did I hear him right? '*Betet für mich.*' What else could it have been? '*Tretet mich*'? 'Kick me'? Ridiculous; that man could not possibly have asked me either to pray for him or to kick him. I have a sudden hysterical vision of the two cherubim leaning towards each other over the Ark of the Covenant, the one saying, 'Pray for me' and the other, 'Kick me'. I don't know what to make of it: this man, this husband of Sophia, this man whom I have just cuckolded, has saved my life, such as it now is.

I am lying on my back alone on the cobblestones, my tunic stuffed into my wound. It is broad day, above me arches the blue sky. High overhead, so very, very, high in the sky, circle a drift of storks, a meditation of storks, circling like those intersecting circles of tiny writing sometimes done by copyists with texts of the Holy Scriptures. They are so high, those storks, that one couldn't say what they are unless one knows, as I do, that every year faithfully come these great dignified black-and-white birds to nest on our rooftops and to circle high in the sky over our town, returning each year in their season.

I smell burning, there is smoke drifting between me and the sky; that will be from the synagogue. Here I must say that I had never been a devout Jew. I owned a skullcap and a prayer shawl and phylacteries; I always turned up at the synagogue for the High Holy Days and I had never before missed Tisha b'Av but my observances were mostly for the sake of appearances; in between I went my own way. God was to me as a parent to whom I had given little obedience and from whom I expected no inheritance.

Now, lying on the cobblestones looking up at the blue sky and smelling the burning I cry out to God in my agony: 'O God!' I say, 'Why is this? What's the use of it? What good is it to anybody?'

God says nothing to me.

'Hear, O Israel,' I cry: 'the Lord our God, the Lord is One. Magnified and sanctified be his great name in the world which he hath created according to his will. What are we? What is our life? What is our piety? What is our righteousness? What our helpfulness? What our strength? What our might? What shall we say before thee, O Lord our God and God of our fathers? Are not all the mighty men as nought before thee, the men of renown as though they had not been, the wise as if without knowledge, and the men of understanding as if without discernment? For most of their works are void, and the days of their lives are vanity before thee, and the pre-eminence of man over the beast is nought, for all is vanity.'

Still no word from God. The blue sky is perfectly blank, the smoke of the burning synagogue drifts in the still morning air; it's going to be a hot day.

'God!' I cry, 'Whatever you are and whatever I am, speak to me! O Lord, do it for thy name's sake. Do it for the sake of thy truth; do it for the sake of thy covenant; do it for the sake of Abraham, Isaac and Jacob; do it for the sake of Moses and Aaron; do it for the sake of David and Solomon. Do it for the sake of Jerusalem, thy holy city; do it for the sake of Zion, the tabernacle of thy glory, do it for the sake of thy Temple's desolation; do it for the sake of the destruction of thy altar; do it for the sake of those slain for thy holy name; do it for the sake of those slaughtered for thy Unity; do it for the sake of those who went through fire and water for the sanctification of thy name. Do it for the sake of sucklings who have not sinned; do it for the sake of weanlings who have not transgressed; do it for the sake of the school-children.

'Answer us, O Lord, answer us; answer us, O our God, answer us; answer us, O our Father, answer us . . .'

It was then that the air began to shimmer and Christ appeared to me. He was tall, lean, and sinewy. One of those fair Jews with his hair further lightened by the bleaching of the sun. Very light blue eyes, perfectly intrepid eyes drooping a little towards the outside of the face, the eyes of a fighter, the eyes of a lion. He was wearing a patched robe, his sandals were worn, his feet looked hard and hard-travelled. He stood there with a silence flung down in front of him. He was no one in whom I had any belief but there he was and there was no mistaking who he was.

I looked at him and listened to his silence for a while. When I was able to speak I said, 'You're not the one I was calling.'

He said, 'I'm the one who came through. I'm the one you'll talk to from now on.'

I saw his lips move but his voice came from inside my head. It made me feel very strange, being on the outside of his voice. I knew that if I were capable of running and were to run away to a distance where I could no longer see his lips move I should still hear his voice inside my head. A woodwind sort of voice with something of the timbre of a modern oboe, it seemed to have in it a capability of vibration that would move the plates of the earth apart; it was a voice that made a great space happen all round it, and all that space was inside my head. Feeling vast and hollow, hearing only a silence all round me and my own voice far, far away inside my head, I said, trying to synchronize my lips with my words, 'Until now I've dealt with your father.'

He said, 'Until now you've dealt with no one and no one's dealt with you.'

I said, 'Is this the Day of Reckoning then?'

He said, 'Every day is the Day of Reckoning.' The way his voice filled all the great echoing vastness inside my head was frightening; I wanted to get away from him but I was afraid to try even to stand up because of the bleeding. I looked all round me; my member and testicles were nowhere in sight. I thought of them thrown away like offal, I thought of them eaten by the Jew-finding sow, I vomited again.

I said, 'I want to talk to your father,' then I held my head and waited for his answer to echo inside me.

He said, 'Humankind is a baby, it always wants a face bending over the cradle.'

I said, 'God's our father, isn't he?'

He said, 'God isn't a he, it's an it.'

I said, 'Where is it, his strong right arm that was stretched out over us?'

He said, 'It's gone.'

I said, 'Have I got to be my own father now?'

He said, 'Be what you like but remember that after me it's the straight action and no more dressing up.'

Neither of us said anything for a little while. I didn't want him to go away but I didn't want to hear his voice inside my head.

'Will there be a Last Judgment?' I said.

He said, 'The straight action *is* the last judgment; there's no face on the front of it, it has no front or back.'

We are walking, I am leaning on Jesus; with his right arm round me he keeps me from falling. I feel the strength in him rising like a column. In the morning sunlight rises the smoke from the synagogue. The fire crackles, the flames are pale in the bright morning. Suddenly there is so much space between the Jewish quarter and the rest of the town! Suddenly the Christian roofs are sharp and distant, they are looking away. In the great space all round the synagogue the bodies of the dead are vivid, the blood fresh and dark on the cobbles that seem to have put themselves into patterns I have not noticed before: there are twisting serpents, shifting pyramids, I see the face of a lion that comes and goes. There are many Jews flattened to the earth, limbs all asprawl, mouths open. The children are just as dead as the grown-ups, it seems precocious. It is a very informal gathering, there have been scenes of intimacy with no attempt at privacy. Here among a scattering of random guests and witnesses is an impromptu bride of the soldiers of Christ. White thighs, black hose, skirt flung over her face. Did they call her *thou*?

'Thou Jew,' I say to Jesus, 'tell me about this conversion of the Jews.'

'What conversion?' says Jesus.

'From life to death,' I say. 'Why does it keep happening? Why is it God's will?'

Jesus turns his face to me and opens wide his eyes. There come upon me such a shuddering and a blackness, such an expanding pleroma, such an intolerable fullness that I am filled to bursting with it. I open, open, open but cannot contain it, I explode in all directions to infinity, I contract to a point, I explode again from the point, I come back together and return shuddering and full of terror.

'Forgive me, Lord,' I say.

There come into my mind thunders and lightnings and a thick cloud on the mountain and the voice of a trumpet exceeding loud. There comes into my mind the sanctified mountain that might not be touched, neither by beast nor man. There comes into my mind a voice saying in Greek:

> For not ye have approached to a mountain being felt and having been ignited with fire and to darkness and to deep gloom and to whirlwind and of trumpet to a sound and to a voice of words, which the ones hearing entreated not to be added to them a word; not they bore for the thing being charged: If even a beast touches the mountain, it shall be stoned; and, so fearful was the thing appearing, Moses said: Terrified I am and trembling . . .

Jesus says, 'Can you contain even the expectation of the full reply of me to you? Can you contain even the silence before my answer to you?'

I say, 'No, Lord, I cannot contain it.'

Jesus says, 'Can you contain even the thought of knowing the will of God? I speak not of the knowing; I speak only of the very thought of knowing.'

I say, 'No, Lord, I cannot even contain that thought.'

Jesus says, 'If it be God's incomprehensible will that the universe shall flower to the end of all things and from that end of all things seed itself anew, will you question the slaughter of Jews? You see on the cobbles the dead who were alive, who sprang from the leap of the lightning that cleaves the dark that waits for the leap after the stillness, the stillness after the leap. You see the dead: backward into their life and forward into their death extends the black-body spectrum of their being; their diffraction is as yours. Will you offer an opinion?'

I say, 'I have no opinion, Lord.'

Jesus incorporates me in his glance and I begin to see him in more than one way. Jesus is the great dead Lion of the World and in his mouth is the live black body of Christ Radiant. The great dead lion is walking the rocks and desert, walking the mountains and the high ground, looking down on deep gorges where rivers serpentine, and in his mouth the live black body of him the one radiant, him the Christ flickering his black-body spectrum, flames all dancing on the live black body of him in the mouth of the great dead lion of himself. The black body opens, it is a sky of lightning, a sea of fire, mountains of ice. The sky grows tiny, contracts to one black dot, absorbs the sea of fire, the mountains of ice. The black dot opens out into the great live Lion of the World. In his mouth the tiny dead golden body of Christ. In the mouth of the tiny dead golden body of Christ is the world, the sun, the moon, the stars, the wheeling heavens of night. Far and far the thunder of his silence rolls, the lion roars, the stars shake, flicker, burn to paleness and morning.

Silence. The lion is a great paper kite, blue and yellow, the paper fluttering in the morning wind. Far, far down goes the string to Jesus winding in the kite. The lion-kite bursts into flame, the flame runs down the string, Jesus is on fire.

All round the three hundred and sixty degrees of the horizon dance the avatars of Burning Jesus, Christ as fire in perfect silence dancing. One for every degree of the circle, three hundred and sixty avatars of Burning Jesus dancing the colour of

Jew, dancing the full black-body spectrum of Jew. One by one the emissions cease, one by one the colours disband, the burning avatars rejoin each one the next and all go back to one, the live black body of Christ Radiant in the centre of the great circle of fire, the burning world-circle. The motion of the dance continues, it is bursting the skin of the sky. The colour of Jew is rent with a great ripping down the centre of the sky.

Leaning on Jesus and held up by him, suddenly I rage at him. Feeble, unmanned, weak from loss of blood I rage at him the Christ, him the anointed one. 'Who are you to put these pictures in my eyes!' I say to him. 'Thou Jew! Hear, O Israel! the Lord our God, the Lord is One! The Lord is not three and you are not the One. What kind of a Jew are you to turn the world against your people? Images are worshipped in your name! In your name Jews are slaughtered!'

'Whatever I am,' says Jesus, 'I'm the one you talk to from now on.'

I think: O God, what if he's right? What if God's gone and I never really had a chance to talk to him. Forgotten prayers crowd my head, I look away from Jesus, I look up to the sky. 'Answer us, O Lord!' I cry, 'answer us on the Fast day of our Affliction, for we are in great trouble; turn not to our wickedness, and hide not thy presence from us, nor conceal thyself from our supplication; be near, we pray, to our cry, let thy kindness we beg, comfort us; answer us, even before we call unto thee, according to that which is said: "And it shall come to pass that, before they call, I will answer; while they are speaking, I will hear!" For thou, O Lord, art the one that answerest in time of trouble, redeemest and deliverest in all times of trouble and distress! Blessed art thou, O Lord (Blessed be he and blessed be his name!) who answerest in time of trouble. (Amen!)'

There was a long silence after my prayer, then Jesus said, 'Did you feel that prayer going anywhere or did it just go out of you?'

'It just went out of me,' I said.

'You're shaking an empty tree,' said Jesus. 'You're letting down your bucket in a dry well. There was no answer when the knife was on your flesh and there'll be no answer now. And for what do you pray now? The thing has already been done and you are cut off from your generations.'

'Thou Christ!' I say, remembering suddenly whom I'm talking to, 'Thou Christ who fed the hungry, cast out demons, healed the sick and raised the dead! Surely thou wilt restore me to my manhood!'

Jesus shook his head. 'The fig tree stayed barren,' he said, 'and you will stay a eunuch; it is what you wished.'

I wasn't sure I'd heard him right, I couldn't believe what he was saying. When he said this we were not walking, I was in my bed, dispersed in two-dimensional sunlit patterns like an infinitely extending oriental carpet. I seemed to have been there for some time. 'What did you say?' I said.

Jesus said, 'I said it is what you wished.'

I said, 'Can you have seen Sophia and say that? I am young, the blood in me runs hot, I lust but I am unmanned. I lust, I long, I yearn, I hunger, I hum like a tuning fork, I flutter like a torn banner in the wind. That which I was I can never be again, that which I am is intolerable, that which I shall be I cannot imagine. I glimmer like a distant candle, I mottle like the sunlight on the carpet, like the shadows of leaves. I am something, I am nothing, I am here, I am gone.'

'It is what you wished,' said Jesus. 'Only now do you hum, flutter, glimmer, mottle, be something, be nothing, be here, be gone with me. Only now are you tuned to me.'

'Never did I wish to be a eunuch,' I said, 'and never did I wish to be tuned to you.'

Jesus said, 'And there are eunuchs who made themselves eunuchs on account of the kingdom of the heavens. The one being able to grasp it let him grasp.'

I said, 'I never made myself a eunuch.'

Jesus said, 'Life moves by exchanges; loss is the price of gain. Some pay with one thing, some with another; whatever is most dear, that is my price.'

I said, 'Why is that your price?'

Jesus said, 'What is dear is what is held dear, and there can be no holding by those who go my road; there can be no holding by those who will be here with me and gone with me.'

I said, 'Never did I ask to go that road, never did I wish to be here with you, gone with you.'

Jesus said, 'Always you wished it, and most of all when you put hand and foot to that ladder of love and pleasure. In your soul you called to me, you longed for me when you climbed that ladder. With eager hands you reached for pleasure and held it fast but whoever holds on wishes to let go because attachment is not wholeness: the only wholeness is in being with everything and attached to nothing; the only wholeness is in letting go, and I am the letting go.'

I said, 'I know nothing of all this.'

'You will know,' said Jesus, 'and your knowing in time to come will make you know it now.'

'What is between us, you and me?' I said.

'Everything,' said Jesus.

'Why me?' I said.

'Why not you?' said Jesus.

I, Pilgermann, poor bare tuned fork, humming with the for-everness of the Word that is always Now. Unbearing the Un-bearable, intolerating the Intolerable, being not enough for the Too-Muchness. I, poor harp of a Jew twanging incessantly in the mouth of Jesus, in the lion-mouth of Christ Pandamator, Christ All-Subduer. There is a point where pattern becomes motion; the pattern has found me and I must move, must be aware of moving, must be a motion, an action of the Word. Poor bare tuned fork.

'Blessed are they that are tuned to me,' said Jesus.

'Why?' I said.

'Because they shall move,' said Jesus. 'They shall go, they shall have action.'

While he was saying that I was thinking: I, poor eunuch of my Lord, neither sheep nor goat, neither of the left hand nor of the right, subject always to Christ the redeemer, the ransom, the sacrifice, victim, torturer, murderer, bringer of death. Iesous Christous Thanatophoros. Kyrios.

Jesus said, 'I am the light of day. Do you believe?'

'I believe,' I said.

Jesus said, 'I am the energy that will not be still. I am a

movement and a rest but at the same time I am all movement and no rest and you will have no rest but in the constant motion of me. Do you believe?'

'I believe,' I said.

'Why do you believe?' said Jesus.

'No belief is necessary,' I said. 'It manifests itself.'

Jesus said, 'Why in your mind do you call me bringer of death? Why in your mind am I Iesous Christous Thanatophoros?'

I said, 'How can I not think of you as Thanatophoros? Whoever wants to kill a Jew does it in your name. In your name they kill the seed that gave you life.'

Jesus said, 'From me came the seed that gave me life.'

4

There arises the question of the tax-collector. Drifting in my oriental-carpet patterns I see him high above me, sitting on his horse and looking down at me the bloody and castrated Jew, the mutilated and unmanned thing that has cuckolded him and entered the golden Jerusalem of his wife. Although he has never taken any notice of me he has seen me often enough in the town, he has me on his records, he knows me for a Jew. Famous as he is for his hatred and loathing of Jews, why has he saved my life? It is true that it is my *castrated* life that he has saved. Can there be some meaning, some message in this? Can he possibly know what has happened between his wife and me? Impossible. It happened only a few hours before he saw me, at a time when he was somewhere else altogether, there was no time for him to be told of it. But is it possible that he never left the town, that he became suspicious of the lurking Jew, pretended to go away but circled back unseen to see what happened? Possible. Or might he simply have instructed a servant to observe carefully and report to him in whatever place he has gone to? Even more possible. Well, which is it then — does he know or doesn't he know? I have no idea. No, I don't believe that he knows, I don't think that he has been suspicious, I don't think that it would ever occur to him as a possibility that a Jew should enter where he has entered.

But wait, maybe he dreams of such a thing constantly; maybe he is utterly consumed by the thought of a Jew by night creeping in through the window to enjoy his wife, maybe it burns in him like a constant lamp, maybe it is the one thing wanting for his happiness and peace. He sees me hanging about, sees the possibility, absents himself in hope. The wife opens the Jerusalem of her body to the lusting Jew, then as an unexpected treat the Jew is caught by the peasant soldiers of Christ, he is flung to the cobbles, stripped, castrated, he lies there shuddering in his blood and vomit while his penis and testicles are eaten by a sow. His fading lust renewed, the husband returns as a giant refreshed to the guilty and submissive wife whose only thought is to anticipate and satisfy his every demand. Is that how it is? God knows.

Can there be, there must be, some reasonable explanation, but what can it be? Here is a Jew, one of the people this man hates, lying bloody on the cobblestones, his death only a moment away. Why should the tax-collector have any interest whatever in saving the life of this man? And why should he say either 'Pray for me' or 'Kick me'?

When I become exhausted with thinking about the tax-collector my mind, like an automaton that cannot be stopped, returns again and again to the castration itself: if only I had taken another way home, if only I had turned and run, if only I had fought harder. Those faces above me in that dawn, I have seen such faces centuries later in the paintings of Hieronymus Bosch. Ah, the tax-collector again! I have seen his face, his particular face, in a particular painting by Bosch, a painting of Christ being crowned with thorns. The tax-collector is that man wearing the spiked red leather collar and a black astrakhan hat on which there is a sprig of oak leaves with an acorn. In his left hand he holds a staff, his right hand is on Christ's right shoulder; almost comforting and consoling that hand seems: 'Bear up, old fellow; be brave; it'll all be over soon' might be the message of that hand. Maybe that man with the tax-collector's face is Pontius Pilate and he's saying, 'I find no fault in you but this is how it must be; I wish it could be otherwise.' A troubled man, Pontius Pilate; he died by his own hand some years later — that same hand, probably, that rests on Christ's shoulder in the painting. There it was on the end of his arm year after year: feeding him, writing letters, caressing his wife, holding whatever there was in life for him to hold. Suddenly it lets go of everything and jumps up and kills him. For how many years did that thought lurk in the hand? Always, perhaps. In this way are human hands made by God; they carry in them always a last mortal judgment. Perhaps it was to protect himself from that hand that Pilate wore such a spiked collar. Is this then a clue to the tax-collector's strange behaviour towards me? Did some time, perhaps in the dead of night, his hand leap up and take him by the throat and say, 'Jews also must live!' Perhaps his hand said this on the very same night that my hand took hold of his naked wife! Only now, as these thoughts move among the waves and particles of me, do I perceive that every hand is the hand of God: hands doing good and hands doing evil, are not they all His (Its) work? Think of the constant action of all the hands of all the world, gathering and scattering, building and destroying and praying, holding on and letting go.

So. And what of my hand, also a hand of God? Did my hand perhaps carry in it a judgment? Did my right hand and its fellow cover my ears and my eyes so that I should be in ignorance of what was happening in the world at the time I climbed that ladder? They did not; I knew that the Pope's appeal had inspired peasants as well as knights to shed the blood of Jews and I knew that we in our town might at any time find ourselves in the path of trouble. Was I then vigilant on behalf of my fellow Jews and myself? Did I keep watch early and late, did I arm myself to defend the Scroll of the Law and God's children in the land of their exile? No. The only weapon I took in hand was the one with which I forgot thee, O Jerusalem, and entered the strange Jerusalem of the tax-collector's wife. Having done what I did in the great house in the Keinjudenstrasse did I then take myself in hand with prudence and with caution to make my way home? I did not; one hand pushed me from behind while the other pointed like a signpost to strange and unlucky streets where I would not have walked the day before; one hand showed the conquering hero the world that lay before him while the other patted him on the back in congratulation. And here I am: the waves and particles of a eunuch.

I talk and I talk and words come out of me in an unending stream but I cannot say the plain truth: I have done wrong, O God. Forgive me for climbing that ladder. For God's sake, Pilgermann, say it straight out: Forgive me, O God, for lusting after Sophia, for loving her, for consummating that love and lust. Forgive me that I have sinned, and forgive me that if I had the cock and balls to do it with I'd do it again this minute. O God! Why cannot I speak with a pure heart? I have done wrong and I know it, but how could you put Sophia into the world and expect me not to do wrong? It would be an insult to your creation not to climb ladders for that woman. Now I see why there must be a tree of knowledge in the garden of Eden: it bears that fruit which cannot possibly be resisted; God did not make it resistible, it must be eaten so that a mystery will be perpetuated, the mystery of the gaining of loss. Before we eat of the fruit we have no knowledge of loss, we don't know that there is anything to lose, nothing has any value; only when we are driven out into the world and the cherubim and the bright blade of a revolving sword stand between us and the forbidden garden, only then are we rich in loss, only then have we salt for the meat of life. Life has no value, means nothing until we have paid for it with the sin of disobedience; only after that original sin does one's proper life begin. What if Adam and Eve hadn't eaten of the fruit of the tree, what then? No Holy Scriptures, no story to tell. Who'd have wanted to know about them? They'd have stayed in their garden obedient and ignorant, bored to death with life and each other and tiresome in the sight of God, they'd have been like a picture that is hung on the wall and after a time not looked at any more. God *made* us such that we would eat of that fruit, God would have been ashamed of us if we hadn't done it. God would never have bothered to make a man and a woman to live out their days dreaming in a garden.

And yet, and yet! I have done wrong, O God, I know it. I made that tax-collector poorer when I enjoyed his wife, I know that. Maybe only on her glorious body could he pray, maybe only with her could he be with you, and I came between him and his prayer. But he was holding on then, wasn't he, being so attached to her, and Jesus said that holding on was no good. No, it's no use, no matter how I try to squirm out of it I've done wrong and reparation must be made. Because I violated that man's privacy, because I burst in upon his quietness. Not that he was all that good a man, certainly I never knew anyone to have a good word to say for him. Maybe his first good action was saving my life that day, maybe that was the first time he'd ever looked kindly upon a Jew, and it only happened after I'd had his wife. Ah! what's the use of twisting and turning, there's something required of me: what? What should I do, where should I go? 'Jerusalem! Thou pilgrim Jew!' I did not speak those words, it was a voice that spoke within me: not so much a voice as the daughter of a voice, what is called in Hebrew a Bath Kol. There was about it the scent of Sophia's voice but I knew that it was expressing God's intention. 'Jerusalem! Thou pilgrim Jew!'

I, a pilgrim! To Jerusalem! This thought entered me, I could already feel the road under my feet. A name, a word, has substance; the word Jerusalem colours the air. Yerushalayim! I say it, and I that have no face, I feel where there used to be a face, I feel that sharp sensation in the nasal passages, the ache in the throat as the tears start into the eyes of that face I no longer have. Yerushalayim! Flesh made word, soul made word, world made word. Yerushalayim! What longings come to a point in that name! Spin, world; be born, people, and die whoring after false gods, shrinking from the one true one. Speak, prophets, and be stoned by the unhearing. Yerushalayim; spinning domes of gold in the sea of the one mind that is God. Ineffable.

Knights in mail, peasants with billhooks were going to Jerusalem. What were the pictures, what were the words in their minds? I could feel the pull as one who stands at the water's edge feels the sea pulling at his feet. The figure of Christ loomed gigantic in my mind, a figure of gold at the heart of a black mountain. The word, the name of Jerusalem revolving in my mind sent out its glints of gold, and my mind revolving with it found a thread of gold spun out into my road away that beckoned me.

Now I knew what Jesus had meant when he said, 'After me it's the straight action and no more dressing up.' God was already gone from us. How much longer would Jesus be with us? If others had done as I had done the time might not be long. There came to me the thought that the world is full of mysterious, unseen, fragile temples; it was in these many temples that God used to dwell among us; they are easily destroyed, these temples, as I had destroyed the temple of the tax-collector's privacy in his wife. How many of them still remained? How many temples between us and Christ's last day, between us and the eternal faceless action of God as It? Quickly, quickly must something be done before all the temples were gone. Now I understood why everyone was rushing to Jerusalem, now I knew why this was a time unique in history: this was the time when people everywhere had all at once had the same thought that I had just had. Perhaps even the Bath Kol had spoken to each of them as it had spoken to me, and all of us were now hurrying to Jerusalem to make with the gathered power of our hearts' desire a church of all souls craving Jesus, a place of rebirth in the place of holy sepulchre and resurrection. True, it was a pope who had first called for this great going of multitudes to Jerusalem but no pope could have moved so many people had not God truly willed it. I determined to begin my pilgrimage as soon as I was strong enough, and when my wound had healed sufficiently I began to walk a little every day to get my strength back.

When I came out once more into the streets I saw everything very small, very sharp. How impossibly small was the blackened stump of the synagogue! How could even one whole Jew have fitted into it! Sometimes all the spaces where I walked seemed empty and I felt left behind, like horse dung on the cobbles. Many of the shops in the Jewish quarter had shut down; the butcher had become a vegetarian, the bookseller had been burnt to the ground. There were not many Jews to be seen; those who remained looked at one another with faces full of shame as if they had been caught in the practice of an unspeakable vice. Everyone wondered what was coming next, or rather when and in what manner would come that same thing that always came.

It was at this time that the Jewish population of the town were astonished — astonished is too weak a word, they were absolutely knocked over — by the appearance in the Jewish quarter of the tax-collector in a long coarse tunic, a scrip hanging from his shoulder and a staff in his hand. Nobody could believe it: the Jews were not called to assemble at the Town Hall to hear his words; he came alone and on foot and humbly asked the Rabbi (the son-in-law of our old Rabbi who had been killed by the sow-led peasants) whether we would be kind enough to come with him to the ruin of the synagogue where, under the open sky and in the plain sight of God, he had a few words he wished to say to us.

To me it was like something in a dream or like something seen in another life. His face as he spoke was no longer closed to us and hard, it was open and trusting. For the first time he looked at us as one looks at other human beings. As he spoke his hand kept straying to his throat. 'Townspeople,' he said, 'friends, if I may call you that although until now I have never been a friend to you, I am here to say that I am truly sorry for any harm that I have done you. The candle tax is hereby abolished and the inspection and stamp of approval for circumcision knives will no longer be required. Any words of mine that may have injured you I take back with my whole heart and I ask God's forgiveness and yours; I have already retracted those words publicly at the Town Hall. I am leaving you now to go on a penitential pilgrimage to Jerusalem. I will pray for you and I hope that you can find it in your hearts to pray for me. Goodbye and fare you well, may God be with you and keep you from all harm.'

Having said those words the pilgrim tax-collector departed as he had arrived, humbly and on foot. All of us were deeply moved and deeply grateful, and yet even while the figure of our new friend was receding humbly in the distance there appeared almost visible question marks in the air over our heads; and in front of the question marks there were questions: What? Why? How? What had brought about this sudden change of heart in a man who had until now been solidly convinced of the rightness of oppressing Jews? Why did he suddenly feel guilty for what he had done over the years? Or was there something new for him to feel guilty about? I saw again his pale face looking down at me as I lay on the cobblestones. He had come so close on the heels of those peasants with the sow; if only he had arrived a little sooner! Perhaps when he saw what they had done ... but with that thought still unfinished there came another thought: what if he had brought them to our town? Those had not been peasants anyone had seen before on market days nor had there been any word, in the days before their arrival, of armed peasants moving towards us.

Yes, that was undoubtedly what had happened: the tax-collector had brought the peasants to our town and then, seeing what they had done, was overcome with remorse. And I had been reproaching myself for destroying the temple of that man's privacy with his wife! Ah! if only I could do it again and again and again! My guilt leapt from my shoulders, there surged up in me the virtue, the power, the innocence of the injured party.

But wait. Our God, the God of the Jews, works in strange ways. What if God, looking down at his world in the days before my castration, has noticed Pilgermann. Maybe Satan also, going to and fro in the world and up and down in it, has noticed Pilgermann lusting after the forbidden Gentile woman, has seen him moving through the darkness towards the forbidden garden. 'Well,' says Satan to God, 'there's one of your chosen down there. What do you think he'll do? Perhaps you'd like to make a little bet?'

'Of course he'll climb the ladder,' says God. 'That's nothing to bet on; any man with balls would climb that ladder, I make them that way to keep the race going. The thing is, will he climb the ladder if God tells him not to?'

'That's nothing to bet on either,' says Satan. 'Of course if he hears your voice he'll do as you say, nobody is going to say no to YHWH if he hears your proper voice.'

'Maybe a Bath Kol,' says God.

'Same thing,' says Satan. 'No bet.'

'A thought,' says God.

'No visions,' says Satan, 'just a thought.'

'A thought is all it takes,' says God. 'To a Jew a thought from God is as a thousand brazen trumpets. The thought of God is as the voice of God, and the voice of God will be obeyed.'

'So what are you betting?' says Satan.

'Anything you like,' says God.

'If you'll excuse my saying so,' says Satan, 'you could well be leaning on a reed.'

'If he's a Jewish reed he'll hear, and if he'll hear he'll obey,' says God.

'Will you bet half of the congregation of his town on it?' says Satan.

'Done!' says God.

It sounds like a joke when I tell it that way but it could well be how all those Jews in my town ended up dead that morning. Some may ask how God in his omniscience could be such a fool as to bet on Pilgermann. And how is it that God who is no longer even manifesting himself as He can have a conversation with Satan? Obviously God in his omnipotence can be absent as a world manifestation while being present in the individual or the collective mind as he chooses. As to his foolishness, it is just by this very willingness to lean on a reed that he shows his divinity, his difference from his mortal children: God does not learn from experience, he has never become cynical, he is innocent as only God can be. He approaches every mortal testing with a clean slate, always expecting from each of us the right action that is in us along with the evil impulse. So. God asked for right, I gave him wrong, and the guilt is back on me again.

I am not alone in my guilt, and it is perhaps at this point that I should begin to widen my narrative by bringing in figures from the great world beyond the gates of my town. Now, while the surviving Jews of the town are active with prayer shawls and with phylacteries in which there are no toads and before my onward road unrolling before me bears me away, I must tell of the Pope's dream. The pope I speak of is of course the very famous one who called for soldiers of Christ to save Jerusalem and the Holy Sepulchre from the Turks. His name is Urgent III or Umbral V, it's just on the tip of what used to be my tongue. Unguent, that's it. Unguent VII. How strange must be the life of such a man who happens to stand at a juncture of virtualities, an impending of immensities: perhaps this man is thinking that he would like to have a little more sky over his garden, and he is thinking this thought at a time when the sky is just getting ready to fall; he pulls at a little corner of the sky, the whole thing comes down, and he is known thereafter as the one who called for a skyfall.

Unguent had his practical side; he undoubtedly had political reasons for calling for the rescue of eastern Christendom, but once the thing had got itself moving his feelings went somewhat deeper: Unguent had a dream. I know about the dream because the waves and particles of me drifted into it. Not at the time when he first dreamt it but much later, quite recently. This dream goes on continuously, and in one corner of it, kneeling with clasped hands and looking upward, is Unguent, very small, like a donor in a painting.

This is the dream: in it are Unguent, a sparrow, and the great golden dome of the Church of the World. This dome is seen only in dreams, it is not to be found in ordinary daily life. The sparrow is sitting like a weathercock on a perch at the top of the dome and like a weathercock it is turning in the wind. It is the only sparrow in the world and Unguent knows it. A great golden voice resounds from the dome, it says, 'Are not two sparrows sold for a farthing?' Unguent has a sling in one hand and a pebble in the other. He puts the pebble in the sling, he whirls the sling knowing that he cannot possibly hit the sparrow, that nobody can be that accurate with a sling at that distance; at the same time he is weeping because he knows that he is going to hit the sparrow. He looses the pebble, sees it hit the sparrow, sees the sparrow topple from its perch, strike the golden dome, slide down the great golden curve of it and disappear. Unguent is flooded with an inexpressible surge of black eternal grief. This black grief is so vast that all of what we call time is included in it; this black grief is what we call space. Unguent has become a great round universe enclosing all the black space. At this moment it comes to him that it was not a pebble that he slung at the sparrow, it was his gold seal-ring on which was engraved Saint Peter in a boat fishing.

For me the centre of this dream is Unguent whirling the sling and weeping. There I find it impossible not to feel for him.

5

Sometimes I don't know anything at all for large spaces; sometimes I know many things all in the same place. My perceptions are uneven, my understanding patchy but I have action; I go. I can't tell this as a story because it isn't a story; a story is what remains when you leave out most of the action; a story is a coherent sequence of picture cards: *One*: Samson in the vineyards of Timnah; *Two*: the lion comes roaring at Samson; *Three*: Samson tears the lion apart. That's a story but actually the main part of the action may have been that there was a butterfly in Samson's field of vision the whole time. The picture cards don't show the butterfly because if they did they would have to explain it. But you can't explain the butterfly.

See in Unguent's dream the great golden dome of the Church of the World. Hear the golden voice resounding, hear Unguent weeping and the swish of the whirling sling, hear the little thump as the body of the sparrow strikes the golden dome. Now while that's still going on — and it always is going on — hear the crackle of the flames: the Temple is burning, the Temple of Yerushalayim burning on the Ninth of Av, A.D. 70. Flames, flames for the Temple of the Jews. From the starved and defeated Jews goes up a cry like a sheet of flame. Titus runs to the Holy of Holies, with his sword he slashes the curtain, he must see for himself whether there are images or not. Hold the two together: Unguent weeping with the sling; Titus peering into that empty room. Empty for him. And the sword that was dry before he slashed the curtain has blood on it.

I am the resurrection and the life,
saith the Lord: he that believeth
in me, though he were dead, yet shall
he live: and whosoever liveth and
believeth in me shall never die.

Well of course the action never stops. Look at me, not famous or anything yet here I am. Is this, then resurrection and life? I suppose so. Although my action continues I don't actually know who I am. By now I am only the energy of an idea; whoever is writing this down puts the name of Pilgermann to the idea, says, 'What if?' and hypothesizes virtualities into actualities.

On some plane of virtuality the Temple stands, the Jews of A.D. 70 sing and dance while the scholars among them ponder God's choices. God is a scientist. He knows everything and, having all the time there is, he demonstrates everything including his actual non-presence. Names colour actualities; forget the names Jew and Christian, call them X and Y. Let X be those who said, 'The blood of him on us and on the children of us.' Let Y be those who sometimes call that to mind when killing X. What is being demonstrated? X is being demonstrated as victim, Y as avenger. X's action as victim shows us something of X's character; Y's action as avenger shows us something of Y's character. Will Y, red of hand with the blood of X through the centuries, ever say, 'The blood of them on us and on the children of us'? It's a matter provocative of thought.

A matter provocative of thought, and new approaches continually offer themselves. For example: God being omnipresent is therefore everywhere at once in what is called time; all slaughter of X is therefore in his awareness simultaneously with the birth of him whose death the slaughter avenges. Might it even be possible that God, in his Hebrew aspect writing from right to left, writes first the slaughter of X and later the crucifixion for which they are slaughtered? If we look at it in that way we might see the slaughter as cause and the crucifixion as effect: the sin of the slaughter being heavy on the sinners, there comes the redeemer to offer his innocence for their guilt, the one for the many. As Pontius Pilate washes his hands X is heard to say (by an evangelist writing some four decades later), 'The blood of him on us and on the children of us', quite accurately predicting that they, X, will be held accountable for the death of that one who gave his life in expiation of the sins committed and yet to be committed against them, X. The purist may argue that God, being everywhere in time at once, would not have written one thing 'before' and another 'after' but that argument is well answered when we point out that the Creator characteristically employs a sequential mode of presentation, even going so far as to work six days one after the other and rest on the seventh.

One seeks, as far as possible, reasonable explanations, but here, speaking as waves and particles freely ranging through what is called time, speaking as a witness to what has been done to six million or so X not so very far from here in what is called time, I must say, though lightning strike me as I speak, that there are moments when I begin to wonder whether God really is omniscient; I begin to think that it may be with him even as with some lowly mortal novelist who, having written a tremendous later scene, must perforce go back to insert an earlier one to account for it. Here of course I'm being arrogant, and maybe that's why God keeps writing slaughter scenes: the character gets out of hand; X, having been called the chosen, presumes too much, grows excessively familiar, requires too much of God, becomes like the relative who turns up uninvited on the doorstep to stay for a month. Maybe it's that simple — God is omnipresent but not omnipatient. He sometimes needs to make a little space around himself and Pfft! there go a few hundred or a few million X. Ah! to be an X, even to be the drifting waves and particles of an X long defunct, is to be not only arrogant but more than half mad. No matter.

> I am the resurrection and the life,
> saith the Lord . . .

So presumably there will always be action of one kind or another, some of us moving in flesh and blood, some of us in waves and particles.

I return now to my flesh-and-blood days. Being now strong enough to travel I prepare to go. I sell all my possessions except my books; my books I give away, I keep only my Holy Scriptures. How shall I dress for my pilgrimage? Not as a Jew, certainly. For the first time in my life I can travel incognito, nobody can prove that I'm a Jew. A wildness comes over me, a giddy sense of freedom. At the same time I think: What have I to live for? It's as if I am at once walking on very thin ice and drowning in the black water beneath. The Bath Kol then speaks to me for the second time. The same words: 'Thou pilgrim Jew!' These words I accept as an answer. Ah! the scent of Sophia in that daughter of a voice!

I dress as did the tax-collector: I put on a long coarse woollen tunic, woollen hose, stout boots. I have an ash staff shod and tipped with iron; a dagger with a Damascus blade; a good thick woollen cloak with my spare underclothes and surgical instruments in a satchel slung on my back; in my scrip bread and cheese and apples; sausages too, I don't intend to be a kosher pilgrim; fifty gold besants in my purse, three hundred more sewn into a special compartment in my satchel; the same amount in diamonds sewn into the hem of my cloak.

I have no debts to pay; I make my farewells. And Sophia? Our hello and our goodbye will be for all time together in that one time we have been together; such as I am I will not climb that ladder again; I will not intrude upon that altar where I cannot offer. The Shechinah was present in our holy sinning, I know that; nothing can be added to it, nothing can be taken from it. All the same, when I leave the town that night I take my way past the great dark house in the Keinjudenstrasse. I look up at that grouping of the lower stars of the Virgin and those three stars between the Virgin and the Lion, that gesture like a hand flung up: What! will you block the road for ever?

I move on.

6

So. Wherefore is this night distinguished from all other nights? It isn't. The barking of a dog, the cry of an owl, the distant burning of the stars, these are of every night. The departure? Also every night. Every night the departure softly closes the door of the house behind it and puts its foot to the dark road; there is a continual walking into the dark on the road away. Other nights I have lain in my bed; tonight I hear my footsteps on the road, tonight I put my feet into my footsteps and I go.

Night, night, night. The owl is the Jew-bird, I have been told. Because we are called the children of darkness. Why children of darkness? Because we clung to the so-called night of our old belief, we turned away in A.D. 30 from the new dawn of Jesus Christ. And who should know better than I that A.D. 30 is, along with everything else, the present moment. It's all here and now, you can choose whatever line you like to follow through the space that is called time. Virtualities and actualities both. Look, here's a virtual time-line entangled with the others. What does it say on it? ROMANS. Very good, I'll follow it a little way, see where it goes. It looks quite interesting, things are altogether turned round: Rome is governed by Jews, Rome is an outpost of the far-flung Jewish Empire.

Rome with a Jewish governor! Maybe it's Jairus, the father of that Eleazar who on another time-line commanded the Sicarii against the Romans at Masada. But on this time-line Masada won't be happening, and in A.D. 30 Jairus is Governor of Rome. So they bring before him this fellow Jesus, he's a wandering preacher from Arezzo or some place up in the hills. He's been getting the people all stirred up with his teaching and his miracles, he's been worrying senators and priests and officialdom in general, they don't know what he might bring down on their heads and they think it would be much better for everybody if he could simply be got out of the way. Mind you, he's no Jew, this Jesus; he's an uncircumcised Italian, he's one of theirs but they want no part of him, he's too dangerous. When Jairus says to them, 'What then may I do to Jesus called Christ?' the assembled senators, officials, priests, and hangers-on all say, 'Let him be crucified.' Jairus is willing to let the Romans sort things out in their own way. He washes his hands before the crowd, he says, 'Innocent am I from the blood of this man; ye will see to it.' And the assembled Romans say, 'On his own head let the blood of him be.' I listen and I listen but no one says, 'The blood of him on us and on the children of us.'

The Jewish legionaries scourge this Italian Jesus and they nail him to a cross on the Capitoline Hill. After his death I mingle with the crowd, I listen to what they are saying.

'Lousy Christ-killers!' says the man next to me.

'Who?' I say.

'Who?' says the man. 'Those murdering Jews! Who else?'

'I thought perhaps you meant the Romans who told the Jews to do it,' I say.

'Never mind that,' he says. 'Who's governing Rome? Who put Jesus on the cross, eh? Who drove in the nails? It was those lousy Christ-killers, it was those murdering Jews.'

I turn to others in the crowd. 'Those lousy Jews!' is what they all say. 'Those Christ-killers!'

Here I leave the Italian Jesus; I don't know whether or not he rose up and made further appearances.

Night, night, night. Perhaps the only realities are night and departure. Everything else is illusion. Staying anywhere in the light of day is illusion. If there were no Jews they would have to be invented.

Yes, I am a child of the night, a child of departures. The barking of dogs is my signpost, the voices of owls mark my road into the darkness. Inside my head I have stopped talking, I am quiet. I give myself to the old, old night that waits within me, the old, old night in the old, old wood. In this night the charcoal-

43

burners crouch listening by their hearths while the trees pray, the wind speaks, the leaves rustle like souls departing with the upward-flying sparks. Quiet, quiet, the mist is rising from the river, the bats are writing the names of darkness, the owl is teaching the mice: 'Hear, O Israel: the Lord our God, the Lord is one.'

I listen for my Bath Kol but I hear only the thumping of my heart and the sound of my footfalls. Why am I on this road through the dark wood? I am afraid. What have I to sustain me? Jesus has appeared to me but what have I to do with Jesus? I think of the tax-collector, perhaps he too has passed through this wood wondering what would sustain him. 'Thou Jew!' whispers the Bath Kol suddenly, whispers the Bath Kol in my ear in the dark wood. 'My Jew!' whispers the Bath Kol.

In fear I go forward. The quietness of the Bath Kol draws itself together in the dark, becomes a point of silence from which a hugeness grows. In the hugeness I perceive this wood, this rising ground to be the Mount of Venus between the opened thighs of the mother-space that is time. The wood is clamorous with the silence of birds and demons and great wordless mouths full of sharp teeth. When I close my eyes I see the colour of the dark: it is a strong purple-blue, very luminous and vibrating like a crystal. In those crystalline vibrations I seem to see a pale green phosphorescence in the shape of a man hanging head downward by one leg. He is hung by one ankle, his other leg is bent, the bent leg crossing the straight to make an upside-down figure four. His arms are bent to make a tri-angle on each side, his hands are behind him. He fades with the purple-blue and I hear the low voice of a bell that nods to the walking of an animal. 'Thou also,' says the rough and broken voice of the bell, so I know it to be the bell hung from the neck of Death's pale horse. I see Death on his horse, all luminous bones that look as if they would clatter but they move in perfect silence. Death beckons and I follow through the dark wood in which he moves like a lantern.

There is a stench of rotting flesh. I am standing in front of a tree; it is an oak tree. In the crystalline vibrations of the purple-blue I see the shapes of oak leaves trembling and I see the man hanging by one leg. He is naked. He has no head, his head has been cut off. Much of the flesh has been eaten off the bones by animals; what remains of the corpse is bloated and writhing with maggots. The swollen male member sticks out stiffly, uncircumcised and tumescent with rot. Death says to me in a low voice, 'This is that man who saved your life when they cut off your manhood.'

I begin to cry with great wracking sobs that shake my whole body. In this stinking maggoty corpse I see a light like a candle in a tabernacle, within the stench I smell a sweetness. Inside the corpse I see Jesus Christ crucified, broken and twisted on his cross that is right-side up in the upside-down body. 'No, no!' I cry, 'It mustn't be like that! Stop it, thou Jew, stop being crucified! Come down off that cross!' I claw at the rotting corpse, trying to pull the crucified Jesus out of the dead flesh so that I can get him off his cross. Jesus smiles and begins to fade. O God! what will there be now? Only the black spin of the universe, only eternal motion without face or voice when Jesus is gone. 'Jesus!' I cry, 'Don't go away!'

'Hurry!' whispers the Bath Kol, 'Hurry to Jerusalem!'

Hearing that urgent whisper I become terribly, terribly afraid that I shall not be able to get to Jerusalem quickly enough, that no one will get to Jerusalem quickly enough to keep Christ from going away. How do I yearn for the haunting dread and joy of his voice in the echoing dark of the world inside me, the comfort and terror of his presence. How do I long for him the virtuality without limit, him the quickener, him the mystery. Remembering no prayer I howl in my fear and I begin to kick the maggoty corpse. 'Jesus!' I cry, 'Come thou out of there! Thou Jew! Be with me!' But there is only darkness and rottenness in the corpse, the light that was within it has gone and the sweetness. The corpse is too high for me to kick properly; kicking it I fall down. Lying there in the wet grass under the corpse I feel maggots under my fingers and among them a gold ring, I feel the goldenness of it in the darkness, it must have fallen from the headless man's gullet when I kicked him.

It is of course the tax-collector's wedding ring, the circlet of gold that proclaims his union with Sophia. There has been a day in the life of this headless carcass when it knelt beside that splendid woman, exchanged vows with her, put a ring on her finger, received this ring on its own finger that is now bloated and glistening. I feel in this dead man's headless memory the touch of her hand, the scent of her breath, the softness of her mouth in the marriage kiss. In the memory of this rotting stump of flesh I hear the rustling of silk that slides away to reveal the dazzle of her naked flesh, the imperious and delicate scroll of her law. This golden circlet has dropped with the maggots out of the dead gullet because the pilgrim tax-collector before his death has swallowed his wedding ring, has renewed his covenant with his wife before being murdered and robbed. What am I to do with this ring from the finger of this maggot feast that was the lawful husband of my wife of one night?

Here I must speak of a particular phenomenon and to do so I must refer again to Hieronymus Bosch, that marvel among painters who never fails to notice the butterfly in Samson's field of vision. Bosch is above all the master of what is seen out of the corner of the mind, the essential reality behind the agreed-on appearance of things. Sometimes I manifest myself as an owl painted by Bosch and in this way I fly through the skies of his paintings and observe what is happening. My owl-by-Bosch manifestation is not a superficial one, it follows virtual lines back to his pencil and charcoal sketches and forward from underpainting to varnishing.

A very good example of the accuracy of Bosch's observation of the real behind the apparent is the upper left-hand side of the central panel of the 'Temptation of Saint Anthony' triptych. It is not necessary to have seen this painting to recognize immediately what I am about to describe; I refer to it only as a convenient example.

The upper right-hand side of the central panel shows a daytime sky; extraordinary things are to be seen in it but none the less it is an ordinary daytime sky; the left-hand side of the central panel shows the night that is always waiting within the day and the fire that is always waiting within the night. It is in this night within the day, this fire within the night, that what I am going to talk about is to be seen. Bosch gives us burning farms and churches, falling steeples and gibbets, winged creatures (one of them with a ladder) flying through the air, companies of horsemen, sundry peasants and animals, and a woman washing clothes in the river by the light of the burning. One sees at once that this fire has not spread gradually from a small beginning; no, it has from its waiting state exploded into being, has burst the skin of night and time that could no longer contain it. On the right-hand edge of this night with the fire in it, in the space between the night on the left and the day on the right, the illumination is like that of a twentieth-century sports stadium in which a night game is being played; only there does one see light of such preternatural brilliance as that through which the creature (is it an angel or a devil?) with the ladder flies. Bosch could have seen such light and shadow only in a flash of lightning. But the light in this picture, this light between the night on the left and the day on the right, is not the flash that is gone in a fraction of a moment, it is lightning sustained and steady. This shows Bosch's virtuality as well as his virtuosity; I have flown beside that creature with the ladder (always uncertain as to its allegiance; it has a tail but I cannot be sure it's a devil) and I can testify that Bosch experienced that sky by quantum-jumping to the strange brilliance of total Now.

This condition of total Now manifests itself in a number of ways and one of them is that extraordinary lucence that I have just described, that epiphany of light immanent in our being and experienced in certain heightened states as the light-as-bright-as-day within the night, the light as bright as lightning. Now as I lie in the darkness on the wet and maggoty grass under the headless naked body of the tax-collector it is not darkness that I see but the crystalline vibrations of the purple-blue. These vibrations I recognize as being of the spectrum of total Now, that moment without beginning or end in which all other moments are contained.

I have spoken before this of the Now of Sophia's nakedness in my mind but it is not with Sophia nor with Jesus that I have seen the light of total Now. No, the headless naked body of the tax-collector has been the first thing that I have seen in this unearthly light. Now lying on the ground under his hanging body I hear in the purple-blue the multitudinous leaves whispering Now in the rising wind.

The purple-blue withdraws, the sky goes black; the thunder

47

rolls, the lightning crashes and the jagged black doors of the sky jump apart to reveal the purple-blue multiplied, intensified to unbearable brilliance. Now I see that the life of humankind, the life of the world even, fits easily into the space of that lightning-flash. And how many lightning-flashes have there been, will there be. It is with the dead tax-collector that I have seen this and I begin to pray for him. The words come into my mind:

> What is man that thou art mindful of him . . .

But no more words come; I don't know to whom or to what I pray. I perceive that what is receiving my prayers is nothing with whom one speaks in words, nothing of whom one asks anything, nothing to whom one tells anything.

The thunder crashes where I am, the lightning cleaves the tree to its roots, the stinking maggoty corpse falls on me. I jump up and run through the dark wood, and as I run I hear the bell that had been nodding slowly now ringing fast, I hear the clatter of bones, the neighing of the pale horse, the low chuckle of Gevatter Tod, Goodman Death himself. The Bath Kol hisses wordlessly in my ear; I stop running and walk forward slowly, feeling with my hand in the darkness before me. My hand finds a wire, a man-snare.

I draw my dagger and go on. In the air on my face I feel the approach of something, I step to the right, a blade rips through my left sleeve, someone grunts as with my left arm I get him in a neck-grip and with my right hand I strike with the dagger. 'O my God!' cries a man's voice. Again and again I strike, there is gurgling, gasping, coughing, he falls to the ground and is silent. I move back off the path into the trees and wait to see if anyone else is coming. I am not afraid and this surprises me; I think: When I had balls I didn't have this much balls.

While I lean against a tree, panting in the dark of that dire wood and listening to the hooting of an owl, the world is full of domes: golden domes and leaden ones; domes with crosses, domes with crescents, great domes and small ones; broken domes and whole ones; domes in Jerusalem, domes in Constantinople. The biggest dome of course is that of the heavens, one can't in this world have a bigger one than that; but there is a human urge to enclose domes of air as large as possible, to shape lesser heavens in domes of human manufacture. So many domes!

It must be borne in mind that one is part of a vast picture the whole of which can never be seen; in this picture, as in Bosch's 'Temptation of Saint Anthony', night and day are side by side — I have seen this myself. The world is two domes put together, the night curves round it, fading into day. Somewhere, while I lean against this tree in the dark, it is already broad day. This little wood of night with its tiny figures, its owls and mice, its rotting corpse, its luminous Death on his pale horse with its nodding bell, its river running beside it humming in the starshine, is a background detail; in the foreground of the central panel flash the gold, the domes, and among them none greater than that one enclosing its vasty heaven of silvery lucence, blue and golden dimness in Constantinople, decked with jewels and hung with lamps and lustres, starred with glimmering suspended candles burning in the air that is smoky with incense: the Church of the Holy Wisdom, Hagia Sophia. This dome that I have never seen has because of its name and the mystery of itself incorporated itself with Sophia in my mind.

Now, however, in my little wood in this little night part of the background, I see nothing of domes, I see only the darkness, hear only the owl, listen for Death, listen for my Bath Kol. I hear nothing for a long time but when I move away from the tree I do hear something; I throw myself to the side, hear a knife smack into the tree. Before I can make a move with my dagger a powerful female voice bellows, 'Don't hurt me! I'm only a poor widow woman, I meant no harm!'

I grab her arm; even as she begs for mercy she is pulling with all her might to get the knife out of the tree for another try. 'Meant no harm!' I say. 'You tried to kill me!'

'Where's the harm in that?' she says, gripping my wrist with her free hand. 'You're a gentleman, aren't you? I wasn't doing anything but sending you early to Heaven.'

'How do you know you'd be sending me to Heaven?' I say. As I say it she twists suddenly and, still gripping my wrist, bends smoothly and throws me over her shoulder to the ground.

I land heavily on my back but I bring her down with me and in the struggle that follows I end up sitting on top of her. She's a well-built woman and I think longingly of times that will never come again. 'Why are we fighting?' she says. 'We're all God's children, aren't we? We're all brothers and sisters in Christ.'

'Not me,' I say. 'I'm a Jew.'

'So was Christ,' she says. 'It makes nothing. Are you just going to sit there, aren't you going to have me?'

'I can't,' I say. 'I'm a eunuch.'

'Yet God be thanked!' she says.

'For what?' I say.

'That they didn't cut out your tongue as well!' she says.

Thus, in our little dark wood in our tiny bit of background on the night side of the picture.

The night is far gone when she takes me to a little hut deep in the wood and well off the travelled path. Hanging from a tripod over the embers of a fire is the head of the tax-collector, somewhat shrivelled and smoke-darkened. 'God in Heaven!' I say.

'Pontius Pilate,' she says. 'He's not quite done but he'll certainly fetch twenty pieces of gold when he's ready. You won't get a Pilate like that anywhere for less than fifty; a Pilate like that will make any church rich, it's really unusual.'

'Why Pilate?' I say.

'I don't know,' she says. 'That's just how it is. When I saw him I said, "Pontius Pilate".'

'Yes,' I say, 'but why would a church want the head of Pontius Pilate?'

'How could they not want him?' she says. 'What kind of relics have they got? They've got Christ's foreskin and Mary's afterbirth and three hairs from Joseph's arse but what about the man who made Christianity possible? What if Pilate hadn't washed his hands? What if he'd turned Jesus loose and let him go on preaching, what then, hey?'

I ponder this.

'Why were you coming through this wood?' she says.

'I'm going to Jerusalem,' I say, suddenly remembering that I'm in a hurry.

'What for?' she says.

'To keep Jesus from going away,' I say.

'He's already gone,' she says. 'If Jesus had stayed buried in Jerusalem he'd have been divided up amongst all the churches in Christendom by now. You must know he was resurrected even if you are a Jew.'

'I know,' I say. 'I've seen him.'

'Did you get any relics of him?' she says.

'I'm not joking,' I say. 'I really saw him.'

'How?' she says. 'Had you a vision?'

'I don't know,' I say. 'I wasn't quite myself at the time. I was leaning on him, he was holding me up.'

'Did he have a smell?' she says.

I put my mind back to when I was with Jesus. 'He smells of stone and sweat and fire,' I say.

'Then Jesus he wasn't,' she says. 'Jesus wouldn't have a smell, that's how you'd know him.'

'Everybody has some kind of a smell,' I say.

'Well I know it,' she says. 'That's just why Jesus would be different; he's the Son of God, isn't he? Do you think things came out of him like out of ordinary people when he was on earth? Do you think he made turds?'

I say, 'Well, he ate and he drank and he bled so I suppose he must have done the rest of it as well the same as anyone else.'

'There you show your heathen ignorance, thou child of darkness,' she says. 'If Jesus had made turds they'd never have corrupted like ordinary ones and they'd be in little golden jewelled caskets in churches.'

This also I ponder.

'Maybe I should come with you,' she says. 'It isn't safe to travel alone these days.'

I look at her. She's not at all a bad-looking woman, she's certainly strong enough to be a helpful companion on the road and she's good company as well. It's true that she's a murderess but in these times that's perfectly acceptable to me as long as she's murdering for me and not against me.

'You owe me something, you know,' she says. 'After all, it was you that widowed me.'

'And it was you that almost made me a relic,' I say. I want her to come with me but it would be a kind of holding on; my pilgrimage requires to be a solitary journey; it is a private matter between Jesus and me and the tax-collector. 'I can't take you with me,' I say, 'I've made a vow.'

'Of what?' she says. 'Chastity?'

'A vow to go alone,' I say. 'You won't be without a man long, a woman like you. You can find yourself a real man instead of a eunuch.'

'Give me that ring on your finger then,' she says. 'For remembrance.'

I look at my hand. There it is, the tax-collector's wedding ring. I put it on her finger.

'If you had your proper parts you'd have taken me,' she says. 'You wouldn't have been able to do without me once you'd had me.'

When she says that it comes to me suddenly that if I had my proper parts I'd not be in this wood, I'd not be on this pilgrimage. If I'd been more careful about what streets I walked in I might still be climbing that ladder while the tax-collector completed his metamorphosis into Pontius Pilate. It occurs to me then that it might have been my castration as much as anything else that started him on his penitential pilgrimage.

The poor maggoty stump of his corpse is still lying on the ground by the lightning-blasted tree while his head hangs from the tripod in the hut. That the head is either assuming or re-assuming the identity of Pontius Pilate seems to me a destiny that is not for me to interfere with. To the body, however, I surely owe a burial.

'Why was he hung up like that?' I say.

'I don't know,' says the woman. 'Udo did that, the one you killed. He didn't like the look of him.'

The woman has of course a shovel among the tools and implements of her trade and with it I dig the grave. We put the body into the grave and I hear the words of the Kaddish coming out of my mouth, I see the black Hebrew letters rising in the morning air: '*Yisgaddal v'yiskadash sh'may rabbo* ... Magnified and sanctified be his great name ...'

Hearing the words, seeing the black letters rising in the air, I find myself paying attention to what I am saying, paying attention to the first words of the prayer:

Magnified and sanctified be his great name in the world which he hath created according to his will.

As I say these words I am looking at a spider's web pearled with the morning dew; the morning sunlight shining through it illuminates every droplet and every strand of the web; the spider, like an initial letter, witnesses the prayer and the fresh morning darkness of the oak leaves above it. My partnership with the tax-collector makes continual astonishment in me: it seems to me that never before have I noticed how much detail there is in the world which he hath created according to his will. That this headless stump with the absent face of Pontius Pilate should lie writhing with maggots under the freshly turned earth while each perfectly-formed drop of dew shines on the purposeful strands of the spider's web and the spider itself is a percipient witness and the oak leaves tremble in awareness of the morning air — all this is as the hand of God upon my eyes even though I know that God will never again limit its manifestation to any such thing as might have a hand to lay upon my eyes.

In the mounded earth of the tax-collector's grave I plant his pilgrim staff and to the staff I tie a sprig of oak leaves. I find myself wondering about the boundaries, the limits of the tax-collector. I find myself wondering whether his face might appear on more than one person. I go to the body of the man I killed, Udo. He is lying on his face where he fell. I turn him over and have a good look. It is not the face of the tax-collector.

'You want to remember him?' says the woman.

'I want to remember everything,' I say.

'You want to remember me also?' she says.

'You also,' I say.

'Here,' she says, giving me her knife and taking Udo's knife for herself. 'It'll bring you luck.'

We stand looking down at Udo. 'What about him?' I say. 'John the Baptist maybe? The prophet Elijah?'

She shakes her head. 'He never was any good for anything but being Udo,' she says.

We bury him and I go. As I'm walking away into the morning I turn and look at her. A big strong murdering woman, but alone.

'What's your name?' I say.

'Sophia,' she says.

7

In a red and smoky dream of Hell full of cranes and scaffolding and ladders, in a dream of Hell where demons and sinners labour constantly to build their flaming towers, Unguent VII, carrying a hod of bricks, climbs a shaky ladder made of bloody bones torn out of live Jews. Once on his scaffolding of stiff Jewish corpses he picks up his trowel, a Jewish shoulder-blade, and lays yet another course to make the wall of his circular tower one brick higher.

Within the circle of his wall rises the circumcised member of Christ Erect. With bricks and mortar made of the clay of Jews, made of the straw, lime, sand, water, and blood of Jews Unguent is trying to build the tower high enough so that he can put a foreskin made of flayed Jews on the member of Christ. As the tower rises so does the member but Unguent toils faster and faster.

Just as he is about to put the foreskin on and tie it down with a rope made of Jewish entrails the bricks dissolve into a sea of Jewish blood in which Unguent swims for thousands of years until he sees under that everlasting red and smoky night the lighthouse of Christ Lucent. It is an iron lighthouse, it is white-hot and the sea boils round it but Unguent must needs cling to it or drown.

Unguent clings and drowns, clings and drowns in the boiling sea of blood for thousands of years more until the sea recedes to reveal the endless empty desert in which rises the pillar of the Salt Christ. Not until Unguent licks the salt pillar down to the ground will the rain fall to slake his thirst. When the rain falls it is the blood of Jews. That is as far as Unguent has got in this dream in all the times he has dreamt it. Like the dream of Unguent related earlier this one goes on all the time and Unguent the donor, modestly small, kneels praying in a corner of it.

The fabric of the world being made as much of dreams and visions as it is of earth and stone, these virtual dreams of Unguent and these actual visions of Bosch centuries after my time are as real as anything else in my pilgrimage: they are as real as the castle on the mountain, as real as the gibbet at the crossroads where the crows flap cawing from the hanged men as I pass, as real as the wolves of the forest that drift like grey ghosts among the trees; the village dogs that guard the dust of the street and bark as I pass; the women at the well; the men outside the inn; the pigeons circling the pantiled roofs; the peasants in the fields; the signpost under a grey sky on the heath. By this same signpost will pass Bosch's gaunt wayfarer of the 'Haywagon' triptych, will pass Schubert's heartbroken young winter traveller; there is only one road for all.

Like the crows flapping up from the hanged men my thoughts scatter and like the crows they return to what they were feeding on. This is a good comparison because for the crows there is life to be got from death and for me there is the life of my present state arising from the death of my past one. If I had my proper parts I'd not be on this road; that's a simple truth, not to be argued with. Had I my proper parts I'd still be prescribing for my patients or sitting cross-legged with my cloth and my needle, plying my trade and in my free hours finding what pleasure I could in life. Climbing that ladder is what I'd be doing as often as I had the chance. But how long could that have continued, my garden of Eden? Even God had to put Adam and Eve on the road before he could get on with the story. Thinking, thinking, and I can't think how I could have gone on living without coming on this pilgrimage, without being as I am being now. When I had my proper parts I must have been blind and deaf, the world had not come alive for me, I had never talked with Christ, had never put my feet into the footsteps of my road away, had never, alone in a dark wood, seen the light of Now. So, Pilgermann, let your heart have balls, and on to Jerusalem.

Under the sun, under the rain I trudged on. On the bank of the

55

river I saw a man hanging a bear from a tree. Not bear meat but a whole live bear. He was hanging it with a rope passed over a branch and a hangman's noose on the end of it the same as if he were hanging a man. A big brown bear and it was coughing and moaning as its own weight slowly strangled it. The man was lean and ragged, his beard was full of twigs and leaves and rubbish, it looked as if it might have birds nesting in it. As he braced himself with his feet against the trunk of the tree and pulled on the rope he cried, 'My God, my God, why hast thou forsaken me!'

Before I could think what I was doing I had cut the rope with the knife given me by the second Sophia. The bear crashed to the ground and lay there without moving. The man turned on me in a fury. 'You murdering fool!' he screamed, 'You've killed God!'

I said, 'I didn't mean to kill him.'

'But you *have* killed him!' he said. 'God was everything to me, he was big and strong and shaggy, he was like a bear.'

'He *was* a bear,' I said.

'Of course he was,' said the man. 'God can be whatever he likes, completely and divinely; he always used to find me honey trees. And you've killed him, you've killed God.' There were a bow and arrows and a hunter's pouch lying on the ground; he picked up the bow and fitted an arrow to the string, aiming it at me. At this moment the bear stood up on his hind legs. He began to low and grunt, making gestures with his paws like a man making a speech.

'Lies!' shouted the man. 'Lies, lies, all lies!' He aimed his arrow at the bear.

The bear made a few more remarks; he put one paw over his heart and shook his head sadly, then he made a gesture clearly expressing that everything was over between him and the man. What a wonderful bear that was! How I wished that I could have him for a friend, what a travelling companion he would be — he clearly had a profound understanding and was one of those people who know when to talk and when to be quiet. While I was thinking this he dropped on to all fours and hurried off towards the trees. The man swung round to loose his arrow, I threw out my hand to knock him off his aim but there fell across my arm something as hard and heavy as an iron bar, a blackness came in front of my eyes and I fell down.

When I came to myself the bear, shot full of arrows, was lying dead and the man was sitting on the ground throwing dirt on his own head and crying, 'O my God, my God, why hast thou forsaken me!'

I said, 'Don't be such a fool, he hasn't forsaken you — you've killed him.'

He said, 'I killed him because he forsook me.'

I said, 'How did he forsake you?'

He said, 'He wouldn't show me any more honey trees.' He sat there rocking to and fro in his grief. It was that sort of a hot still day when one seems particularly to hear the buzzing of flies. I left him to his lamentations and went on my way.

I was thinking about the bear, how good it would have been to have him with me, how I should have heard the padding of his feet and seen out of the corner of my eye his shaggy brown back rocking along beside me through the long miles. Big and strong he was too, a match for half a dozen men in a fight; one would feel easy anywhere with such a friend. Perhaps he might even have danced a little now and then for our supper and a night's lodging. Pilgermann and his bear would have become famous on the pilgrim road.

There was a low chuckle in my ear and a hard hand clapped me on the shoulder in great good fellowship. It was that bony personage who had been riding his horse in the wood where the headless body of the tax-collector was hanging from the tree. This time he was on foot; he was dressed as a monk and like me he carried a pilgrim's staff. It was very shadowy under his hood, one couldn't properly say that there were eyes in the eyeholes of his skull-face but there was definitely a look fixed upon me; it was that peculiarly attentive sidelong look seen in self-portraits.

'Am I a mirror in which you see yourself?' I said.

'Everybody is,' he said. 'I am so infinitely varied that I never tire of myself. Mortals looking in a mirror see only me but I see all the faces that ever were and I love myself in all of them.'

'You think well of yourself!' I said.

He hugged himself in a transport of self-delight. 'When I say, "Sleep with me!" nobody says no,' he said. 'Kings and queens, I have them all, no inch of them is forbidden to me; nuns and popes, ah! There's good loving! I am the world's great lover, that's a simple fact though I say it myself. Well, there's no need for me to blow my own trumpet — you'll see when you sleep with me.'

He kept turning his face to me as he spoke, and his breath did not reek of corruption as one might suppose: it was like the morning wind by the sea. 'Call me Bruder Pförtner,' he said, 'it's a name I fancy: Brother Gatekeeper. It has a kind of monastic humility but at the same time it goes with a swing.'

'Bruder Pförtner,' I said. I thought about the gates he kept.

'You've no idea,' he said. 'No idea at all.' He made a graceful gesture and there opened upon my vision the brilliant lucent purple-blue of the crystalline vibrations of Now. His arm swept back, the gate was closed, the day seemed dark. We went on a little way in silence. His face was looking straight ahead and I saw only his cowl moving companionably beside me. 'You know why I was chuckling when I first appeared to you?' he said.

'Why?' I said.

'I was chuckling at your bear thoughts,' he said. 'Really, you're no better than that other fellow, you know. Had the bear been your friend you'd not have been content to let him be, you'd have had him dancing for your supper, and you with all that money on you. That's how people are: they're trade-minded, they can't let anything be simply what it is. It was I that knocked your arm down when you tried to stop that fellow from shooting the bear.'

'Why?' I said.

'That bear was finished,' he said. 'He had nothing left to live with. Did you understand what he was saying when he made his little speech?'

'No,' I said.

'This is what he said to that man,' said Bruder Pförtner: '"I never wanted to be anything but a friend to you. The only use I wanted to make of you was to be with you sometimes; nothing more than that, and I didn't want any use to be made of me more than that. The first time I gave you honey it was just because honey was there, so we both had some of it, sharing like friends. But then you had to boast to everyone that you had a bear who found honey for you and I had to boast to everyone that I had a man who followed me to where the honey was. Then

58

I showed you where the silence was and you thought I was God and I let you think it. We corrupted each other and so there had to be an end to it. Now I don't think I can even find the silence for myself, I don't think I even know how to be simply myself any more, and I want to go away and not be with anybody." That's what the bear said just before the man shot him.'

'Poor fellow,' I said.

'People can't let anything be,' said Bruder Pförtner. 'They can't even let me be.'

'What do you mean?' I said.

'This very moment while we're talking,' he said, 'you're feeling more and more friendly towards me. Very soon you'll be wanting to call me *thou*; next thing you'll be wanting me to dance for your supper. Have no fear, I'll dance for you; but not yet, not yet a little while. You mustn't presume on this slight acquaintance just because I said you were going to sleep with me, you mustn't become too familiar. Friendly, yes; but not too familiar.' With that he disappeared.

I thought about Bruder Pförtner a little. I thought him visible again, trudging beside me companionably. 'Why am I here?' he said.

'I just want you to know how things stand between us,' I said. 'I have no control over your actions but I am master of your appearances to me; my perception is the substance of your apparition, so you too must mind your manners if you want to go on being seen by me.'

Bruder Pförtner chuckled. Quite a remarkable sound, his chuckle: bony and brutish. 'Anything you like,' he said, and disappeared again. The manner of his chuckling made me unsure that I was master of his appearances to me; I thought him visible again but he did not appear, only his bony chuckle returned to jog along with me.

Ahead of me I heard the thin and straggling voices of children singing:

Christ Jesus sweet,
Guide thou our feet,
Our light in darkness be;

Make straight the way
By night, by day
That brings us, Lord, to thee.

The day, as I have said, was hot and still. Behind me in that heat and stillness were the dead bear and the crying man; farther back in the little dark wood in a shallow grave rotted the maggoty headless corpse of the tax-collector while the second Sophia prepared his head for the role of Pontius Pilate; in another grave lay the relic-gatherer whose life I had gathered up; and ahead of me the children sang with silvery voices in the dust of the dry road.

The humps and hollows of the landscape tend always towards the human: on this day the horizontal head of Christ was clearly visible in woods and fields and rocky outcrops. It was the head of the dead Christ brought down from the cross, his eyes closed, his passion complete. I sensed that it was important not to tilt my own head to the horizontal the better to see his face; while I had no wish to make with the vertical of my head and the horizontal of his a cross, neither could I in good conscience avoid it.

Nor mountains steep
Nor waters deep
Turn back the faithful soul;
Nor fire nor sword,
Christ Jesus Lord,
Jerusalem our goal.

So feeble, so wan those voices, like a candle flame in the sunlight. The dry and dusty road was ascending the brow of the horizontal head of Christ; the children would not be in sight until I reached the top of the hill. Long and long I toiled up the brow of Christ in the heat and the stillness of the day. When I reached the top I saw the children. They were moving very slowly in the glimmering heat and in the dust that rose up from their going. Peasant boys and girls they were, between twenty and thirty of them, the oldest of them twelve or thirteen but most of them younger, all of them thin and ragged, carrying their pitiful little bundles and singing thinly as they walked in the dry and dusty road.

As I watched them I heard again that bony and brutish chuckle: not only Bruder Pförtner but a whole company of him, a bony mob of him came trotting past me throwing off their monks' robes and showing the tattered parchment of their skins stretched taut over their bones. All of them had great long bony members wagging erect before them so that it was difficult for them to run; all of them were giggling and chuckling as they stretched out their bony hands towards the children. When they reached the children they pushed them down on to their hands and knees in the dusty road, mounted them like dogs and coupled with them, grunting in their ardour, screaming in their orgasms. The children crept forward slowly on their hands and knees, singing as they were violated:

Christ Jesus mild,
Sweet Mary's child
That hung upon the tree,
Thy cross we bear,
Thy death we share,
To rise again with thee.

When the skeletons had sated their lust they fell away from the children and lay sighing and snoring in the road with limbs outflung. The children, their hands and knees bloody, stood up again and trudged on.

Of the Rock that begot thee thou art unmindful,
and hast forgotten God that formed thee.

This has come into my mind as I ascend the stone brow, the horizontal broken rock of Christ who is of the broken Rock of God, the Rock that was shattered by the unfaith of its people, the Rock that was drained of its strength by the lust for the seen and by the whoring after no-gods. I remember how our old Rabbi has said that only once in the Holy Scriptures is the unpronounceable tetragrammation of God written with a small *yod*, and it is here in Deuteronomy that it is written so to show God's loss of strength from Yeshurun's disrespect:

61

But Yeshurun grew fat, and kicked:
thou art grown fat, thou art become thick,
thou art covered with fatness;
then he forsook God who made him,
and lightly esteemed the Rock of his salvation.
They provoked him to jealousy with strange gods,
with abominations they provoked him to anger.
They sacrificed to powerless spirits;
to gods whom they knew not,
to new gods that came newly up,
whom your fathers feared not.
Of the Rock that begot thee thou art unmindful,
and hast forgotten God that formed thee.

What is called time passes and yet all time is present; one has only to turn one's head to see the happening of all things: there I am going up the ladder while Satan smiles and God perhaps weeps. God being omnipotent has the power, even while apparently absent, to manifest the idea of a weeping God. But God as It, God without personification — can it truly be that this God can be lessened and made weak by any human action, by my disrespect, by my adultery? I don't know, I am full of doubt and worry as I ascend the broken rock of the horizontal brow of Christ.

When one is a child, when one is young, when one has not yet reached the age of recognition, one thinks that the world is strong, that the strength of God is endless and unchanging. But after the thing has happened — whatever that thing might be — that brings recognition, then one knows irrevocably how very fragile is the world, how very, very fragile; it is like one of those ideas that one has in dreams: so clear and so self-explaining are they that we make no special effort to remember. Then of course they vanish as we wake and there is nothing there but the awareness that something very clear has altogether vanished.

And God, we think that because he is all-powerful the amount of available power is always the same; but it changes, it wavers, it shifts from the kinetic to the potential, varying with the action of the universe, the action of the world, the action of the individual. Earlier I have had the thought of many mysterious unseen fragile temples in which God used to dwell among us; now I perceive that these temples are each of us however unreliable, each of us for good or ill, each of us as the total of our actions and our being. It is because of such as I that God is absent and Christ horizontal; it is because of such as I that these children are raped by skeletons on the road to Jerusalem.

I hurry to catch up with the children, I kick snoring skeletons out of my way, I trample their mouldy bones and filthy parchment skins, I tread on their great phalli and their ponderous testicles. They don't care, they grunt and sigh and roll over in their sleep.

The children with bloody hands and knees trudge on. They are so very thin, their arms and legs are like sticks, their cheeks are hollow, their eyes sunken, truly they seem Death's own children as they sing:

> Our faith our shield,
> Thy word we wield
> Of love and Christian pity.
> The seas will part
> That pure in heart
> May reach Thy golden city.

'Brother pilgrim!' cry the children when they see me, 'Brother pilgrim! Have you anything to eat?' I give them all the food I have, sausage and bread; it isn't very much for so many. A boy who seems to be the leader thanks me and divides it with great precision. There is no more than a mouthful for everyone, they chew it slowly and with great care.

'Have you nothing more?' says the boy. 'You can have, you know, any one of us you like.'

'Look at your bloody hands, your bloody knees!' I cry. 'Look where your clothes are torn! You've just now been had by skeletons!'

The boy looks at his hands, his knees. 'It's a rough road,' he says. 'One stumbles.'

'Selling yourselves for food,' I say, 'is that how you've been making your way to Jerusalem?'

'We beg, we steal, we sell what we have to sell,' says the boy. 'God wills it.'

'How can God will such a thing as that?' I say.

'If God wills that we should be on the road to Jerusalem then He wills the rest of it as well,' says the boy. 'Dead people can't walk to Jerusalem, and one must eat to live.'

'Do you know where Jerusalem is?' I say to him. 'Do you know how far it is to Jerusalem?'

The boy turns his face towards me and looks at me for a moment without saying anything. Looking at me out of his eyes I see the lion-eyes of Christ, and I am frightened. I hold my head because I know that when he speaks his voice will be a woodwind voice that comes from inside my head and resonates there. 'Jerusalem will be wherever we are when we come to the end.'

I look away, ashamed. I look down at the tawny dusty road. I feel as I did when as a child I was ill and did not go to my lessons. Lying in my bed I heard the voices of the other children as they passed my window. Over those voices I now hear the singing of these Christian children:

Christ Jesus sweet,
Guide thou our feet,
Our light in darkness be.
Make straight the way
By night, by day,
That brings us, Lord, to thee.

I walk on quickly, the children are left behind, the voices fade away. The road continues on high ground; below me I see peasants making hay, their voices float up to me singing and talking. Beyond them is a wood, a hamlet, houses, a church, a village green, a craggy height, the river winding in the distance. Men and women pass me with baskets of fruit and vegetables on their heads. For them this road does not go to Jerusalem, it goes to farm and cottage, to ease at the day's end, the evening meal and a good night's sleep, nothing required the next day but the next day's work in the same sure place. See the man on top of the hay-wain: for him at this moment the world is soft and fragrant. Perhaps not. Perhaps in his soul he walks barefoot on sharp stones.

'Rubbish,' says Bruder Pförtner at my elbow. 'Do you see that woman with the rake, the one that's bending over? In his soul he's lifting her skirt and he's giving it to her, Uh! Uh! Uh! Uh!' Pförtner is grunting and he's thrusting with his great bony pimmel as he thinks about what he thinks the peasant is thinking about.

'That's not in his soul,' I say. 'That's in his mind.'

'Don't talk nonsense,' he says, 'that man hasn't got a mind, he's perfectly healthy; minds are a sickness. All he's got is a soul and his soul is in his scrotum.'

'Filthy brute,' I say. 'Is that all you think of?'

'It's my whole purpose in life,' he says. 'I like to do it with thin girls best, you can get closer to them. Ah! I'm getting excited thinking about it!' His monstrous member is stiff again, he strokes it lovingly.

'Those children you've just done it with, they'll die now, won't they?' I say.

'My seed is in them,' he says. 'They'll give birth when the death in them comes full term.' He begins to sing and dance, stamping his bony feet and raising the dust on the dry road:

'Golden, golden, ring the bell,
Go to Heaven, go to Hell,
Go on land and go on sea,
Go with Jesus, come with me.'

'You're so full of jokes and fun,' I say. 'What happened to your more dignified manifestation as Goodman Death riding slowly on your pale horse with the slowly ringing bell?'

'That's for strangers,' he says. 'You're not a stranger now. I'll see you at the inn.' And he's gone again.

Through the long day I walk my road to Jerusalem while the world on both sides of me makes hay, drinks beer, mends thatch, shoes horses, draws water, carries burdens, crows from its dunghill, grunts in its sty, grazes on its hillside. With evening I arrive at an inn, The Black Boar. In the inn yard are horses, carts, wagons, sledges, billhooks, scythes, rakes, pitchforks, dogs, peasants, pilgrims, and a sow wearing a red cross.

The sow is looking at me from under her blonde eyelashes. She turns her snout towards me and begins to grunt urgently, perhaps ecstatically. I say ecstatically because I note that she has been mounted by the ever-potent Bruder Pförtner who is himself grunting ardently as he makes love to her. 'Uh! Uh! Uh! Uh!' grunts Bruder Pförtner. 'Hoogh! Hoogh! Hoogh! Hoogh!' grunts the sow. The sow is on one end of a rope; on the other end is that peasant who said, 'Cut it off and make a Christian of him.' He is looking at me narrowly as if trying to remember where he has seen me before.

I kneel beside the sow listening attentively to her grunts. 'Quick!' I say to the peasant, 'Get a basin!'

'What for?' he says.

'To catch the blood,' I say as I cut the sow's throat. Her blood spurts out and in the same moment with her dying squeal I hear Bruder Pförtner screaming as he comes. The peasant grabs a billhook but before he can take a step towards me Bruder Pförtner, his great bony pimmel still erect, has leapt upon him and is enjoying him. The peasant utters a choked cry, gives birth to his death immediately, and falls on his face on the ground.

I am left standing there with the knife of the second Sophia in my hand and in my mind the thought: Jerusalem is wherever I am when the end comes. The other peasants are looking from the dead man to me and back again. They make the sign one makes against the evil eye. The pilgrims as well are looking at the dead man and looking at me.

I look at them from one to the next. I look at them all. In the air in front of me I draw the two mingled triangles of a six-pointed star. I don't know why I do this, it simply comes to me to do it. They look at what I have drawn in the air, I wait for them to take up their knives, billhooks, scythes, rakes, pitchforks and staves and kill me. No one moves, no one says a word.

'You saw me listening to the sow,' I say. 'She was confessing to me, she was telling me her last will and testament. She was telling me of her many sins, how she repented of them; she had no wish to go on living. She leaves her corporeal being, her bacon, her ribs, her chops, her crackling, all of her sweet flesh and nourishing juices to you her countrymen and to you her fellow pilgrims on the road to Jerusalem, that golden city that is at the same time in the Holy Land far away and in the heart of each of us. May Jesus Christ how savoury be with you and keep you from all harm.'

I let my eyes pass over all of them. I do not expect to leave this place alive. No one moves, no one says a word. Stepping very carefully, as if I am walking on crystal goblets, I go out of the inn yard and back to the road.

8

'Jesus Christ how savoury'! Almost I said, 'Jesus Christ our Saviour', almost those words leapt out of my mouth. Strange, how eager those words are to be said, and stranger still how busy is the idea of being saved. As a boy I was told that there is a big book in which every deed is recorded; on the Day of Judgment one is shown this record, must examine it carefully and sign it. I was told that the righteous go to Gan Eden and the wicked to Gehinnom but even as a child I never believed it; even as a child I sensed that the arrangement of one place for the good souls and another place for the bad ones was simply not such a thing as would happen in a universe of sun and moon and stars, of night and day and the wheel of the seasons. God said a great many things in the time when it was manifesting itself as YHWH; some of them may well have been misunderstood or written down wrong. Or it may be that he put things in a very simple and vivid way so as not to require too much of the general understanding. Space and time have in them no Gan Eden and Gehinnom, no Heaven and Hell as what could be called places, and I cannot believe that anyone can now take seriously the idea of a soul that is simply righteous or wicked. Even the souls of such creatures as Torquemada and Hitler are not simply wicked although the weight of their actions is mostly in the gehinnom of things — I use the word as one might say right or left, up or down, plus or minus. It is in the rotation of eden and gehinnom that we feel the cosmic dance that is the motion of the universe, and in the play of these energies come punishment and reward. My punishment is that such evil as I have done has tuned me to the gehinnom frequency where I vibrate to the memories of all who have done evil; I share their being as well as their memories, and what I remember I remember as a doer remembers. My reward for being no worse than I am is that I remember no more than I do.

And what is this *I* that speaks now? Only a fiction, a name of convenience, a *poste restante* for whatever addresses itself to the persistence of memory and the force of idea: there is no Pilgermann distinct from anything else; why should there be? It is difficult for me now to understand why anyone should want a continuance of identity in a life after death. All those ancient mouldering kings entombed with their murdered wives, with their servants and soldiers and horses, with their weapons and chariots, their stone bread, their stony dregs of long-departed wine! Imagine the burial of a mouse with weapons, an ant with concubines! The arrogance, the greed of it! Even now the space all round me is thick with the fat globules of undissolved souls blinking and bleeping their greed for more! more! until the signals fade to silence and the lights go dark. More indeed! Not only human souls — the dying Earth itself moans like a stunned ox; the deeps of space are clamorous with its panting, its unwillingness to be absorbed into the allness from which it came. I have lost my humanity, I have been waves and particles too long to feel what humans feel. And yet, and yet . . . I remember with something like a pang how I wanted God to come back, how I wanted Jesus not to go away.

I am on the road again. Life is so strange! It is nothing I have ever been able to take for granted, just simply being alive with the world in front of my eyes and looking out through those eyes at the world. And when the eyes are closed, the colours, the patterns, the flashes and flickers; pictures even. How can it be that pictures can be seen with the eyes closed? Dreams! Maybe there were dreams before there was anything else; maybe there were dreams before there were people to dream them. Maybe dream life is the real living and our waking life is just the necessary exercising of our bodily functions in the time between dreams.

I am on the road again, trying to remember the last thing Jesus said to me. 'From me came the seed that gave me life,' he said.

He may be right. Look at what he does with stone, it sets time at naught completely; give him any stone and any stonecarver whatever and he can make it happen, he can make his living and his dying be Now, for ever this very moment. He has no need of flesh and blood, he can live in stone as others live in flesh and blood. Partly I understand it: what one thinks of as the hardness of stone is actually its memory, its retention, its capability of holding images and thoughts. That's why Christ has always been so easy with stone, he comes to it so willingly because it goes with him so willingly; he likes to be long in stone, short in stone, likes to live out his story large and small in shapes of stone. Christ comes for any stonecarver who calls him with his chisel, calls him with his iron to the stone. He has no vanity, does not push himself forward, he takes his place modestly with the other figures, acting out his story as bidden. Because of this the stone is eager to please him, it's always thinking of new little touches that will put something more into the story. In my drift through what is called time I have my favourites here and there, and as often as not they are after my own time. What an odd thing to say: my own time! That time during which I lived is what I mean, and that sounds equally odd because I have always been somewhere in one form or another; precision with words is impossible.

But I wanted to say something about a particular stone Christ-story, the one in Naumburg Cathedral in the west rood-loft. I believe that it was done in the twelfth or thirteenth century, I don't know who the sculptor was. There are seven scenes in it: the first is the Last Supper, perhaps it is that moment when Christ is saying, in the Gospel of Mark, 'Take ye; this is the body of me.' As Christ speaks these stone words — they are not cut into the stone but they are there in the air of that stone scene — he puts into the mouth of Judas a piece of bread while Judas still dips with his own hand in the dish. The stone and the carver are good with this scene as they are throughout: as Christ with his right hand puts the bread into the mouth of Judas he draws back with his left hand his right sleeve to keep it out of the gravy and in this way the eye is led from the bread to the hand, wrist, and arm of Christ that extend the bread, showing the oneness of the bread with the self of him who gives it. Or it may be — and I rather believe it is — that the moment shown is that one in the Gospel of John when Jesus, having been asked who will be the betrayer, answers, 'That one it is to whom I shall dip the morsel and shall give him.' And John goes on to say, 'And after the morsel then entered into that one Satan.' Yes, that for me is what is happening in that stone moment. Because all eucharists are double—this is what I know now, this is why I am easy now between the grinding of eden and gehinnom in the mill of the universe. When God was a he he never told us everything; where is it written that he told us all there was to tell? Nowhere. Nor did Jesus tell us everything. He never told—did he, is it written somewhere? I think not—that all eucharists are double; but they are. 'Take ye; this is the body of me.' 'And after the morsel then entered into that one Satan.'

What chance has Judas? He eats the bread of Christ as would a dog given a crust by his master, and with the bread comes Satan. There sits Christ, stolid and stocky in the Naumburg stone, solid as the stone itself. There is no fault to be found in him, he will betray no one. Ay! Judas, Adam and Eve, the Jews—what was to be expected of them? What did God as He, God as Logos, God as Christ, want of any or all of them? How were Adam and Eve to resist the fruit that God had created irresistible? How were the Jews to be other than imperfect and deviant from the will of that same God who created them imperfect and deviant from his will? How were they not to make a golden calf in the shadow of that holy, that terrifying and untouchable mountain of the Law? How was Judas not to betray Jesus after Satan had entered him in that double eucharist? Jesus was the one who could withstand Satan, he was the strong one; he required of Judas that betrayal that Judas, powerless to do otherwise, already a dead man and Satan-entered, enacted as his necessary part of the story.

What are we but creatures of the God who made us as we are? Either God is omnipotent, omniscient, and omnipresent or he isn't. If he isn't then he must take his chance with the rest of us and not demand special treatment; if he *is* all-powerful, all-knowing, and everywhere-present then he has nothing to complain of except that the universe would come to a halt without the dynamic asymmetry of Adam and Eve's original sin, of the Jews' whoring after false gods, of Judas's betrayal of Jesus, of Pilgermann's adultery and every other act of wrongdoing since the human race first took upon itself the task of maintaining universal spin and motion according to the will of God. Try to conceive of things as other than they are — it can't be done. While humankind exists there can only be the rotation of God's impossible requirements and humankind's repeated failures. Indeed, what *is* God but an impossible requirement? Any possible requirement would not be God.

So. Stone Judas, fed by his stone master, eats his stone bread while dipping his hand into the stone meats of the last supper. The stone, friend and brother to Christ and stonecarver and all of us alike, remembers this because the iron has told it to remember and it obeys.

In the next scene of the Naumburg stone story Judas gets his thirty pieces of silver from the high priest. Here we see the full power of that stone memory, that stone retention. This stone knows what it knows: Judas, his face that of a stunned brute, is not his own master, and this is not forgotten by the stone. But if Judas is thus sold even as he sells Jesus, what of this high priest through whose listless fingers slide the clinking silver coins into the fold of the cloak Judas holds out to catch them. Is this Caiaphas? It must be he. And what is in his face, this face that seems of all of them to be the most thoughtfully observed? Does Caiaphas choose to be Caiaphas? Why does he look out at us like this from the stone? Such a tired face. 'There is left to me only this!' says that face.

Why? Why only this? What words of Caiaphas does John give us, what has Caiaphas to say of Jesus? 'If we leave him thus, all men will believe in him, and will come the Romans and will take away both the place and the nation.' What else does Caiaphas say to the council of the chief priests and the Pharisees? 'Ye know not anything, nor reckon that it is expedient for us that one man should die for the people and not all the nation perish.' And this, John tells us, Caiaphas 'from himself he said not, but being high priest of that year he prophesied that Jesus was about to die for the nation, and not for the nation only, but that the children of God having been scattered he might gather into one. From that day therefore they took counsel that they might kill him.'

So. Judas is entered by Satan, Caiaphas is doomed by reason and prophecy. How much freedom of choice has Caiaphas? He, like the rest of us, is free within the limits of his understanding. As I have said before, a story is what remains when you leave out most of the action. Vulgar tradition, like a painter who does not know how to render shadows, has filled in the sparseness of the Gospels with a sugary muck that makes the empty spaces dark and sticky. In the coloured picture cards in which Jesus now lives he and his twelve disciples move softly in their marzipan robes but the Jesus I saw was not a soft mover, and Caiaphas's concern indicates that Jesus's following was such as could well have moved Rome to take away both place and nation from the Jews.

Thus Caiaphas, acting for the good of his people, ensures their everlasting infamy. God as He, God as It has done this, has shown in this the never-to-be-understood mystery of his action in which Judas must betray Jesus and Caiaphas his people. All we can know is that there must be betrayal. Is not life betrayed by death? Is not up betrayed by down? Is not space-time betrayed by that recurrent contraction to the singularity from which it must burst anew? The Jesusness of Jesus cannot live without the Judasness of Judas, the Caiaphasness of Caiaphas, the Pilateness of Pilate. Ponderous wheel!

In the next scene Judas kisses Jesus while Peter with a sword cuts off the ear of the high priest's servant. Christ stares out in perpetual innocence from the stone while the guilty betrayer, submissive to the forces moving him, presses close like a dog to his master. In the Gospel of Matthew Jesus says to Judas, 'Comrade, do that on what thou art here.' In Mark he says nothing. In Luke he says, 'Judas, with a kiss the Son of man betrayest thou?' In John again he says nothing. There it is: the Gospels say what they say and the stone remembers what it is told. Very good. Who is this Pilgermann, this drifting wave-and-particle vestige of a castrated Jew, who is this Pilgermann to have an opinion on the matter? From where I am now I see the universe isotropically receding in all directions. I am, equally with all other waves and particles, its centre. From that centre I speak as I find, and I find that I have questions for which neither the Gospels nor the Holy Scriptures offer answers. Theologians and fathers of the Church cannot confound me, they have no firmer ground on which to stand than I. So. Here is Christ, the one who makes the blind see, makes the crippled walk; here is Christ, the one who raises the dead, walks on the water, feeds the thousands with his loaves and fishes. Christ the Word made flesh, Christ the Son of God. And what says he to this mortal lump, this uncorrected sinner, this strayed sheep and Satan-entered? What says Christ, the Good Shepherd? 'Judas, with a kiss the Son of man betrayest thou? Comrade, do that on what thou art here.' Because Christ will have, must have his betrayal. 'Comrade, do that on what thou art here.' Do it that the cosmos may uncoil its onward energy, that the wheel may go on turning: night and day, plus and minus, eden and gehinnom, matter and anti-matter, Jesus and Judas.

Now I wonder, yes I wonder, on whom is it to forgive whom? Who is the sacrifice, the one for the many, the ransom, the redeemer? Who is to represent us all? Is it Jesus the betrayed, the crucified, or is it Judas the betrayer and his own hangman? Or is it the binary entity of Jesus/Judas alternating and inseparable? How the thunder rolls when certain words are put together! When certain mysteries are named! Not to be understood, not to be attempted even! Roll, thou eden and gehinnom of the rolling universe! Hurry on, thou road to Jerusalem, thou road returning! A rushing and a plodding, a palimpsest of footsteps rising from the ground under my feet up into the air high over my head so that I feel myself to be drowning in the going and the ghosts of going of those footsteps, footsteps upon footsteps and ghosts upon ghosts, a madness of going that moves both ways on this road. This road is the treadmill on which we walk day into night and night into day, eden into gehinnom into eden, Jesus into Judas into Jesus.

Jesus does not tell us everything but he has much to show us. In the next scene of the Naumburg stone story we see Peter on the left-hand slant of the roof of the porch of the rood-screen doorway. He is turning away from the high priest's maidservant who questions him; he is making one of the three denials he will make before the cock crows. Ah! the genius of that Naumburg stone, that Naumburg master! Look at the face of that maidservant, the eternal directness of the soul behind the stone eyes that are turned away from Peter as she looks towards what is not carved in the stone, towards Jesus brought before the high priest, chief priests, elders and scribes. She looks away from Peter but she stretches out her left hand, it is almost touching Peter's shoulder as she says, 'And thou with the Nazarene wast — Jesus.' Peter says, 'Neither I know nor understand what thou sayest.' What is meant by this triple denial of Christ? Is not each part of the Holy Trinity being denied once in it? As if Christ is telling us: 'Look at this mortal lump, this thrice-denier; yet will he be my rock.' Because mortal lumps are all humanity can offer, and if rocks are needed these must suffice. Having only mortal lumps to choose from, Christ will use this one for a betrayer, that one for a rock. Just as his father before him used this one to receive the tablets of the Law, that one to make a golden calf. Matter and anti-matter, yes and no of the treadmill that walks the rolling earth from night to day. Here stands in the stone Peter the rock in baffled recognition of what he is and what he is not in the numbers of eden and gehinnom. That the stone and the carver could produce these two faces, the maidservant and Peter, that is certainly in the eden side of the balance for all of us. Such a brutal innocence, that maidservant! An innocence not possible for Jesus, the innocence of the pure lump of mortality with no connexions in high places. And Peter! that face of his! The light of understanding that floods the stone of him!

Peter and the maidservant are on one side of the roof of the porch of the rood-screen doorway; on the other side are two soldiers of the watch. Underneath them in the rood-screen doorway and twice as large as they is Christ crucified, Mary on one side of him and John on the other.

After the maidservant and Peter and the soldiers of the watch here is Jesus before Pilate. Oh! that meekness of Jesus, that stone meekness. It is the meekness of plutonium. He is so very docile, like some absent-minded celebrity asked to pose in a group photograph. 'Here? Is this all right, is this where you want me to stand?' Waiting patiently for the time when he will explode himself upon the world. Pilate holds out his left hand while a servant pours water over it into a basin. Pilate is thunderstruck and so is the servant; to both of them at once has come the realization that this moment is what it is for ever — it has never been before, it will never be again; it is Now and they are living it, never in life, never in death to escape from it. Pilate's mouth is open wide, it is as if a great thick invisible vine is growing out of it; or a snake. 'Innocent I am from the blood of this man,' he says; 'ye will see to it.' Of the two faces that of the servant shows the deeper feeling; Pilate's perception of this moment is confused by his official identity but the servant can take it in just as it is and he knows that never in the history of the human race will there be any going back from this moment. Here is the hump of the story, here is the last of the uphill part; after this it rolls like a monstrous and implacable wheel through the ages, crushing everything in its path and preparing the way of the Lord, the gone, the never-again-coming.

Christ is scourged then, and in the next and last scene of the rood-loft reliefs he goes off dragging his cross. These last two scenes, like the Crucifixion below, are not from the hand of the master who carved the first five scenes; it was the destiny of the original stone of the last two scenes not to endure with those other faces and gestures that are fixed for us upon the mirror of time. These last two scenes and the Crucifixion, all of them in wood and by a centuries-later hand, have not the power of the original stone. As I have said, Christ has a special way of being with stone and the Naumburg master knew how to let that special way of being happen.

I am on the road, this road through time and space to Jerusalem, but I am no longer alone: the sow I killed and her peasant master now walk with me; they are my new colleagues, and not only they: the bear who was slain by his worshipper also walks with me; Udo the relic-gatherer whom I killed in the wood is here, and the tax-collector. Yes, the tax-collector — how not?

The sow is walking upright, she minces on her trotters like a heavy woman in tiny shoes, her flesh shaking and wobbling erotically, her flesh that is naked among us; there is a scarlet necklace of beaded drops round her throat and a thin trickle of blood from her mouth. She is confused by her present condition and shakes her head as she walks. 'Little love!' she says to her peasant master. 'O my treasure!' she says, pressing close to him, 'What gives it here?'

'He killed you, this one,' says the peasant. 'Smell him. Is he a Jew?'

'I don't know,' she says. 'I don't think I can tell the difference any more.' She turns to me. 'Ay!' she says, 'how the life rushed out of me on to your blade, it was like an orgasm. Such a knifeman are you, such a thruster!'

'Such a sow are you,' I say. 'Such a Jew-finder, such a leaver-behind of dead bodies.'

'How sweet she is!' This is Bruder Pförtner, he too is with us. 'How I love her!' He throws himself upon the dead sow, forcing her down on all fours and entering her zestfully.

'Ah!' cries the sow to Pförtner, 'you were always the best, you were always the most man of them all!'

'Get off her,' says the peasant to Pförtner. 'She's mine.'

'There's enough of her for everybody,' says Pförtner contentedly. 'She's inexhaustible. You must be patient and wait your turn.' He reaches orgasm quickly, screams with joy as the sow squeals under him, then falls off her and lies snoring in the road behind us as we go on.

'Tell me about yourself,' I say to the sow. 'Tell me your story.'

'Ah!' she says. 'There's so much to tell! There's more to tell than even I myself know. You know of course that I'm descended from the Moon Goddess, from Diana herself; yes, everyone knows that. That's why, you see, I'm so eternally desirable — I have that quality of virginity. Every time a man takes me it feels to him as if it's my very first time; it makes him feel so outrageous, so naughty, so triumphantly and impeccably male. Why don't you have me, you'll see what I mean.'

'Not just now,' I said. 'I want to hear more about you.' Wondering at the same time whether a penis and testicles might have such a thing as a ghost, and whether a live eunuch might couple with a dead sow by means of the ghost of a penis. Never in my life had there been so many sexual invitations as now when I was castrated.

'My sowhood,' said the sow, 'has not been like that of other

77

sows. I am fecund, I am fertile, but I have never farrowed. I have not multiplied, have not increased myself; my essential virtue is intact, I have not gone beyond the original limits of myself. Only men have known me, I have never felt upon me the rough and bristly weight of a boar.'

'How was that?' I said, remembering suddenly that it was probably she who had eaten the lost parts of me. There she was mincing beside me on her little trotters, looking at me sidelong from under her blonde eyelashes. The trickle of blood from her mouth and the red line round her throat made her seem a creature enslaved by lust.

'I seen to that,' said the peasant. He was a big man, dirty, tattered, patched, and unshaven. In his face was a darkness other than the dirt and beard. The darkness of his eye sockets was such that his eyes could not be distinctly seen. I thought of all the years of his life in which he had looked at the world from out of that darkness. 'I seen to that,' he said. 'I kept her safe. I made for her a harness with spikes on it. I knowed early on I weren't never going to have no wife, I knowed I'd have to provide for myself the best I could. I seen her when she were only a little thing and I fancied her.'

'Fancy!' said the sow with a snort. 'It was more than fancy, it was love; it was the same as what the high-born folk make songs about and play on lutes. Say it right out: it was love. Ah! what a little enchantress I was in those first days!'

'But you became a huntress,' I said. 'You became a smeller-out of Jews.'

'How that happened,' said the peasant, 'it were like this: it were three or four year back the spring crop failed and the autumn as well. We run out of grain and beans, we run out of everything. Bodwild here, I had to keep her hid or she'd have been ate sure. There been a little girl went missing from the next village and folk were saying one thing and another, most of them thought that girl been ate. Such things been heard of before and it were always Jews done it. Sacrifices, you see. They drunk them children's blood for their rituals. A dog in our village dug up some bones, they was from a human child.'

'There were folk in our village looking at my little Konrad and muttering this and that,' said Bodwild. 'He'd always lived alone and kept to himself. They knew we were in love and they begrudged us our happiness.'

'Like I said,' said Konrad, 'I had to keep Bodwild hid or she'd have been turning on someone's spit. I found a hole in amongst some big rocks it were in the wood by the common. I put some straw in there for her, I done my best to keep her comfortable. Mind you, I weren't too comfortable myself what with people pointing the finger at me like they was because of them bones and some said they seen me burning that little girl's clothes. There's always people will try to take away your good name but they couldn't prove nothing.'

'How well I remember that time!' said Bodwild. 'How well I remember a particular November evening: it was dusk, it was raining; I remember the smell of the rain on the dead leaves, I remember the smell of the damp straw. Suddenly there came a fresh smell: it was strong, it was sharp, it excited me, it made me want to nip and cuddle, it made me quiver with lust. There crept into the hole with me a man, such white skin he had, such black hair, such red cheeks!'

'He were a clipcock,' said Konrad. 'He were some kind of Jew magician, he had papers on him with that kind of secret writing they do. He weren't from our part of the country; some of them in our village they seen him sneaking through the wood and they begun to chase him.'

'It was his fear I smelt,' said Bodwild. 'So strong and sharp it was, almost like doppelkorn, almost like schnapps. It made me wild with desire. I kissed him and called him sweet names, I pressed close to him and offered myself, my pinkness and the sugar of me, I was like marzipan; who could refuse me?'

'They won't get near pork,' said Konrad, 'them children of darkness, them Jewish devils. They call up Asmodeus, they drink the blood of Christian children, they say the Lord's Prayer backwards, them Christ-killers. He pushed her away.'

'Me!' said Bodwild. 'He pushed *me* away. Men have paid good money to sleep with me, but he pushed me away.'

'They haven't paid money but they'd give me a sausage or maybe a chicken or some doppelkorn,' said Konrad.

'I was outraged,' said Bodwild. 'I had never been insulted like that, I wept bitterly.'

'She were squealing her head off,' said Konrad. 'I heard her half a mile away and I come running. We burnt the Jew that night, there were human child bones found in his pouch.'

'Clever little Konrad!' said Bodwild. 'It all worked out so well, everyone was satisfied. How he writhed and crackled in the flames, his bones cracked and the marrow boiled out. I remembered the smell of his fear as I saw him twisting in the flames, it was almost better than making love. Watching him burn I came again and again.'

'I had you under my cloak and I was playing with you,' said Konrad. 'I could feel how you loved it, how hot you were.'

'Did you smell the Jew's fear when he was burning?' I asked Bodwild.

'No,' she said, 'I had to remember it from before to call up my excitement. He was singing but that did nothing for me.'

'He were trying to save his self with his Jew magic what they call up devils with,' said Konrad. 'There's a spell they sing, it's called "Schemmah Yisrowail"; I've heard it often when I've caught Jews. They sing it when they're burning but it never puts out the fire.'

'Do you remember when you smelled me out?' I said to Bodwild. 'Do you remember when you told the others to castrate me?' I said to Konrad.

'I *thought* it were you!' said Konrad. 'I *thought* I remembered your ugly Jew face looking up at me when we had you spread out on the ground. Well, you won't be making no more little Jew brats, will you.'

Bodwild came close to me, nuzzling and sniffing me. At her touch I felt the ghost of an erection spring up, I felt myself rocking like a chip on the torrent of lust that flowed through the first Sophia, the second Sophia, and this sow with her scarlet necklace of blood. Even now as I have these words in my mind I am confused by the presence among them of my lost God, my remembered Christ. How I am flooded with the humming and the roaring of great waters, with the music of the great currents in which rock and dance the Great Mother, the Father, the Son, the Virgin and the Lion! Unseen! Chosen I am, chosen are my people to be the thrall of the multitudinous, of the humming and roaring unseen manyness that whirled the Jews like a bull-roarer round the head of its manifestation as YHWH, made of them a sounding of the unseeable, the unknowable, the utterly ungraspable. How it raged, that idea, when it was YHWH and the Jews whored after stocks and stones and golden calves! How it would not tolerate any limitation of form, of image, of substance! How the every-thingness of it commands every flash and glimmer of the mind, how all thoughts that ever were or ever will be run beneath its hand like sheep beneath the hand of the shepherd! Lion-sheep, star-sheep, ocean-sheep! '*Now* I remember you!' murmured Bodwild with her snout brushing my ear. 'Now I remember the smell of your fear, it was dark and full, it was like music and strong drink to me. I didn't smell it when I saw you in the inn yard just before you killed me; you had no fear then, I smelled nothing.'

'So it was the fear you smelled when you hunted Jews,' I said, 'it wasn't the Jewishness.'

'It's all the same,' said Konrad. 'When you're hunting Jews and you smell fear that'll be a Jew sure enough.'

'If they don't know you're hunting them they won't be afraid,' I said.

'They know that a time will come when they will be hunted,' said Bodwild; 'that was what I could always smell.'

'It doesn't seem to bother you any more that I'm a Jew,' I said.

'Everything seems different now that I'm dead,' she said. 'I feel as if I'm letting go of things. And I've told you I wanted to make love with that first Jew; I've wanted to make love with all of them but I've had to content myself with their dying. I'm just like anyone else, I take my pleasure where I can.'

'Here we're talking like old friends,' I said, 'and yet you must be full of rage because I killed you.'

'Why should I be full of rage more than you?' she said. 'I sniffed you out, they castrated you and I ate your male parts. So you killed me, that's reasonable. A little time one way or the other, it seems a big thing when you're alive but when you're dead you wonder what all the fuss was about. When I was alive we hunted you down; now we're dead and you're alive and already we're friends. Very soon you'll be dead also and you too will wonder why it ever mattered so much who was what and who did what.'

'And you?' I said to Konrad. 'You were the master of this sow, it was you who used her to sniff out the Jews that you tortured and killed. What have you to say for yourself?'

'What have I to say for myself?' said Konrad. 'You lousy Jew eunuch with your soft white hands, in your whole life you probably never done nothing heavier than count your money. You're all usurers, the whole filthy lot of you, trying to get the whole world in your pocket. Knights going to Jerusalem, they have to pawn their castles to you. Many's the Christian lady you've crept into bed with, I'll bet, and her lawful husband gone to fight the heathen. Not that it don't serve them right, they're nothing but thieves and murderers and their foot on the neck of the poor from the time we're born till the time we die. Look at my hands next to yours, eh? Mine are more like hooves, ain't they. They're that hard. Here I am dead from your Jew magic and how much did I ever have in these hands. Tools to work another man's land with mostly. Heavy soil and a heavy plough and a six-ox team, you probably wouldn't have the strength in them white hands of yours to turn a plough like that. How much Christian blood have you drunk?'

'I wonder what makes Christians think that anybody would want to drink their blood,' I said.

'If you don't drink it you do other things with it,' said Konrad. 'Everybody knows about Jew magic.'

'You're a Christian, are you?' I said.

'What else would I be, you Jew Antichrist-worshipper,' he said, 'I been baptized, haven't I.'

'And died with your sins heavy on you,' I said. 'Died all unshriven.'

'What difference does that make,' he said. 'I ain't burning in Hell nor nothing like that, am I.'

'Maybe your Hell will be to walk to Jerusalem with the Jew you castrated,' I said.

'Whatever I have to do,' he said, 'I'll do it like a man, I've nothing to fear. It's yourself you'd better be worrying about; the Last Days are coming and then you'll see what burning is. There's been signs in the sky, you know — great flaming clouds in the shape of Christ with a sword in his hand fighting the Jewish Antichrist with three heads and seven horns.'

'Who won?' I said.

'You'll see soon enough, clipcock,' he said. 'I forgot, you ain't even that no more, you're a no-cock clipcock.'

'I'm so sorry you're dead,' I said. 'It's a great loss to me that you could only die once; it would be such a pleasure to kill you.' Thinking, as I said it, that these dead ones were already like a family to me.

'It means nothing at all,' said the bear, 'whatever you see in the sky.' The arrows that had killed him were still in him, they nodded as he walked upright with the others. 'There's been a Great Bear in the sky all these years and even a Lesser Bear as well and nothing's come of it, nothing at all.'

'Did you think anything would come of it?' I said.

'Of course not,' he said. 'Why should I. You can see anything you like in the sky, anything at all. And what it means is anything at all.'

'That man who killed you,' I said. 'What do you think he's doing now?'

'He's looking for another bear,' said the bear. 'He's hopeless, he's incapable of learning.'

'You think you're quite the thing, don't you,' said Udo the relic-gatherer to the bear. 'You think you're better than us. I seen you slipping through the woods now and again when you been alive. You wouldn't say nothing to us then, you wouldn't stop and pass the time of day, you were too good for us.'

'If I'd stopped you'd have shot me full of arrows,' said the bear.

'Yes I would,' said Udo. 'Yes I would just *because* you wouldn't stop and talk. If you'd talked with me we could have been friends, you could have showed me where the honey trees were.'

'Another one,' said the bear.

'Don't take that tone with me,' said Udo. 'How much honey have you had in your life and how much have I had in mine?'

'Whatever I've had I've found for myself,' said the bear.

'Oh yes,' said Udo. 'Naturally. The wood is your village, isn't it. So you know where to find things the same as I did in my village. If you'd come to my village looking for the well or the inn or whatever I'd have shown you where to find it, I'd have had time to stop and talk, wouldn't I. But when I come to your wood a runaway and a stranger trying to stay uncaught for my year and a day it's not a word from you I get, is it. It's nothing, nothing, nothing I get from everybody. The lord and his lot they treat you like an animal till you run off and you think at least if the animals will treat you like an animal that's not so bad, you'll be a brother to them. But they won't, they turn their backs on you. Die, serf! Die, slave! Into the ground with you and give the maggots what they're waiting for.'

'Excuse me,' said the headless tax-collector. A thrill ran through me when I heard his voice, the voice of my brother in Sophia, the voice of my brother pilgrim whose temple I had destroyed, whose world I had blackened and made empty. These new colleagues of mine, these dead men and animals, all of them appeared to me as I had last seen them. So the tax-collector was of course naked and headless and writhing with the terrible swift energy of the maggots that continually consumed him but never diminished his dreadful corpse. I couldn't bear to look at him but my eyes were again and again magnetically drawn to the horror of him while in my mouth I tasted writhing maggots.

'Excuse me,' said the tax-collector to Udo. 'I don't want to offend a respectable murderer but when you talk of giving the maggots what they're waiting for, then I really must say something, I really must put in a word, must mention that you were eager enough to give me to the maggots. You seem to feel very sorry for yourself but you didn't feel sorry for me when you caught me with your wire and took my head off with your sword.'

'That were business,' said Udo. 'I never wished you nothing ill. Anyhow what's one pilgrim more or less; you've died on the road but here's Herr Keinpimmel will go to Jerusalem for you; he'll make the journey for you and say however many prayers you like. So there's nothing lost, you've give the world up for Jesus and I say well done and Amen.'

'Ah, yes,' said the tax-collector. 'My good friend Herr Keinpimmel, the illustrious Jew adulterer. The one takes my wife and the other takes my life. And my head will bear the name of that one who washed his hands and said that he was innocent of

84

the blood of Christ. What more could I ask for? I am happy, I am content to dance with the maggots until . . . '

'Judgment Day?' I said. I couldn't keep silence, I had to speak to his absent face, I had to look at where his face would have been if he had had a head.

'Ah!' he said, 'At last! The first words spoken by you to me! And it is the Day of Judgment about which you speak to me. It is with this thought, this question, that you break your silence. You cannot look me in the eye because my head is elsewhere but I think that even if my head were here you might not be able to look me in the eye, isn't that so?'

'Yes,' I said, 'that's true enough. But might not you also find it difficult to look me in the eye? Me and a few other Jews who lost their lives to the soldiers of Christ.'

'I have already begged your forgiveness, have I not,' said the tax-collector. 'In front of your synagogue under the open sky in the sight of God have I humbled myself to the Jews.'

'We were under the open sky because there was no roof to stand under,' I said. 'The synagogue had been burnt to the ground, and there were many Jews who could not attend because they were busy dancing with the maggots.'

'Forgive me,' he said. 'Please, please forgive me. I would do it again if I had the chance.'

'Do what?' I said.

'What I did,' he said.

'Ah!' I said, 'Do you now tell me that you brought those peasants to our town?'

'Naturally I did,' he said. 'How was I not to do it?'

'It was because of you that there were all those dead Jews on the cobblestones!' I said, listening with dread and with fascination for the words that I knew must come next.

'Indeed,' he said. 'Because of me and because of you.'

Hearing this I found that my throat was affected in such a way that I could not swallow. My mouth was so dry, my tongue so thick that I could scarcely speak. 'Because of what I did,' I said.

'Yes,' he said. 'You are that Jew who finished me off. You are the last in a long succession of Jews who took away my life. Do you shake your head? No, you don't, you know what I'm

85

talking about. I was already dead some little while before this lout here took my head off, dead and Jew-killed. I saw you hanging about in the Keinjudenstrasse, I knew what was in your mind, I knew what would happen when I rode away. I made my arrangements, and once you were on that ladder death was on its way to the Jews of our town.'

'Why the others?' I said. 'Why didn't you just kill me?'

'Killing you alone wouldn't have been enough,' he said. 'Did you think you were the only one? There were always Jews, they were like owls that one hears calling in the dark: one close by, one farther away; you never see them but they know where you are. They smelt out Sophia the way Bodwild smelt you out, they smelt her lust and her appetite for the other, for the circumcised, for the lurking Jew. Could you possibly have thought you were the first one?'

Looking at that headless mass of maggots I felt the stare of his absent eyes, I began to see in the empty air the eyes of the dead man, his desperate eyes looking into my desperate eyes. 'Yes,' I said, 'I thought that I was the first one.'

'You weren't,' he said. 'I could smell them always, smell them on her skin and on the silk she wore next to her skin, I could smell them in the bedclothes and in the folds of curtains, I could smell them in the passages of my house. They required no words, she and they, they made their wants known without language, like animals that go on all fours. Only a look, only a smell and they followed, like dogs running to mount a bitch in heat. A bitch in heat or a wild ass:

'A wild ass used to the wilderness,
That snuffeth up the wind in her desire;
Her lust, who can hinder it?
All they that seek her will not weary themselves;
In her month they shall find her.'

That desperate man with no head had found the right words, the words that with a rush made Sophia freshly real in my mind, the desert animalness of her in the hidden flesh, the covered nakedness. Gone from me for ever, I knew that I was never to see her again. For a moment the loss of her closed in upon me so crushingly that I thought I might kill myself on the spot; it seemed all at once that there was no space, no time for me to live in. Yet here before me was her husband: he too had lost her and death had given him no rest; the memory of her was a wheel on which he was broken again and again. When was there an end of pain, I wondered. Never. The cup was golden and it would not pass from me. While I was alive I should have to drink it empty and when I was dead it would be there to drink afresh. And still I drink it now, newly bitter after all the centuries. But the pain is the life, the pain is what separates the animate from the inanimate, the human from the stone. What is human may long for the stone of its innocence, the stone of its ease, of no pain; but the pain is the life. Even after death the pain is the life. This pain is not a simple one, it is complex.

Was there pain before there was a world? Was the world brought forth in pain? Yes, I am sure of this, I am convinced that it is so. What knowledge can there be of this? As these words come on to the paper by way of what goes by the name of Pilgermann I note that theoretical science has worked its way back deductively to the very first moments of the universe and the bursting forth of everything from the time-space singularity which had contained it just before that moment. All of this is imprinted on the waves and particles of me, it is in the mystical black letters that rise above all flames, it is the Word that is at once the birth-scream and the death-cry of the cosmic animal that is God, the It that is both creator and created. How should there not be pain? One has only to listen to music run backwards to sense the reversing cycles of consummation and creation, the continual ordering and re-ordering of the disturbance that is the endless idea that continually thinks itself into and out of the manyness of its being.

It is not from the loss of Sophia, the loss of Christ and the loss of God as He that the pain comes, no. It is from the pain that God comes, that Christ with his lion-eyes comes, that Sophia in all her beauty, her splendour, and her passion comes. It is from the cosmic intolerable of the nothing-in-everything alternating with the everything-in-nothing that all things come. This great pain, this ur-pain, swims its monstrous bulk in deeps far down, down, down below that agony of loss in which I grind my teeth remembering the golden bell of Sophia's nakedness and the sharpness of the knife of joy.

Knife of joy. At this thought almost do the waves and particles of me laugh. Perhaps this almost-laugh is seen somewhere as the shaking of a leaf in the evening wind, the shaking of a leaf seen in the light of a street lamp under a humpbacked moon in a modern place where the few trees speak to the dry stone. 'Knife of joy,' I said, and immediately there came to mind the knife of unjoy, the knife that drew the line for me. Now of course I know what I did not know then: I know that the pain waits in the joy as the dragonfly waits in the nymph. Almost I sense that the joy, as the nymph to the dragonfly, is a necessary stage in the development of the pain.

With my dead colleagues I was on the road to Jerusalem: with the sow Bodwild and her peasant master Konrad; with the bear shot full of arrows by his worshipper; with Udo the relic-gatherer; with the tax-collector the husband of Sophia, and with us was Bruder Pförtner in his appearances and his disappearances. And now I became aware of perhaps someone else, it was only the faintest light and shadow as it were sketched on the air, a ghostly chiaroscuro walking familiarly with the rest of us as if by right. This sketchy figure was in truth familiar, uncertain of feature as it was: it was immediately recognizable to me as an early state of my death. I felt drawn to it as a father to a son. This simulacrum was in no way childlike, it was a fully-grown duplicate of me but not yet fully defined, not yet fully realized, and therefore it was to me as a child to be looked after.

Child! Looking at my immature death, feeling protective towards it as if it were my son, I found myself thinking: What if Sophia and I have made a child! What if in her womb is growing new life from our sin, our adultery, our triumph! I laughed aloud as this thought leapt up in me. I looked sidewise at the tax-collector, my brother in Sophia. 'In her month they shall find her,' I said.

Strange, talking to a headless dead man. No face to look at, but from somewhere he was staring at me hard. 'Judgment Day,' he said. 'You spoke of it just a little while ago. You must know in your heart, as I knew in my heart while I was alive, that the Day of Judgment is the only day there is. In our mortal life we play at dividing this one everlasting day into many tiny days and we say, "Tomorrow I shall perhaps do better." But there is only this one day in which we live our whole lives and from which we fade as consciousness fades. It is where I am now but in a little while I shall fade out of it and be gone while you for as long as you live must remain in it.'

'Is that why you told those peasants to let me live?' I said. 'So that I could suffer it continually?'

'I told them to let you live because I felt myself judged in that moment when I looked down at you lying in your blood and vomit,' he said.

We said nothing more. Bruder Pförtner was with us again, he was walking close beside my young death and fondling it from time to time.

Walking the road to Jerusalem I find myself weeping. This is because my mind has shown me a connexion that it was just beginning to perceive when I was leaning against the tree in the little dark wood after I killed Udo the relic-gatherer. It was then that there came into my mind the great dome that I had never seen, the dome of Hagia Sophia in Constantinople. Ah! now as I walk I know that there is no separateness in the world, I know that the souls of things and the souls of people are inextricably commingled; I know that the dome and the woman both are manifestations of something elemental that is both beauty and wisdom and it is for ever in danger, for ever being lost, torn out of our hands, violated. It is impossible to keep it safe. That heaven shapen by human hands, that blue dome hung with lights and lustres, starred with flames and dim with incense, that spirit-bowl, that God-mother and Mother Goddess, that Wisdom of stone and gold, how should it not be violated, how should rough hands not be laid upon it, how should the holy silence not be broken by the thudding of hooves, how should war horses not be ridden up to that altar, how should the altar not be smashed? Altars are made for smashing. That thing in us that waits to jump up and smash, it stands looking over our shoulder as we build the altar. It rages, it smiles, it laughs deep in its belly, it dances on cloven hooves at the consecration of the altar, it looks ahead to the time of the smashing. More, more is

89

there in this: that of which the dome is a visible aspect, the great Wisdom, golden Wisdom itself, is the mother of both the altar and the thing that smashes the altar. The Wisdom in its wisdom thus provides that beauty and wisdom shall never be within our grasp, shall only be a light upon our eyes and passing.

Passing, passing! *Echah*! O how! O how is the beauty passing, how is it departed, gone, gone! It is gone because the Wisdom in its wisdom has ordained that beauty is that which passes, it is that which will not stay; beauty is a continual departing, a continual going away. Sophia is one with the dome in my mind that arches over me like the Egyptian sky goddess arching over her earth-god brother who penetrates her and must be separated from her.

In the making of Sophia's beauty was the violation of it by separation, by departure, by shouts of impiety under the great dome of it, by the castration of its consort and the beheading of its protector. The great dome echoes with the clatter and the clamour of the horsemen, with the smashing of the altar, the tearing of the silken hangings. Listen, listen to the trampling of impious feet on sacred books, listen to this trampling that is the most constant road in history, the trampling of murderous feet on sacred books. In the writing, in the copying, in the binding of the books, in the very ink and paper, in the blood and bones of the original writer and in the blood and bones of every copyist thereafter lives coevally the trampler and the burner of the books of God and the God of books, lives the trampler and the burner of books and people, of beauty and domes.

I am on the road to Jerusalem with my dead colleagues, with Bruder Pförtner, with my death that is not yet ripened to term. The year is 1096 in the Christian calendar, *Anno Mundi* 4857, two thousand, four hundred and eight years since Moses brought down from the mountain the second tablets on the tenth day of Tishri. It will not be until A.D. 1204 that violent men mouthing Christ will sail from Venice to sack Constantinople. In the adzes and hammers of Venetian shipwrights not yet born, in their blood and bones, in the blood and bones of their mothers who will bear them waits to be born the sack of Constantinople and the fall of an emperor unborn, and all of this is under the dome of that Sophia who is or is not carrying my child, that Sophia who revealed her nakedness to me, gave it splendidly and lavishly to me, that Sophia, that nakedness that I shall no more see. *Echah!*

The above is my *kina*, my dirge, my lament that is suddenly in my mind as I recall walking with my colleagues on the road to Jerusalem. In my mind at the end of my lament on the inseparability of Sophia and Hagia Sophia is another thought: the enemy matters nothing; truly it is not the apparent enemy that sacks Constantinople, it is that which crouches always at the feet of beauty and in its season leaps up to destroy. It is the impulse that leaps up, and it gathers to itself whoever comes to hand whether it be Christians or Muslims; it clothes itself with whatever costume it finds. The fall of Constantinople that begins in 1204 with the French and the Flemings is consummated by the Turks in 1453; what is required is not that a particular enemy shall attack the dome, only that by sword and fire beauty shall be brought low, only that the holy books shall be trampled. *Echah!*

9

Now must I begin to speak of war, now must I make ready for dust and blood, for the smoke and flame of siege and battle, for the ringing of dinted iron, the quivering of severed limbs. Now must I see in my mind the secret colours of entrails sliding from the opened bellies of warriors while their eyes look down in disbelief. Now must I see Bruder Pförtner and his ready companions making sport while swords clang and arrows hiss all round them; now must I hear them screaming in their pleasure as they have the tumbling of heroes Christian and Muslim both.

What a ponderous labour is war, what preparations must be made years and years before the first blow is struck! Decades before the first battle must the first engines of war be brought into play: the first engines of war are men and women, they are the hammer and the anvil that in the heat of their action make soldiers. In order that the dead may be heaped on the walls and roofs and in the streets and houses of Jerusalem in 1099 there must be heavy coupling from about 1060 onwards among Christians and Muslims both. For the making of each soldier must a man and a woman labour in their lust, for the making of each soldier must an egg and a sperm conjoin to write their word of flesh, must a woman carry that word for nine months until her great-grown belly fulfils its term and is delivered of a man-child. Then must the boy be given suck, must he be kept alive to grow strong and active, must he be led safely past the ills of infancy and the perils of childhood to the day when he can take in his hands the weapons of war and go out to the place of killing.

Fields of grain and vegetables, herds of cattle must be grown to feed these ripening warriors. Wool of sheep, thread of flax, fur of fox and rabbit, hide of cattle must be grown to clothe and shoe the soldiers of Christ and Muhammad, and for this the sheep, the foxes and the rabbits, and the cattle must also couple tirelessly while the earth grows the sown seed in its belly. What chance would Mars have without the help of Venus? What hard breathing, what amorous sighing, what grunts of ardour and cries of joy sound in the gathered darkness of those soldier-making, soldier-feeding, soldier-clothing, soldier-shoeing nights!

And the arming of them! While these boys ripen like peaches on the tree of war there are heard, first here, then there, then everywhere the clink of hammers and the windy breath of bellows. All through the Christian world and all through Islam rise and fall the brawny arms of smiths beating out the passing moments into days and weeks and years of swords, spearheads and arrowheads, lances, pikes, maces, axes, mail shirts and iron helmets, spurs, stirrups, bits, and horseshoes. Hammers and anvils of flesh, hammers and anvils of iron striking the years! Fires of war in forges east and west, their red coals purring! Red-hot iron, red-hot steel and a leaping up of golden sparks under the hammer blows! Hungry iron, hungry steel, hungering for flesh!

And I too, Pilgermann! I too, with prayer-shawl, with fringes and phylacteries, with books and surgical instruments, I too have been ripening on this tree of war. But I am wrong to say 'tree of war'; if one speaks of trees then there is only one tree: of war and peace and everything else; not only do soldiers ripen on it but all who live in this world; it is a wondrous tree and it bears different fruits in different seasons to be shaken down by the winds of necessity, plucked by the hand of circumstance. The dead Jews on the cobblestones before the synagogue, the dead girl with her skirt over her face, they too have grown on this same tree with the soldier-fruits. And my Sophias first and second. And these dead who walk with me. And my own young death as well. How difficult it is to speak of any single thing — one takes notice of a stone at the foot of a mountain, steps back to look at the mountain, walks far enough away to see the top of it, climbs another mountain to see the plain beyond the first one, and little by little widening the view sees from a very long way off our little cloud-wreathed planet swimming in the sea of space, and it is only one thing after all.

Stones! When the hammers are heard on the anvils of war the stones will not be found unready; they will come to hand equally for those who besiege and those who defend. Built up into strong walls they await the rumble of the seige tower, the shock of the ram, the crash of the stone that comes whistling from the mangonel. War sets one stone against another, calls this one a missile, that one a stronghold. But the freemasonry of the stones is stronger than the temporary loyalties imposed on them; they do what is required of them but in their hardness they retain their one essential fact: they know that they are all one thing. What do the stones say? 'We have no enemy.' This I have not read in a book, this I have heard them say and I know it to be true. Muslims build them up and Christians knock them down or Christians build them up and Muslims knock them down; war and peace and the passage of what is called time shake and throw them like dice and in the throws read winning and losing. But the stones of Jerusalem laughed when the Temple was destroyed. 'Full quittance!' they shouted. 'Full quittance for the sins of the Jews!'

And what were the sins of the Jews? The graven images, the idols, the high places, the Baalim and the Ashtaroth, the adulteries of spirit and of flesh. And why did God rage so because of these acts, why were they not to be tolerated by Him? Because the insult was too monstrous to be borne. Because He had chosen the Jews for His vessel, He had chosen them to be the ark of the idea of Him and of It, the idea of the Unseen, the Ungraspable, the Unknowable, the idea never to be contained by the mind that is contained by it. He had chosen them to be mind-heroes, to open their minds to the idea that could not be held by any mind, and what did they do? They fouled themselves, they rolled in the dung and the degradation of the seeable, the knowable, the ordinary. They said to stocks and stones, 'Be thou our God.'

I do not forget thee, O Jerusalem. But what is Jerusalem but the seeable and the knowable? What is Jerusalem but the stones that have no enemy? The stones on which Christ walked, the stones over which he dragged his cross, the stones of that Western Wall that alone remain of the Second Temple, are they to be held sacred, are they to fill the eye with the seen? It is the Jerusalem of the heart that must not be forgotten because in the Jerusalem of the heart is the heart of the mystery where lives the idea of the Unknowable that is God.

I say that now when I have been dead for centuries, I say it now that I am more or less full-grown. But in this time that I have been speaking of, in this time called A.D. 1096 when I trudged my road to Jerusalem I was going to a Jerusalem that lived in my mind as coarsely painted and as vividly coloured as an inn sign, a Jerusalem of blazing eastern sun and buzzing flies, of awninged blue-shadowed bazaars in the narrow streets walled in by tawny stone far, far away at the end of many days, many nights of perilous roads and long dusty approaches. When I thought of the gates of Jerusalem I thought of sunlight dazzling in its white brilliance, I thought of blue and purple shadows among which had moved the shadow of the very hand of God, a *seen* shadow. And it was a seen Christ that I was travelling towards, a Christ who had already appeared to me and had spoken to me.

Now help me, Memory! Let me find again that road of youth and pain, let me hear again the tramp of thousands to Jerusalem:

> Thy dead shall live, my dead bodies shall arise —
> Awake and sing, ye that dwell in the dust —
> For Thy dew is as the dew of light,
> And the earth shall bring to life the shades.

Marzipan. Manticore. Mazery. Manzikert. Manzikert, yes. And the name of that pope isn't Unguent VII, it's Urban II. But I was saying Manzikert. Nobody can deny that after the Battle of Manzikert in 1071 Byzantium was no longer what it had been. The Emperor Romanus, taken prisoner at Manzikert, was blinded; and it was a Jew who was forced to perform this office. I hear the voices of Romanus and his Jewish executioner mingled in a constant faint murmur barely audible among the stronger transmissions in the hum and crackle, the roar and whine and whistle of the cosmos; it's astonishing how many individual voices can be distinguished in what one would think of as a general uproar.

Any sequence of events is interesting because of its positive and negative shapes. Take a pair of scissors and cut something out. Anything. Why not a devil with horns and a tail and cloven hooves. So. There is your paper with a devil-shaped hole in it. Two devil-shapes, one positive, one negative, and both of them made at the very same moment. Was the Battle of Manzikert the shape of the paper or the shape of the hole? It's as I've said before: there is always a twoness in the oneness, and for this reason it's almost impossible to know what is happening in the space-time configuration. Not only that: as soon as an effort is made to look at any particular thing the aspect of that thing becomes other than what it was — that event that happened in full view when unlooked-at covers itself when observed, spins around itself one of those wonderful encrusted eggs with a peephole in one end of it; I the observer, receding reactively from the gaze that proceeds from my eyes, find myself shot into the distance thousands of miles away from the peephole. Inch by inch I think my way back; closer, closer, closer I come and here it is all tiny — the tiny, tiny Battle of Manzikert. Closer still and I am in the dust and the trampling of it, hearing the grunts and the shouts of the living and the sighs of the dying.

How nothing is simply one thing! There comes to mind unaccountably an order of the day from Jenghis Khan to his horsemen at some distance from 1071, a century or two perhaps. In this order he commands his men to leave their horses unbridled on the march — they are to have their mouths free, they are not to be galloped on the march.

Where was I when the Battle of Manzikert was fought in 1071, *Anno Mundi* 4831 in the Jewish calendar? That was the year of my birth; on some frequency still sounds my birth-cry in the hum and crackle, the roar and whine and whistle where lives the mingled murmur of Romanus and his Jewish executioner. Questions arise continually, everything must be kept in mind at once — at least one must try, must do one's best. Because everything is with us. Even now the fading heat of the universe's explosion into being warms the deeps of space, still it fades there, the echo of that first blind bursting shout of beginning. I note that everything that has ever happened is imprinted on me. I can feel it even though I cannot by my own volition recall most of it. With the bursting of the original explosion in me I am again in the year 1096, moving with the many, moving with the thousands towards the fall of Jerusalem, that golden city that I never lived to see. The fall of Jerusalem is at the centre of its space-time; the centre of anything is the centre of everything; how may it be looked at? Could the siege of Jerusalem have been painted by Vermeer? Can such a thing be looked at in such a way? Can the sunlight on mail shirts and blood and severed limbs be looked at as one looks at the daylight from a neat Dutch window in which a quiet woman weighs gold? A better painting to think of is the 'Head of a Young Girl': the look that looks out from the face of that young beauty, such asking is there in that look! 'Are you love? Are you death? Are you the beginning of everything, are you the end?' Not only does this young girl with her look see all of these but all of these look out at us from her face.

And the look with which Vermeer looked upon her face, that is the look with which everything must be seen; yes, even the severed limbs. Everything that is, everything that happens must be seen with the eye that is in love with seeing. All must be seen with a willing look. From the face of Vermeer's young girl looks out at us the heart of the mystery, the moving stillness in which again and again explodes, in which even now at this very moment explodes the beginning of all things. From her eyes the unseen looks out at us, and through our eyes looking back into hers also looks the unseen.

This unseen that sometimes we call God, has it a purpose or a destiny? What is its present work? Elephants, whales, mice, cockroaches, humans — from a single cell of any of them can be made the whole creature complete; there is in the cell that reservoir of potentiality. With what we call time the potentiality is unlimited: each moment has in it the matrix of all moments, the possibility of all action. Is it God's destiny to turn the wheel until every potentiality has become an actuality? For this has God come to hate the world? For this does God weep and curse continually as the wheel turns and there approach him over and over again popes, Jews, warriors, idiots, kings, queens, beggars, lepers, lions, dogs, and monkeys, each busy with its tiny mortal history and each tiny mortal history different from all the others. Even if each one were to try to live out that history exactly the same as the one before it can't be done; variations and permutations will always come into it.

Will there ever be an end to it all, is the end one of the possibilities? God doesn't know. God created all the possibilities of variation and permutation but he cannot calculate them. How can this be? Is not God omniscient and omnipotent? Yes, and being so he was able to conceive and create possibilities beyond his understanding and beyond his capability to deal with as agent, as doer. If he were not able to do this he would be less than all-powerful. There is of course a paradox here: if God has not the power to understand everything he is not omniscient, and equally if he has not the power to create something beyond his understanding he is not omnipotent. It is my belief that God is of an artistic temperament and has therefore chosen to let his own work be beyond his understanding; I think this may well be why he has abandoned the He identity and has moved into the It where he is both subject and object, the doer and the done. God is no longer available to receive or transmit personal messages; he has been absorbed into process and toils ignorantly at the wheel with the rest of us.

In this general process some potential actions are actualized, some not. In the channel of action where I moved with the thousands towards Jerusalem there moved also the unlived action of earlier popes who were unsuccessful in their attempts at what is now called a Crusade, *Kreuzzug* in German. The most direct translation of this word is Cross-pull, and indeed the Cross did exert a pull. Pope Sergius IV in 1011, Leo IX in 1053, Gregory VII in 1074 had tried but had not been able to set these thousands moving towards Jerusalem. Time after time had violent men sharpened the cross into a sword and made their silken vestments into banners; time after time had they spat out the wafer and the wine and shouted for real blood and real bodies. Again and again had this moment tried to come into being; blown out each time like a candle its light sprang up again whenever any flame approached the smoking wick.

Looking at it all from where I am now, looking at faraway events from this great distance I see them as if jumbled together or dancing in a ring, unseparated by time: Crusades, plagues, massacres of Jews, dancing madness, peasant revolts — a dance of life and a dance of death. A dance of life that spins itself into death like gold being spun into straw. Life cannot tolerate itself, life wants to become death. Almost one might say that the function of life is to manifest death. Perhaps death is the gold, life the straw. Death is the natural expression of life. See the swift and fluent dance of maggots in a dead mouse, such a relief, as when a smoking log bursts into flame. And of course it was in my country that the Dancing Madness arose, following hot on the heels of the Black Death which followed on the Crusades.

Because of what happened, because of what was done in the name of Christ, Jerusalem ceased to exist. What remained was not Jerusalem, it was an image fixed on a dead retina. An image retained on the dead retina of an idea. An idea is an eye given by God for the seeing of God. Some of these eyes we cannot bear to look out of, we blind them as quickly as possible.

I must be more precise: Jerusalem has not ceased to exist any more than bread has ceased to exist; the bread that has been eaten is gone, now there is more bread. The Jerusalem that was is gone, now there is more Jerusalem, other Jerusalem. One assumes that the world simply is and is and is but it isn't, it is like music that we hear a moment at a time and put together in our heads. But this music, unlike other music, cannot be performed again.

With the ear of the mind I hear the army of the Franks on the march, I hear the massed clinking of their tread, I hear the horses snort and whinny, the rattling of leaves of iron. With the eye of the mind I see spokes of sunlight revolving through marching figures, I see the night gleam of armour, I see the Orontes River. As I recall life now I sometimes think of it as a sort of raisin-cake with vast distances between the raisins. As I send the idea of my being questing back it is from raisin to raisin that it makes its way, like the line connecting the dots that make the constellations of the Virgin and the Lion on the star charts.

Or the route of the Franks across plains and mountains as they headed, with the harmless migrant storks high above them, for the water-crossing at the Bosporus. The line seeks the image, it smells out the image-making dots as a salmon returning from the sea smells out the river of its birth, swims upstream, spawns and dies. So with the line: it swims upstream, spawns a dot, and dies. The action of the spawning and the death make a dot; what was smelled was the place wanting the dot. Why did the place want a dot, how could a place want a dot, what was the need of the place, whose need? The line's? The place's? God's?

No. We assume always too much, we assume what cannot be assumed. We see dots so we connect them with lines and we claim to know what the lines and dots signify. There is a marching, there is a galloping, there is a hissing of arrows, a clashing of swords; or it may be that there is simply a stretching forth of the neck to the sword, there is a wrapping in the Torah scroll, there is a burning alive and we assume (always the assumptions) that these things are happening to different people. We assume that the Frank is distinct from the Jew who is distinct from the Turk but I cannot now think of it as being like that. It seems to me now that that busy line, that motion in the circuitry, did not leap from one dot to another: from the leap of its original impulse its being continued on its way to flash into Christian, Jew, Muslim, fortresses, rivers, dawns, full moons, battles, crows, the wind in the trees, anything you like. Mountains in the dawn; the shock of Thing-in-Itself, the enormity of Now. So it is that although my being is in one way or another continuous I cannot present to you Pilgermann as continuous, only flashes here and there.

How there are vortices in the space-time! My mind keeps spinning down to Manzikert where in actuality I as Pilgermann never have been. It was one of the big dots, one of the juicier raisins. The dust! So much dust stirred up by those hooves, by those feet that trampled out, that trod the grapes of mortality into the wine of history for the Byzantine Empire. Wine! Wine and dust at the same time, at the same time the hot and dry and the cold and wet.

No. Not Manzikert. I mean to tell of Antioch. Yes, where the walls undulated like a serpent on the mountains, where the four hundred towers waited for the line to flash into a dot. Four hundred towers!

Before Antioch there were the Anti-Taurus Mountains. Perhaps I was not a Jew then, because I remember the heat and the weight of the mail shirt that rusted the skin and chafed the body bloody, I remember the donkeys plunging over the edge roped one to the other, the black letters of their braying frozen in the silence of their deaths.

10

'Now help me, Memory!' Only a little space from here have I heard myself speak these words. But as the words and pictures of my thoughts go out on those few millimetres of waveband assigned to me I begin to understand that I myself am a tiny particle of Memory. I am a microscopic chip in that vast circuitry in which are recorded all of the variations and permutations thus far. Not all of my experience is available for recall by my Pilgermann identity, only that in which the energy of the input was above a certain level. Thus it is that I can at any time call up that veiled owl to whom I said, 'Hear, O Israel!' but most of my education is lost to me.

Like any parent I wanted the best for my death, I remember that well. Walking beside me he was scarcely more visible than breath on glass but the manifestation of him was continually more detailed and refined although his face was obscure. He was not as yet ready to speak, perhaps he never would speak, but he looked at me with a look that said plainly, 'I know that I can trust you to do the right thing.' I nodded with a false heartiness, trying to look reliable. When the time came I did the best I could. I don't know where he is now, I don't know what's become of him. One does what one can; the rest is a matter of luck and chance.

My recall is offering me Antioch but the last dot was still in Germany. How did I get to Antioch? Pirates. I was on a ship from Genoa bound for Jaffa when they appeared. Even now I must smile when I see with the eye of the mind the hungry triangle of that red sail cleaving the white dazzle of the sunlight on the dark blue sea. Larger, larger and more and more urgent it becomes and I smile because there is no surprise in it, perhaps even I am not unwilling that this should happen.

When I came down to Genoa out of the north there was the sea dividing with its horizon the picture in my eyes. Everything on this side of the horizon was in the world of HERE, everything beyond it was THERE. Here was a fresh and salty breeze from the sea, here were the clustered masts nodding in the harbour and the gulls soaring, circling, crying, crying, 'Where are you going, Herr Keinpimmel? What is Jerusalem, that you should go from HERE to THERE?' This of course was the voice of the Mittelteufel, the halfway devil; I came to know it later but at that time I had not yet learned to recognize it. I was suddenly cowed by the overwhelming and undeniable reality of the sea, I was reduced to nothing by the objectivity of the gulls, I could not think why I wanted to go anywhere or do anything. In that particular Now that comes just before one embarks only the sea seemed real; not Christ; not God; not sin. I looked round for Bodwild and Konrad, for the bear, for Udo, for the tax-collector and my young death and Bruder Pförtner. There was no one, I was utterly alone.

In front of me stood a fat brown-faced shipmaster with a gold circlet in one ear, a look of contempt on his face, and his palm outstretched. He looked as if he might, after taking their money, chop one lot of pilgrims into pieces and salt them away in barrels for the feeding of the next lot. Behind him were the sea and the circling gulls and his ship tied up at the quay. The ship was a wallowing-shaped thing with its brown sail furled on the yard and its deck all a-clutter with wineskins, bales and bundles, chickens, pigs, and goats. I looked to see what the name of it was: *Balena, Whale.* 'If this ship is a whale,' I said to the master in Italian (I had studied medicine in Salerno), 'I hope that doesn't make me ... '

The master laid his finger across his lips. 'Don't say it,' he said. 'Bad luck.'

I paid him fifty ducats and abandoned all hope. That is, I thought that I had abandoned all hope until I went below decks and smelled the smell there; then I found that there was yet more hope to abandon. I paid five more ducats to be allowed to sleep on deck with the chickens and the pigs and the goats.

When it was time to sail the seamen all lurched aboard fit for nothing but vomiting and sleeping. Some did one, some did both. When woken up to raise the sail and haul up the anchor they all began to sing. Their singing had that peculiar falseness sometimes heard in the choruses of provincial opera companies; it made one lose all confidence in any kind of human effort whatever; it made one doubt that the ship, the anchor, the ocean or indeed the world was real. The ocean proved to be real enough and the ship wallowed in it in a way that was sickening as only reality can be.

So it was that when that red sail appeared three days out I nodded with a sense of the fitness of things. Clearly such a ship as that *Balena*, such a master as that one, and such a crew as that crew had never been meant, in the general design of things, to move a load of pilgrims from an unholy to a Holy Land. There were about fifty pilgrims on board, and when some of the more experienced ones said that they thought the fast-moving red sail might be pirates we all asked the master for weapons with which to defend ourselves and the ship. 'Softly, softly, good sirs,' he said. 'Be tranquil, there's no use pissing into the wind.' The crew then produced swords, pikes, and clubs and herded us into the after part of the ship where we watched the red sail growing ever larger until the pirates closed with us, lines were thrown from them to us, and the two ships linked arms like strolling sweethearts.

The pirate captain then came aboard without much ostentation but it was clear that he was accustomed to being treated with respect. He was a tall lean Muslim and as he stood facing the short fat Christian master of our vessel he seemed to embody some necessary complementarity; together they were obviously spin-maintainers. The two of them exchanged greetings with great civility and then began to haggle spiritedly in Arabic. We pilgrims naturally watched and listened with some interest, and it seemed to us that the master of the *Balena* was saying that we were very valuable while the pirate captain thought perhaps that we were not so very valuable. The negotiations concluded, money changed hands and we pilgrims changed ships. As we stepped over into the pirate vessel the pilgrim just ahead of me turned to me and said, 'What's the name of this ship, did you notice?'

'*Nineveh*,' I said, pleased with my own joke; I had noticed the name but could not read the Arabic characters. But later I asked a Greek-speaking pirate what the name was.

'*Nineveh*,' he said.

To be sold for a slave is a startling experience. The rest of the world knows so little about one and yet it is they who set the price. We were all stripped and examined and relieved of our luggage and whatever was in our pockets or sewn into our clothes. The pirate captain was delighted to find that I was a eunuch in good condition; he made that gesture of kissing the fingers made by all vendors who reckon that they have something especially fine to sell. In the slave market in Tripoli, standing in the cool and coloured shade of awnings, smelling the smoke of water pipes and a variety of Middle Eastern cooking that invited one to abandon introspection and embrace such pleasures of the senses as now offered, hearing Arabic, Syriac, Armenian, Turkish, and Greek spoken all round me I was not so distressed as one might think; it had never before happened to me that I was valued, and highly valued, for my visible qualities alone. It occurred to me that I might be bought for harem duty and I felt a little stir of pleasure; orchards are pleasant even if one can't climb the trees.

A succession of prospective buyers stood before me and tilted their heads to one side, trying, I suppose, to imagine me in their houses as one imagines a table or a chair or a wall hanging. Would I go with the rest of it. A variety of people-buying faces looked at me from under turbans, fezzes, and kaffiyas. The pirate captain found many things to say about me, none of which I understood because he spoke in Arabic. He was at pains to show interested viewers that I had good teeth and he seemed particularly pleased by the arch of my foot, drawing attention to it frequently. In my mind I saw myself standing hour after hour outside the closed doors of a harem listening to laughter and low murmurings while little by little my feet grew flat.

There was standing before me a tall and noble-looking Turk

with heroic moustaches, a red fez, a scarlet and purple jacket worked with gold. I judged him to be sixty or so. He put a large hand on my shoulder and drew me a few steps away from the others. He looked at me in such a way that I knew he was going to say something that would make me his friend. He said to me in Greek, 'What if I say to you that the universe is a three-legged horse, eh? What then? What will you say to me?'

I said to him, 'It is because the universe is a three-legged horse that the journey to the red heifer is so slow.'

'Ah!' he said, 'You're a Jew then.'

'How does that follow?' I said.

'A Jew will consider anything,' he said. 'Are you or aren't you?'

'I am,' I said.

'I need you,' he said. 'Do you need me?'

'Yes,' I said.

'Done!' he said. My price was twenty-five dinars but he counted out fifty gold dinars and gave them to the pirate captain.

'This is twice as much as I have asked,' said the pirate captain in Greek to the Turk. This pirate's name, by the way, was Prodigality. He had formerly been a slave named Thrift who had in trading for his merchant master put by enough money to buy his freedom, and having done so he changed his name and went into piracy. 'Why are you doing this?' he said to the Turk.

'I am afraid not to,' said my new owner. 'I want Allah to take notice that I am taking notice of my good fortune.'

'If Allah's taking notice I don't want to look bad,' said Prodigality, and counting out twenty-five dinars he put them into my hand.

Both men looked at me with expectation.

'Can I buy myself back?' I said to my new owner.

'Just as you like,' he said. Prodigality wrote out a bill of sale to him and he wrote out a bill of sale to me. I then gave him the gold that Prodigality had given me.

'Now you're a free man,' said my former owner. 'What will you do?'

'I'll come with you freely,' I said, 'as we need each other.'

'Thus does the will of Allah manifest itself in human transactions,' said my new friend.

106

'Wait!' said Prodigality as we turned to go, and taking my hand he put into it the remaining twenty-five dinars of the double payment.

'What's this?' I said.

'Allah wills what Allah wills,' said Prodigality. 'Let it be altogether circular.'

'I am obedient to the will of Allah,' I said, and put the gold back into the hand from which it had originally come.

'Let it be noticed by all who have eyes to see,' said my new friend as he received the gold, 'that Allah *has* taken notice.'

'It's a pleasure doing business with you,' said Prodigality. 'It's spiritually refreshing. It's only a pity I can't afford this sort of thing more often.'

With many expressions of mutual esteem we parted, and as I walked away with my former owner and new friend I marvelled at how Prodigality had been able to rise above the practical considerations of commerce. Certainly with my gold and diamonds and the plunder from the other pilgrims in his coffers he could afford to be generous but even so it seemed remarkable to me that gold and silver and gems could produce in him that degree of moral sensitivity that enabled him to behave so handsomely.

My new friend's name was Bembel Rudzuk; he was a wealthy merchant who lived in Antioch. I went with him to the khan where he and his party were staying, and the next morning we departed for Suwaydiyya on one of his dhows. 'How strange that was yesterday!' I said to him. 'How extraordinary!'

'Now more than other things,' said Bembel Rudzuk. 'To me everything is extraordinary and nothing is. Aeschylus was killed when he was hit on the head by a tortoise dropped by an eagle but that's not extraordinary when you consider that he was sitting directly below the eagle when it dropped the tortoise from a considerable height. On the other hand, that there *was* Aeschylus, *that* to me is extraordinary: that the world appeared in his eyes, that the world lived in him like the light in a lantern, that there are continually new lanterns for the world to live in, that you and I are two of them, yes, that to me is extraordinary.'

'That the universe should be a three-legged horse,' I said, 'is that extraordinary, do you think?'

'I don't know what to think about that,' said Bembel Rudzuk. 'Although I said those words and know them to be true I have no idea what they signify. They came into my head when I first saw you yesterday. Perhaps they signify that for us our meeting is the fourth leg. What colour is the horse for you?'

'Red,' I said, 'like the heifer.'

'For me also it is red,' he said.

'Why do you need a Jew?' I said.

'Do you know that story of Abraham that is not to be found in the Holy Scriptures?' he said. 'How Nimrod put him into the fiery furnace and God took him out?'

'Yes,' I said, 'I know that story.'

'Do you perceive,' he said, 'that there is alchemy in this story?'

'Ah!' I said. 'He was put into the furnace, he was taken out again.'

'He will go in again,' said Bembel Rudzuk.

'I believe you,' I said. 'And when will his base metal be transmuted to gold, how long will that take?'

'Ah!' he said. 'It's the metal of those who put him into the fire that must be transmuted.'

'Are there years enough for that?' I said.

'Whether there are or there aren't,' he said, 'that's nothing I can do anything about. But I'm curious about Abraham. Have you heard of the sulphur-mercury process?'

'I think I've seen diagrams of two triangles point to point,' I said.

'That's right,' he said. 'In the diagrams one sees them point to point — the sulphur triangle with its hotness and dryness, the mercury triangle with its coldness and wetness. Look!' He flung out his arm towards the sea where the sun-points danced. 'The hot and dry is dancing on the cold and wet; in everything can we see these combinations working. These two triangles that we see in the diagrams, they want to mingle their natures as they did in that veiled story in which the cold and wet of Abraham's water-nature was activated to neutralize the hot and dry of his fire-nature. Abraham, you know, is claimed by Jews and Arabs both. I myself believe that in this story he personifies the elemental complementarity that moves the universe. It is in the Holy Scriptures of your people that Abraham is first written of, and for this reason I want to avail myself of the action of your mind.'

'How?' I said.

'There is a work that I have been thinking about for some time,' he said. 'I don't want to talk about it quite yet.'

'Are you an alchemist?' I said.

'You mean with pots and furnaces?' he said.

'Yes,' I said.

'No,' he said. 'That to me is greedy, it is a sweating after something to hold in the hand and look at, it is not a true giving, it is not an honest offering of the self to the Unity from which all multiplicity comes.'

'But your two triangles,' I said, 'your sulphur-mercury process?'

'Look!' he said again. The crew were wearing the vessel round before the wind. The helmsman put the tiller over to bring the wind aft, the great triangle of the mainsail was let fly, the old windward shrouds were eased off and the new windward shrouds set up as we came about; the mainsail was sheeted home again and we filled away on the new tack. 'Wind alchemy,' said Bembel Rudzuk. 'The triangle of the sail fills first on one side then on the other to drive us forward. Two triangles. My alchemy seeks no yellow metal; it is a continual offering to the Unity at the heart of the multiplicity. It makes no distinction between what is called something and what is called nothing, it knows such words to be without meaning.' The sail swelled as if with the breath of God, the dhow pitched forward and reared back as if nodding in agreement with the words of Bembel Rudzuk, the sun-points danced on the water, the dark crew, some in white and some in faded colours, ranged themselves along the windward rail. I felt such a Nowness in the light of the day that Christ leapt into my mind like the visual echo of his unheard voice. 'Ah!' I said, 'This, this, this!' He was gone, there were only the sun-points on the water, the breath of God in the sail.

'Yes,' said Bembel Rudzuk, 'you see!'

We made our way up the coast in short stages, calling at Tortosa, Marquiya, Baniyas, and Ladhiqiyya to discharge and

take on a variety of cargoes. Each port in the changing lights of
the day would grow smoothly and mysteriously larger and more
detailed in the eye as we approached: first the massed groupings
of light and shadow of the moored vessels, the low waterside
buildings, the domes and minarets of the town behind; then the
slow shifting of the grouped lights and shadows into separate
and varied lights and shadows growing larger, more clear,
becoming individually defined masts and sails and rigging,
painted boats rocking at their moorings, figures aboard them
standing and moving, faces looking across the green and
sheltered, the shining and the shadowed water above which
drifted the smells of cooking, the smoke of charcoal fires against
a background of warehouse roofs and windows and open doors,
cordage and tackle, bales, barrels, carts and wagons of the
waterside. And always in front of this the motion of vessels
arriving, vessels departing, and aboard these vessels faces passing, passing, locked in unknownness, growing smaller,
becoming unseen.

Although our business in Ladhiqiyya was finished early in
the evening we did not leave until much later; Suwaydiyya was
only three or four hours away and Bembel Rudzuk wanted to
arrive with the dawn rather than in the middle of the night.
'Dawn is the best time for coming into port,' he said, 'and I
always allow myself this pleasure when coming home.'

The feeble lamp-glimmers of the coast shifted subtly in our
passing and were swallowed in obscurity. I looked up at the sky
but the Virgin and the Lion were not to be seen, there were no
stars, the night was opaque; this was already November and the
rainy season. 'Would the Virgin and the Lion be visible if the
sky were clear?' I asked Bembel Rudzuk.

'No,' he said, 'they are below the horizon now.'

Towards morning it began to rain, and it was in the grey
rainlight that Suwaydiyya offered to us the shapes of dawn all
dark and huddled, the low waterside buildings curtained with
rain, the water of the harbour leaping up in points to meet the
downpour, the dawn boats rocking to the morning slap of the
water on their sides, furled sails wet with dawn and rain and still
heavy with night, crews sheltering under awnings, the smoke of
their breakfast fires ghostly in the rain. And as always all of it,

the whole picture in the eyes, had without seeming to come closer grown smoothly bigger in that particular way in which things reveal themselves when approached by sea, opening to the approacher more and more detail, more and more imminence of what is to come. And always, thus approaching, one feels the new day, the new place, coming forward to read the face of the approacher. Always the held breath, the questioning look of the grey morning, the seclusion of the rain.

On boarding Bembel Rudzuk's dhow I had noticed the name painted on the bows in Arabic characters but I had not asked what that name was; I didn't want to know. Having already been transferred from the *Balena* to *Nineveh* and having so far proclaimed nothing whatever on behalf of the Lord I preferred not to be aware of any further names of significance for a time; I wished if possible to be reabsorbed into the ordinary. But no sooner had we stepped ashore than I noticed again the Arabic characters painted on the bows, my mouth opened and was already asking Bembel Rudzuk what the name was before I could stop it.

'*Sophia*,' he said.

Horses were brought and we rode to Antioch, a dozen or so miles up the Orontes. The rain lessened into a dull brightness, that particular dull brightness that is always a little frightening in its blank revelation: one perceives that there is nowhere anything ordinary; there is only the extraordinary. It was from miles away that I first saw Mount Silpius and the many-towered walls ascending from the plain where stood the houses, domes, and minarets of Antioch on the River Orontes. Bigger and bigger in my eyes grew the mountain and the towered walls, the tawny towered walls and high up on the mountain the tawny citadel with its green-and-gold banner hanging motionless in the dull brightness. The mountain itself was browny purple, then blue-green tawny. Everything in that land was tawny either over or under whatever colour else it had. A lion-coloured land.

The mountain! Even a small mountain is always a surprise, it is always so much itself. The first sight of any mountain is the actuality of its strangeness. Let Mount Silpius stand for all strange mountains as it manifests itself in the grey light of morning, as it shows its purple shadows and its tawny dust darkened by the rain, as it shows its strangeness and its dread. That Moses was given the Tables of the Law on a mountain is significant: every mountain is the dreadful mountain of the Law, there move over it the thunder and the lightnings, there move on it the smoke and fire, there sounds from it the trumpet of the dreadful summons. The dread is that now is Now, that here is Here, that everything that is actually is, and everything is irrevocably moving.

With the mountain continually in my eyes I entered that city quick with life, with sound and motion and colour; that city quick with wealth, quick with thought. I understood immediately what it was: it was what in one form or another comes between the pilgrim and Jerusalem. One says, '"If I forget thee, O Jerusalem!"' and then one forgets Jerusalem and life for a time is sweet in Antioch. I wanted to embrace everything—domes and minarets and the shadows of awnings, even the cynical camels with their swaying loads of the goods of this world. In my heart I embraced the Mittelteufel, I said, 'Perhaps there is no Jerusalem, perhaps nothing is required of me. Perhaps there is only Antioch.'

Bembel Rudzuk said, 'There *is* Jerusalem, and whatever is required of you is required; but in this present moment is Antioch and you are here to do what will be done by you here.' The air in the courtyard of Bembel Rudzuk's house was misted by a fountain, passing, passing, not for ever. 'We are brothers,' said Bembel Rudzuk, and embraced me.

'What am I?' I said. 'I am a eunuch, I am cut off from my generations, I am not a man, I am nothing.' I wept by the silvery plashing of the fountain.

Bembel Rudzuk said, 'What say your Holy Scriptures? "Let not the eunuch say, I am a dry tree."'

'But I *am* a dry tree,' I said.

'Listen!' said Bembel Rudzuk. He had got a Greek Bible and was reading to me:

'Thus saith the Lord to the eunuchs,
as many as shall keep my sabbaths,
and choose the things which I take pleasure in,

and take hold of my covenant; I will give to them
in my house and within my walls an honourable place,
better than sons and daughters: I will give them an everlasting name, and it shall not fail.'

'In the Hebrew it doesn't say "fail",' I said. 'In the Hebrew it
says "be cut off" ':

'Even unto them will I give in my house
and within my walls a monument and a memorial
better than sons and daughters;
I will give them an everlasting memorial,
that shall not be cut off.

'Tell me if you can, what everlasting memorial is there better
than sons and daughters? And how shall it not be cut off?'

'Better than sons and daughters is to be with the stillness that
is always becoming motion,' said Bembel Rudzuk. 'And in
being with this stillness-into-motion there is a continuity that is
not cut off.'

The words rattled on my head like pebbles on a roof. 'Where
am I?' I said.

'What do you mean?' said Bembel Rudzuk.

'In the dark wood with murderers, with the headless corpse
of the tax-collector and the maggots I knew where I was,' I said.
'I had a whereness to be in. Now I don't know where I am, I
don't have where to be.'

'Let me show you something,' he said. Taking me into the
house he pointed to a geometric pattern of tiles ornamenting the
front of a dais. 'Look,' he said.

I looked. The pattern went its way as such patterns do.

'This pattern is contiguous with infinity,' said Bembel
Rudzuk. 'Once the mode of repetition is established the thing
goes on for ever. It is apparently stopped by its border but in
actuality it never stops.'

I said, 'You mean in potentiality, don't you? Potentially it
could continue although actually it stops.'

'Tell me,' he said, 'where does one draw the line between
potentiality and actuality? It isn't as if we're looking at a rain
cloud and we say, "Potentially it could rain but actually it isn't
raining." This is something else: with patterns when you say

113

what can be, you're describing what already is. Patterns cannot be originated, they can only be taken notice of. When a pattern shows itself in tiles or on paper or in your mind and says, "This is the mode of my repetition; in this manner can I extend myself to infinity," it has already done so, it has already been infinite from the very first moment of its being; the potentiality and the actuality are one thing. If two and two can be four then they already *are* four, you can only perceive it, you have no part in making it happen by writing it down in numbers or telling it out in pebbles. When we draw on paper or lay out in tiles a pattern that we have not seen before we are only recording something that has always been happening; the air all around us, the earth we stand on, the very particles of our being are continually active with an unimaginable multiplicity of patterns, all of them contiguous with infinity.'

'That's no help to me,' I said.

'Yes it is,' he said. 'It's a great help to everyone.'

'How?' I said.

'For one thing it gives you a whereness to be in,' he said. 'The patterns traversing one place intersect the patterns traversing another place, and by this webbing of pattern all places are connected. Wherever you are at this moment you are connected with all places where you have ever been, all places where you will ever be, and all places where you never have been and never will be.'

I held out my hand in front of me and looked at it. I thought of the patterns of veins and arteries, of muscles and bones beneath the skin. I thought of the patterns within the bone and muscle, I thought of the patterns contained in the sperm and the egg and the pattern of their combination, the thought of God, the word of flesh.

'People also are connected,' said Bembel Rudzuk, 'all people of every time and every place.'

I thought of Sophia, I thought of the way in which we could never again be connected. 'You and I,' I said, 'how are we connected?'

'We are brothers,' he said.

'Yes,' I said, 'but how was it that we became brothers? You've said that you want to avail yourself of the action of my mind for a work you've had in your mind. Can you now tell me what this work is?'

'I want you to devise a pattern,' he said.

'What kind of a pattern?' I said.

'With tiles,' he said.

'A pattern with tiles,' I said. 'For this have you come to the slave market in Tripoli to find yourself a castrated Jew.'

'That's not how it was,' said Bembel Rudzuk. 'I was there on my ordinary business, receiving a cargo and trading in the markets. Having done my business I came to the slave market as one does, strolling here and there. Prodigality was shouting, "Jerusalem pilgrims! Jerusalem pilgrims! Very lucky! Don't miss this chance!"

'I said to him, "How are Jerusalem pilgrims lucky?"

'He said, "They'll bring luck."

'I said, "How?"

'He said, "Who am I to know such things?"

'I said, "Why, then? Why do you say they'll bring luck?"

'He said, "Only think! Possessed by their Christ, driven by a mystical force, they swim rivers, they climb mountains, they strive with brigands who would take their lives, all to travel to Jerusalem! Buy a Jerusalem pilgrim and all this mystical force can be yours!"

'I said, "Won't it rather bring ill luck, to come like this between a pilgrim and his goal?"

'"Not at all," said Prodigality. "Obviously the Christ of these pilgrims has willed that they should become the slaves of the believers of the one true faith."

'Walking slowly and pondering these things,' said Bembel Rudzuk, 'I found myself standing before you. It was then that there came to me the words that I spoke to you.'

I said, 'But why do you want me to make a pattern with tiles?'

He said, 'This idea came into my mind. An idea is an eye given by God for the seeing of God.'

'Is that really so?' I said. 'The idea of murdering someone comes into the mind of the murderer; is this also an eye given by God for the seeing of God?'

'The murderer too sees God,' said Bembel Rudzuk, 'and

perhaps more than others. In any case this idea cannot possibly harm anyone as far as I can see. Can you see any harm in it?'

'No,' I said, 'I cannot.'

This conversation was taking place at the close of day, after the sunset prayer. Behind Bembel Rudzuk's words I heard the falling water of the fountain, the cooing of doves. There came into my mind the twilight at Manzikert on the day of the battle in 1071, the year of my birth. This twilight I knew in my soul, I knew it to be Bruder Pförtner's courtyard, the quiet place where plashes the fountain of his reverie. At the close of that August day at Manzikert the Byzantine Emperor Romanus IV Diogenes must have felt what he had become as the day waned: no longer a man but a line on a map, the ebbing tide-line of Byzantium, ebbing from the sharp edge of the present like blood from a knife. Andronicus and the rear line gone and the Turks all round like murderous stinging bees. Romanus must have smelt Bruder Pförtner's breath, fresh and salty like the wind from the sea, he must have felt himself at that turning centre of all things where stillness revolves into motion and motion into stillness. Aiyee! must have cried the life in him as his blinding and his death moved towards him in that twilight at Manzikert. As Byzantium receded with him towards the allness of everything.

I found myself weeping for Romanus Diogenes and for that Jew who was made to be his executioner. In that twilight in the courtyard of Bembel Rudzuk in Antioch I thought also of Alexius Comnenus, now in 1096 Emperor of Byzantium. The reality of his empire presented itself to me all at once like a naked idiot: he was emperor of the passing of Byzantium, his empire was becoming moment by moment the illusion of, the non-reality of, the unpotentiality of Byzantium. At some point the naked idiot of this actuality became the naked truth of it and I saw, or perhaps I am only just now seeing, or perhaps I have not yet seen and I am at some time going to see that the names of things, of times, of places, of events, are useful for reference and they have some subjective meaning but as often as not they obscure the actuality of the thing they attempt to describe. Now as I think about it I see that we don't always know what it is that we are putting a name to. We are, for example, clever enough to know that a year is a measure of passage, not permanence; we call the seasons spring, summer, autumn, and winter, knowing that they are continually passing one into the other. We are not surprised at this but when we give to seasons of another sort the names Rome, Byzantium, Islam, or Mongol Empire we are astonished to see that each one refuses to remain what it is.

'Why are you weeping?' said Bembel Rudzuk.

'I am suffering from an attack of history,' I said.

'It will pass,' said Bembel Rudzuk.

'Where is this tile pattern to be done?' I said.

'I have bought a piece of land just inside the wall at the foot of Mount Silpius not far from the Tower of the Two Sisters,' he said.

'And you're having a house built on it?' I said.

'No,' he said, 'I have had it prepared as a plane for tiling. I have had the ground cleared and paved with stone so that it's perfectly flat. It's one hundred and twenty feet by one hundred and twenty feet.'

'That's fourteen thousand four hundred square feet of pattern,' I said. 'Why does it have to be so big?'

'Ask rather why it's no bigger,' he said. 'And the answer to that is that this was the biggest piece of land available within the wall. Ideally the plane would extend to the horizon on all sides.'

'Why is that?' I said.

'Because in this case the ideal is the maximum effort possible,' he said, 'and the horizon is the outer limit of how much of the pattern can be taken in by the eye.'

'It wouldn't do to draw it on a piece of paper to hold in the hand?' I said.

'No,' he said, 'As you must know in your heart, it is not only the apparent quantity of a thing that changes with the degree of effort, the manifest character of it changes also as Thing-in-Itself reveals more of itself.'

'Is that what the pattern is for?' I said: 'To show Thing-in-Itself?'

'You know as well as I do,' he said, 'that Thing-in-Itself is not to be seen nor is it to be sought directly. My desires are modest; there are simply one or two things I should like to observe, one or two things I should like to think about.'

'Can you tell me what they are?' I said.

'Motion is one of them,' he said. 'There is transitive motion and there is intransitive motion: the motion of a galloping horse is transitive, it passes through our field of vision and continues on to wherever it is going; the motion in a tile pattern is intransitive, it does not pass; it moves but it stays in our field of vision. It arises from stillness, and I should like to think about the point at which stillness becomes motion. Another thing I should like to think about is the point at which pattern becomes consciousness.'

'Does it?' I said. 'Can this be proved?'

'I know in my innermost being that it does,' he said, 'and I know that we ourselves are the proof of it, but whether this proof can be demonstrated I don't know. It may well be that the proof is being demonstrated constantly but in our ignorance we cannot recognize it.'

'This design that you want me to make,' I said, 'how should it look?'

'That will come from you,' he said. 'It will come from your hand at the moment when you begin to draw. Try not to think about it beforehand, don't let your mind become busy with it.'

'My mind is already busy with it,' I said. 'How could it not be?'

'In that case you should do it now,' he said, 'and we must go to the place where it is to be done.' From a cabinet he took a straight-edge and a large wooden compass fitted with a piece of chalk and we left the house.

Through the darkening murmurous evening, past the lamps of evening and the smells of cooking we made our way to the paved space at the foot of Mount Silpius near the Tower of the Two Sisters. The town was still murmurous but all the voices of the day that had been close were now distant. Before us Mount Silpius gathered itself into night. The lamplight in the windows of the towers made the stone around them bulk darker against the sky. Someone was playing an oud, someone was singing; it was a woman's voice rising and falling in a pattern of repetition contiguous with infinity. Warm and sad the voice, a woman of flesh and bone, contiguous with infinity! On Bembel Rudzuk's paved square some boys were kicking a blown-up bladder that rasped with a skittering rush across the stone, each thump of the kicking like the unsequent beat of a disembodied heart; the voices of the boys appeared at sudden places in the gathering night, now near, now far; their feet scuffled mysteriously on the stone.

That evening Bembel Rudzuk and I felt ourselves to be inside the walls of Antioch, how could we not? There were the walls of stone all strong and thick and guarded by soldiers, there were the towers with their lamplit windows girdling the city in the encircling night. Yet even then, so contiguous was my mind, is my mind, with infinity that my thoughts found themselves here in this present space in which only broken remnants of those strong walls stand and the inside is seen to be one with the outside. My consciousness that evening in 1096 came forward to the present and the toothless broken stones of now, and my present consciousness goes back to the great thick towered walls forty feet high and paced by weaponed men.

Strong walls, always have strong walls been walked by weaponed men. And those who came and took Antioch, such stones they captured in their strong places up and down the land, such stones they put together in their Latin Kingdom, those strong men and those who came after them! As Pilgermann the owl I fly on silent wings above them looking down. Lion-stones, warrior stones, now they have peace. How they sing in their silence, how they are easy, the great strong stones, the lion-stones, the tawny. Even they, the strong stones of the great Jew-killers, even they have longed for ruin and the stillness, for the wind sighing over them, for the grass growing on roofless walls and alone-standing arches. Even when the arrows hissed from the loopholes the stones were singing the stillness to come, the clopping of cows' hooves up and down the stone steps where those iron-ringing men walked in their time. Now the stones have arrived at the strong life of the stillness of them, their strong song, their stillness dancing in the sun.

Warrior lords, those great and fierce men, recruiters of stone, of walls and towers on high ground, of strongholds commanding borders, river crossings, approaches. They said to the stones, as other warrior lords before them had said to the stones of Antioch, 'Be thou firm against the enemy.' And what did the stones say? The stones said, 'We have no enemy.' Lying in the sun they sing the stillness; toppling and rolling they shout, 'God is motion!'

So. Bembel Rudzuk and I in the deepening night in Antioch. Bats fretting the darkness into little points and the woman's voice rising and falling in her song as we stood on the stone paving that was waiting for my design.

The centre of the square was marked by a wooden rod standing upright in the stone. It seemed to me that I could feel the power of the centre there, feel the radii going out from it and coming into it. There was no moon, there were no stars but we could see well enough for our purpose. We had brought no lantern nor did I want one; it seemed right that the design should come out of obscurity, and I wanted to be unobserved, I wanted the shelter of the dark.

Bembel Rudzuk was saying very quietly in Arabic:

'*Labbaika, Allahumma, labbaika.*'

Then he said to me in Greek, 'What I said was: "At Thy service, O Lord, at Thy service." These words are to be spoken only on pilgrimage to Mecca but I could not refrain from saying them.' He took the rod out of its socket, inserted a wooden plug that he had brought with him, and stepped back.

I opened the legs of the compass, stuck the point of the centre leg into the plug and swept the outer leg round to make my first circle. It went just like that; I had no hesitation in deciding on the length of the radius; one action followed another, and as the compass leg swept round there followed it obediently through the darkness a white chalk line that closed itself into a circle as if the impulse had been already there waiting in the stone until, now summoned by the compass, it rose up to the surface.

Keeping the same radius I made the overlapping circles that divided the circumference of my first circle into six parts and produced a flower of six petals luminous in the white chalk. Connecting the points of the petals made a hexagon. From the six points of the hexagon came the two interlocking triangles of the six-pointed star within the hexagon. Connecting the points of intersection divided the two interlocking triangles into twelve small triangles. Extending the lines of the hexagon made the two large interlocking triangles of a second six-pointed star that contained the hexagon containing the first six-pointed star. Lines balanced on the points of the outer star gave an outer hexagon in which eighteen equilateral triangles enclosed the inner hexagon. This completed the unit that would repeat itself in my tile pattern.

'What is the name of this design?' said Bembel Rudzuk.
'I don't know,' I said.

'Think on it,' he said. 'It will come to you.'

We went back to Bembel Rudzuk's house. He gave me paper and coloured inks and drawing instruments and I made a drawing in which I repeated the unit twelve times in the pattern in which the tiles would be arranged. Then I coloured it, making the large and small triangles of the large and small six-pointed stars alternately red and black. The triangles contiguous with the right-hand sides of the star-points (which, going round like the blades of a waterwheel, became left-hand sides then right-hand sides again) were coloured red or black in contrast to the star-points. All other triangles were tawny-coloured.

My pattern was certainly a simple one, primitive even; I was surprised therefore to see how much action there was in it and how many different kinds of action there were: there were twisting serpents, there were shadowed pyramids, and when I tilted my head at the necessary angle the twelve small triangles of the inner stars became the deeply shadowed face of a red lion. When I tilted my head back to the vertical the triangles went blank, an empty mask looked at me instead of a lion. However one looked at the pattern there could be no doubt that the stillness had become motion but I hadn't noticed at what point it had happened. Sometimes the larger triangles revolved around the inner stars, sometimes they took angular courses, pausing occasionally to group themselves in pyramids before continuing on their way. The pattern was altogether regular and predictable but from time to time there came to the eye enclaves of apparent disorder that in a moment disappeared; this had to do with the alternation of the red and the black; the periodicity of the colours was not synchronized with that of the shapes.

'Can you tell me now what the name of this design is?' said Bembel Rudzuk.

I tilted my head, the shadowed lion looked at me; I tilted my head back, the triangles went blank. 'The name of this design is Hidden Lion,' I said. There leapt up in me a wild surge of terror and joy as virtuality, correctly named, leapt into actuality.

11

One wakes up in the morning and puts on oneself. Everyone has experienced this: the self must be put on before any garment, and there is inevitably a pause as it were a caesura in the going forward of things before the self is put on. Why is this? It is because our mortal identity is not the primary one, not the profound, not the deep one. No, what wakes up from sleep is not Tiglath-Pileser or Peter Schlemiel or Pilgermann; it is simply raw undifferentiated being, brute being with nothing driving it but the forward motion imparted to it by the original explosion into being of the universe. For a fraction of a moment it is itself only; then must it with joy or terror put on that identity taken on with mortal birth, that identity that each morning is the cumulative total of its mortal days and nights, that self old or young, sick or well, brave or cowardly, beautiful or ugly, whole or mutilated, that is one's lot.

Every morning when I woke up I had perforce to put on the identity of Eunuch. I had to make to myself a little oration that always began with, 'Yes, but ... '. As the raw being of me drew back from the identity that was offered I would say, 'Yes, but still there are things to be done, still there is life and world, still there is action required of me.' On the morning after drawing Hidden Lion on the stone and on the paper I woke up and said, 'Yes, but there is Hidden Lion,' and just at that moment there came moving upon the morning air the call of the mu'addhin. It seemed to me that his voice, contiguous with infinity, was tracing on the air the pattern I had drawn upon the stone and upon the paper, and I moved forward eagerly into the day.

The hum of the day arose from the city, the work of the day began: the beating of hammers, the baking of bread, the voices of buying and selling. Through these streets of the action of every day we walked to our paved square of stillness that was waiting to become what it would become. The morning sun slanted its light across the paving-stones, the wooden rod in the centre with its morning shadow told the time. The chalk lines drawn by me in darkness were shocking in the light of morning, strange and surprising in their actuality, like a mountain.

'Does it seem to you,' said Bembel Rudzuk, 'that this design was already waiting in the stone for the time when it would become visible?'

'Yes,' I said. 'I think that all possible patterns were in these stones even before they were cut and dressed and made into paving-stones.'

We both stood looking at the chalk lines on the tawny stone. Having spoken the words we had just spoken we now found in our minds the next thought: the actions that would take place on those tiles that were not yet made, were those actions also waiting in the paving-stones that would then be under the tiles?

Bembel Rudzuk measured the three different triangles that in their multiples made up Hidden Lion and wrote down his measurements on a sheet of paper which he put into his document case.

'When can we start?' I said.

As I spoke the shadow of the wooden rod faded into the tawniness of the stone. We both looked up at the grey sky.

'In the spring,' said Bembel Rudzuk, 'when the rains are over.'

I felt like a child deprived of a treat. I wanted something to happen immediately, I felt that such manhood as now remained to me could only live so long as there was action to nourish it. I stretched out my arms towards the corners of the stone square, trying to pull into myself the power that radiated from the centre and passed beyond the outer limits of the paving to infinity.

A small boy walked on to the stone at a corner of the square.

He looked sharp and hungry, like a fox. Like a fox, wary and watchful, he came slowly step by step from the corner towards the centre, walking as one walks on thin ice; perhaps he was counting. At a certain point he stopped, knelt on the stone, and began to draw on it, first with a bit of charcoal then with red ochre. What he drew was a triangle with a short base and long sides; it was irregularly divided into pointed red and black shapes, some triangular, some diamond-shaped, unevenly massed and drawn all skewed and crooked, like scales on a deformed serpent; from base to apex there ran up the middle, like spines, a line of black diamond shapes. Near the triangle he drew a lopsided circle made up of other black and red shapes, masses of black, slivers of red; it suggested the giant eye of an unimagined insect. From this eye emanated red and black arrows.

I walked over to the boy. I had learned to say in Arabic, 'What is this called?' and now I pointed to his design and said this to him.

He looked up at me attentively and shook his head.

I said in Greek, 'What is this called? What is it meant to be?'

Again he shook his head, still looking at me attentively.

'Did you understand me?' I said.

He nodded.

'Are you able to speak?' I said.

He shook his head. Had his speech been castrated? Had his tongue been cut out? I didn't want to ask why he was unable to speak. Had he made a vow of silence?

Still looking at me with that same serious attention he held out his left hand with the fingers outspread and curved as if holding a sphere, then he slowly rotated his wrist. Having done this he stood up and walked back as he had come: first to the corner of the paved square then away into the town.

Then the grey sky opened and down came the rain. As it poured down and drenched me to the skin my heart leapt up to meet it, I didn't know why. That rain, the prospect of which had only a moment before filled me with despair, was now bringing me ease and refreshment.

Under that drenching rain we went to the brickyard. There was little to be seen but an expanse of mud leaping up in points, a little square mud-brick building with a dome, and two or three little square ziggurats that I took to be kilns. In the doorway of the mud-brick building lounged a little moon-faced man of fifty or so; his face was contemplative and serene.

'This brickmaster,' said Bembel Rudzuk, 'this lord of the bricks, his name is Bab el-Burj, Tower Gate. He used to be a slave and his name was Efficiency.'

'Why is his name now Tower Gate?' I said. 'I prefer to avoid people and boats with symbolic names if I can.'

'There's no symbolism in it that I know of,' said Bembel Rudzuk; 'he simply liked the wordplay of Bab el-Tower, that's all.'

'No bricks,' said Tower Gate when we stood before him. 'As you see, I have no bricks whatever, I have only the emptiness left behind by a great many bricks. I am contemplating this emptiness.'

'May we contemplate it as well?' said Bembel Rudzuk.

'I don't think there's enough for the three of us,' said Tower Gate. 'Let me offer you rather some coffee.'

The interior of the little mud-brick building was sumptuously carpeted and adorned with gorgeous hangings and cushions. Bembel Rudzuk and I sat down while a puddle formed around us and Tower Gate prepared coffee. He had no servant with him nor were there any workmen to be seen.

'Strange, is it not,' said Tower Gate, 'that in the Quran there is no chapter called "The Kiln" or "The Oven"? It's such a good metaphor, it lends itself so well to metaphysics.'

'There's the Jonas chapter,' said Bembel Rudzuk: 'he went into the whale and came out of the whale as a brick goes into and comes out of the kiln.'

'Jonas was half-baked,' said Tower Gate; 'he was still unfinished and without wisdom when the whale vomited him up. No, as a metaphor Jonas is not in a class with bricks.' Tower Gate was given to making what might be called 'Aha!' and 'Oho!' gestures with his hands, and so he gestured now. 'Neither is bread,' he said ('Oho!' said his hands): 'bread is baked and eaten and becomes excrement. Brick, which is bread of earth, bread of our origins, is also baked — like Abraham it is put into the fire and like him it emerges hard and enduring, ready to shelter the humble and the mighty both.' ('Aha!' said his hands.) 'It is eaten by time but only slowly, slowly through the alternating dawns and darks of this continuous demonstration that we call the world. No excrement.'

'You have given me so much to think about that I cannot remember what I came to see you about,' said Bembel Rudzuk.

'Bricks?' said Tower Gate.

'Ah!' said Bembel Rudzuk. 'You read my mind.' He took out of his document case the drawing in which I had repeated the Hidden Lion pattern and showed it to Tower Gate.

'Oho!' said Tower Gate with his voice and his hands both. 'The Willing Virgin!'

'What willing virgin?' said Bembel Rudzuk.

'This pattern that you show me,' said Tower Gate, 'it's called "The Willing Virgin".'

'Why?' I said.

'Because the next time you look there's something different about it,' he said. 'Of course that's true of many patterns but this is the one with that name. Had you another name for it?'

'Hidden Lion,' I said. I wasn't able not to say it although I had wanted the name to be known only to Bembel Rudzuk and me.

'Aha!' said Tower Gate. 'Very good indeed! The lion is hidden in the willing virgin; after all who can say no to a lion?'

All of us pondered this for several moments.

'How big are the big triangles?' said Tower Gate.

'Nine and a half inches to a side,' said Bembel Rudzuk.

Tower Gate took my right hand, spread it out, and measured the span with an ivory ruler. 'Aha!' he said. 'Nine and a half inches! Had you noticed that?'

'No,' I said.

'Your design?' he said to me.

'Yes,' I said.

'You're going to put this pattern on that empty square of yours?' said Tower Gate to Bembel Rudzuk.

'Yes,' said Bembel Rudzuk.

'It's good that you come to me now,' said Tower Gate. 'I can think about it over the winter and I'll tell you in the spring.'

'Tell us what?' I said.

'Whether I want to have anything to do with it,' he said.

'Why does it need so much thinking?' I said.

Tower Gate looked at me as if he thought that talking to me might be a waste of time. 'You're dealing with infinity,' he said. 'I suppose you know that?'

'Yes,' I said.

'This pattern,' said Tower Gate to Bembel Rudzuk, 'this square of yours, it's not to be the floor of a building or the courtyard of a khan or anything like that, is it?'

'No,' said Bembel Rudzuk, 'it's just to be itself, it's not a part of something else.'

Tower Gate tilted his head to one side and made with his mouth a sound expressive of doubt, misgiving, and deprecation. 'That's it, you see,' he said. 'That's what gives me pause, that's what's putting the wind up me. Any other pattern I've seen has been ornamenting something, it's been *part* of something, it has not in itself been something. Do you see what I mean? To incorporate a pattern of infinity in a house is not immodest, one's eyes are in a sense averted from the nakedness of Thing-in-Itself. But here you're doing something else altogether: you're making this pattern with no other purpose than to look at Thing-in-Itself. This to me seems unlucky.'

'On the other hand,' said Bembel Rudzuk, 'who has put this idea into my head if not Allah? And who has guided the hand of my friend if not Allah?'

'What a question!' said Tower Gate. 'Do we not read in the Quran that whatever good happens to thee is from Allah but whatever evil happens to thee is from thy own soul?'

'And from where does my soul come if not from Allah?' said Bembel Rudzuk.

'What do we know? Who are we to say?' said Tower Gate's hands. With his voice he said nothing.

As we walked home through the rain Bembel Rudzuk seemed to be carrying on an interior conversation with himself. Sometimes he shook his head, sometimes he nodded, sometimes he shrugged.

'What is it?' I said.

'This matter of the tiles,' he said, 'there's nothing simple about it — one can so easily go about it the wrong way. At first I had in mind to make them of sun-dried mud; I wanted nothing too permanent, I wanted clay from the river bank that would endure only its little season as artifact before it returned to itself. Then there came to me a dream: I was standing on Hidden Lion near the centre of it. The pattern was complete. At the centre of it stood a little tower and at the top of the tower stood a hooded figure who pointed with his finger to the tiles. They were fired and glazed. This hooded personage said nothing but in my mind were the words: "They have lasted this long because they have passed through the fire."'

How strange it was to me, that rainy season through which passed the year 1096 into the year 1097. It was strange in the way in which it associated itself with a name and an image. Through the winter rains there echoed cavernously under the main street of Antioch a great rolling rush of waters in which could be heard the heavy sliding of earth and sand and gravel. This was the winter torrent that little by little was carrying Mount Silpius away into the river and the sea. Down through the cleft in Silpius ran the torrent, through the Bab el-Hadid, the Iron Gate, then under the city it rumbled through its vaulted channel to the Orontes. Onopniktes was the name of this torrent: Onopniktes, the Donkey-Drowner. When I first heard that name a thrill of recognition ran through me, there appeared in my mind the dark and echoing caverns of that churning flood in which rolled over and over dead donkeys in the wild foam. Because of its name, because of the idea of those dead donkeys rolling in the racing flood, because of the idea of the mountain rushing particle by particle under the city to the river and the sea, Onopniktes became in my mind one with the rush of history and the rising of a darkness in the name of Christ.

While that greater Onopniktes that coursed its wild way under the cities of the world brought the Franks upon its flood to Antioch, Bembel Rudzuk carried on his business from day to day but ranged less widely than he used to, both in his shipments and in his travels; he was wealthy enough to be as busy or as unbusy as he chose, and for the present he confined his trading to the stretch of coast from Suwaydiyya south to Ghaza. Professionally well-informed by his correspondents, he noted that pirates were active more than usual; he also had news of the departures of the various armies of Christ on their way to our part of the world. Bembel Rudzuk traded mostly in silk and he found the rise and fall of the price of a standard bale a reliable index to the Mediterranean state of mind. 'Today the market is like a firm and well-shaped pair of buttocks,' he said, 'but tomorrow it could be like burnt stubble. Risk is salt to the meat of commerce but I don't like the smell of the world just now; it has the smell of disorder, it has the smell of a leaking ship in which sea water has got into the silk and the crew have opened the wineskins and are looting the cargo; it has the smell of mildew and rotting oranges.'

Strolling in his warehouse, snuffing up the scents of commerce from the corded canvas bales, Bembel Rudzuk clinked in his hand a sealed purse of gold dinars. 'This purse is sealed,' he said: 'I cannot see what is in it but I believe the number and the weight of the coins written on it; I know that these coins are not made of glass or iron or brass because I know that I can trust the assayer who tested and weighed them and sealed them and the merchant who sent them and the slave who delivered them. Trust is what commerce is founded on; we merchants put our trust in God and in one another. We have no idea what God will do with his winds and weather, his storms and seas, we can't know whether he wills profit or loss until we have either profited or lost. We are in his hand, knowing nothing. When anyone tells me that God wills this or that, whether he be Christian or Muslim I grow uneasy.'

Onopniktes the Donkey-Drowner bellowed like a minotaur in its caverns. Franks put their feet into their footsteps moving towards an Antioch and a Jerusalem full of corpses not yet ripe for the glory of Christ, corpses still green and walking about. December came and Chanukah to Antioch in Syria that had once been the kingdom of that Antiochus Epiphanes against

131

whom fought and prevailed the Maccabees. The Jews of the Antioch of 1096, dyers and glass-blowers mostly, lit their daily candles, gave Chanukah money to their children; the children spun their dreidels on which the letters Nun, Gimel, Hey, and Shin stood for the words NAIS GADOL HAYAH SHOM: A GREAT MIRACLE WAS PERFORMED THERE. On the rain-glistening tawny stones of Antioch they spun their dreidels, the spinning contiguous with the rain and infinity.

Because non-Muslims were required to register and to pay the djizya or poll-tax, my Jewish presence had been known to the Nagid, the leader of the Jewish community, to the Rabbi of the congregation, and to every other Jew in Antioch almost as soon as I had arrived. The Nagid and the Rabbi welcomed me to the Jewish community and the Rabbi wanted to welcome me to the congregation as well. I had perforce to tell him that I was not eligible for this privilege, citing Deuteronomy 23:2:

> He that is crushed or maimed in his privy parts
> shall not enter into the assembly of the Lord.

'Pardon me,' said the Rabbi (his name was Akiba ben Eliezer; he was stocky, muscular, red-haired, quarrelsome-looking), 'now I'm confused — am I the eunuch and you're the Rabbi or are you the eunuch and I'm the Rabbi?'

'I'm the eunuch,' I said.

'Good,' he said. 'I'm glad we got that straight. This is interesting for me because this is the first time I've been instructed by a Jewish eunuch. You're sure you're not an Egyptian and maybe you've been asleep in some pharaoh's tomb all these years?'

'I'm sorry I spoke,' I said.

'Please,' he said, 'no excuses. If one member can't wag then let it be another, who am I to say no.'

'Thank you,' I said, 'for your forbearance. I don't mean to be taking up your time like this.'

'I've got more time than I have eunuchs,' he said; 'so at the moment my demand exceeds your supply and you're precious.'

'Not according to the Holy Scriptures,' I said.

132

'Big scholar, are you?' he said. He had a thrusting sort of face with light blue eyes, and now he eyed me thrustingly.

'No scholar,' I said.

'Lucky for me,' he said. 'I have enough big scholars already, I don't need more. Let me point out that this Deuteronomy business is not that simple. After all, if God thought that His word needed nothing more to be said about it He wouldn't have created rabbis, would He. No. So let me justify my existence.'

'You don't have to,' I said. 'Live and be well.'

'Don't try to push me away,' he said. 'Listen, do you know about Noah?'

'What about him?' I said.

'Noah ended up castrated,' he said. 'Did you know that?'

'No,' I said. 'Who did it?'

'Some say it was a lion, some say it was his own son, Ham,' he said. 'The important thing is that this Noah who built the ark, who also built the first altar, this big shipper and worshipper, he ended up like you but we don't hear anything about his being thrown out of the congregation. I myself think that the crux of the matter is whether you start out as a eunuch or only end up as one. Did you start out complete?'

'Yes,' I said. 'At least physically.'

'Think,' he said, buttoning me on to his hard blue eye as if I were a buttonhole, 'think of this tradition of a castrated Noah. What do you think about it?'

'I'm not yet able to take it in,' I said. I imagined thunder and lightning, the ark rolling in heavy seas, Noah naked with blood streaming from his castration, Noah shaking his first at God. I wanted to put my hands on the Rabbi's throat and cut off the supply of wind with which he continually made words.

'Tradition,' he said with his red hair standing out all round his face like Saint Elmo's fire, 'puts things together like a good cook: a little of this and a little of that. Tradition is a balancer, a bookkeeper, an accountant. Debits and credits, yes?'

'Which?' I said.

'This is why Noah, who was given so much, has something taken away,' said the Rabbi, and folded his arms across his chest as does a man who has utterly dried up his opponent in debate.

'And to what conclusion does this bring us?' I said.

'That is for you alone to know,' said the Rabbi. 'I cannot tell you because I don't know what the Lord has given you in exchange for what has been taken from you.'

I opened my mouth to speak. What could I tell him? That God was no longer He and had become It? That from Jesus himself came the seed that gave life to Jesus? Could I tell him about the tiny dead golden body of Christ in the mouth of the Lion of the World? Could I tell him of the maggot-writhing headless tax-collector and the other companions of my road? Could I tell him of Sophia?

'You don't have to say it aloud,' said the Rabbi; 'I don't have to know; God already knows and if you also know then that's enough.'

'So what do you want from me?' I said.

'I want you to come to the synagogue and pray with your fellow Jews,' he said.

The Nagid had so far been maintaining a dignified silence as befitted someone who was not a seeker-out of others but the sought-out of many; none the less it was a bustling kind of silence. This Nagid, whom I think of as Worldly ben Worldly although he had a name that I ought to remember, was a tall, grand-looking man who seemed to embody the principle of making arangements and the idea that the ponderous wheel of time and history might not roll too crushingly on if one knew the right people. Now he made with his hands that gesture of holding a large invisible melon or model world so characteristic of top arrangers everywhere — I have often thought that the idea of the roundness of the world first came to scientific observers from seeing this gesture, so suggestive of a Platonic ideal that the existence of a physically real counterpart could not seriously be doubted — and said, 'We Jews are scattered over the face of the earth; let us at least be united in those places to which we have been scattered.'

Both the Nagid and the Rabbi, being classified as dhimmis, beneficiaries of Muslim hospitality, wore yellow turbans and belts and were not allowed to ride horses or carry weapons. Perhaps because I was already castrated I found this further diminution galling. I had not so far flouted the law by carrying

134

weapons or riding a horse but I had not put on a yellow belt and turban. In my mind I tried to, but could not, put into words my reasons for not wanting to be welcomed into a community of yellow turbans. Nor would I ever again be a member of any congregation other than that vast and erring one called the human race.

'Matters between God and me have gone beyond synagogues and congregations,' I said to the Rabbi and the Nagid. 'I have no prayers.'

'It's not as if you can pass for a Muslim by denying us,' said the Rabbi; 'you will simply be known as the eunuch Jew who does not wear the yellow belt and turban.'

'So be it,' I said.

Soon after Chanukah came the First Muharram, the new Muslim year, the Hijra year 490. On the Tenth Muharram Bembel Rudzuk fasted. 'Not everyone fasts on this day which is akin to your Day of Atonement,' he said. 'And of course there are those who on this day pitch black tents and mourn the death of Husain at Kerbela. I am not devout in the usual sense of the word but I find that fasting refreshes my attention; so I do it because my attention is always flagging and there are times when I fail to see the she-camel.'

'Tell me about this she-camel,' I said.

'In the Quran we read of a people called the Thamud,' said Bembel Rudzuk. 'They dwelt in rocky places, they had their dwellings in the rock. There came to them a prophet, his name was Salih. He told the Thamud that he was bringing to them the Word of God but they asked him for proof. Salih then called upon Allah and there appeared from out of the solid rock a she-camel, pregnant.

'This she-camel was an exemplary camel; she grazed and she found her way to water and in this way she showed that God's gifts are meant for all of God's creatures, that pasturage and water should not be held fast by the rich and kept from the poor, they should be freely shared.'

'What happened with this camel?' I said.

'Those people of the rocks, those hard and stony people, Salih told them that the eye of God was upon them; he told them to be hospitable to the stranger-camel, to let it graze where it liked and not to withhold water from it. They laughed at him, the Thamud, and after the camel had given birth they hamstrung both the mother and the foal. They killed the camel and her child and they dared Salih to call down punishment upon them.

'"Go to your houses," he told them. "You have three days in which to prepare yourselves." After three days the earth shook, thunderbolts crashed down among those people, the ground opened up, the rocks melted and ran down into the abyss, the people were annihilated; the Thamud people were no more.

'Those foolish Thamud people are often referred to in the Quran and thus are we reminded that not only is every she-camel the she-camel of God, but every other animal and all of us as well, we are all creatures of God. In every configuration of time and circumstance there is the she-camel of the matter to be discerned by those whose attention is strong and constant. All of us dwell in the stone and when the stone brings forth a she-camel we must take notice of it and respond appropriately. But it is so easy to see only the stone and not the camel; I am always afraid that I shall fail to see that she-camel of God.'

All through the rains there was no word from Tower Gate. 'Is he going to make the tiles or not?' I said to Bembel Rudzuk.

'I think he's going to do it,' said Bembel Rudzuk: 'he hasn't said no.'

Passover that year came at the end of March. The day before the Eve of Passover Jews were to be seen selling their leaven to Muslims, and this little act of accommodation touched me. See, I thought, everyone does not wish us dead! and my eyes filled with tears. I remembered the Gentiles buying the leaven of the Jews in my town, the town of my boyhood and my young manhood, the town where I had climbed the ladder to Sophia. So far away it was already in space and time!

On Passover Eve when Jews were reading the Haggadah at the Seder, when the door was left open and a cup of wine was poured for Elijah, I walked in the rain to Bembel Rudzuk's empty stone square. Freed from the traditional observance of the festival my mind widened into the rain, into the night, widened across the space of time to Pharaoh's Egypt, to the killing of the lamb without blemish, to the dipping of the hyssop in the blood, to the striking of the lintel and the sideposts with the blood, to the passing of dread wings in the night and the smiting of the first-born of Egypt, both man and beast. Ah, God! I thought, when will you learn! Why must your arm be stretched out against anyone? Why must you choose us to be yours and to be punished for ever by you and by the world? Then I remembered that God was no longer He. Perhaps as It he remembered nothing, perhaps like blind Samson he simply felt for the pillars and put forth his strength against them.

And then, thinking those heavy thoughts in the rainy night I found myself laughing because it suddenly came to me that it was not only Passover for the Jews but Easter for the Christians; Christ having been crucified at Passover the two moon-coupled festivals were for all time chained together. In Antioch that night the Christians would be reciting the eternal crime of the Jews and worshipping their tortured Jew on his cross while that same cross in cloth of scarlet was moving eastwards on the shoulders of the Franks. While the Jewish doors of Antioch stood open for Elijah. When God was He there was nobody like Him for jokes.

Spring came, the Franks arrived in Constantinople and the price of a bale of silk went up by three dinars in Tripoli. 'As when the leaves of the olive trees show their undersides before the rain comes,' said Bembel Rudzuk. 'These Franks inspire uncertainty, everyone is wondering what will happen next. Some think that fewer ships and caravans will be arriving and everything will be in short supply.'

The weather grew fine, the wooden rod at the centre of the square cast a strong young shadow. My original chalk drawing and the drawing made by the speechless boy had both been washed away by the winter rains; the empty stone presented itself to the eye as if for the first time and the sun shone down as if there would never again be cold and wet, there would only be hot and dry. With the passing of days there began to arrive donkey-loads and camel-loads of triangular tiles, as startling in their actuality as Silpius, red and black and tawny as I had seen them in my mind. With the tiles there arrived workmen who unloaded the camels and the donkeys, sorted the tiles according to size and colour, stacked them on the paving stones, and began to mix mortar.

In my hand was the wooden compass with which I had made my first drawing, and now I opened it once more to the radius that would summon to the surface of the stone that same circle I had first drawn in the darkness.

I removed the rod, inserted the plug, placed the compass foot, and then it was as if the chalk line moved the outer compass leg before it as it closed itself into a circle. Again I developed the flower of six petals, and line by line out of it grew the hexagons and triangles of Hidden Lion.

It was then that there appeared a fully armed man walking across the paved square towards us. 'This man,' said Bembel Rudzuk, 'is Firouz. He used to be a Christian, now he is a Muslim. He is an emir and he is close to our governor, Yaghi-Siyan. The Tower of the Two Sisters is under his command and two other towers as well.'

I watched Firouz walking towards us and I found myself not liking the man. He had a way of half-turning as he walked: a half-turn this way, a half-turn that way. 'He's a turning sort of man,' I said to Bembel Rudzuk.

'He is indeed a turning sort of man,' said Bembel Rudzuk, 'and more likely to take a bad turn than a good one. Try not to let yourself be drawn into a quarrel with him.'

Firouz walked to the centre of the paved square; his shadow fell across my circles, triangles, and hexagons. He touched the central six-pointed star with his foot. 'This is the star of the Jews, is it not?' he said to Bembel Rudzuk. (By this time I had sufficient Arabic to follow the conversation.)

'You have seen this star in Islamic patterns without number,' said Bembel Rudzuk. 'You have seen it in mosques and palaces and in houses everywhere; even is it stamped by some of our Muslim merchants on the canvas coverings of bales.'

'That may well be,' said Firouz, 'but at the same time it is a device used by the Jews, is it not?'

'It is one of many devices used by many people,' said Bembel Rudzuk.

'Was it drawn by you?' said Firouz.

'Yes,' said Bembel Rudzuk, 'it was.'

Firouz's demeanour was such that I knew it could only be a moment or two until he asked me if I was a Jew. I think that he already knew that I was but did not want to appear to have taken the trouble to inform himself of such a trifling event as my Jewish arrival in Antioch; he preferred rather to go through this play-acting in which he pretended only now to have his curiosity aroused by the six-pointed star.

Such an interesting moment, that moment before someone who is not a Jew asks you if you are a Jew! The world being as it is, any live Jew is a survivor in that there will always be other Jews within living memory who are dead only because they were Jews. So whoever asks, 'Are you a Jew?' is saying at the same time, 'Are you one of those who has not so far been slaughtered?' To answer yes to this question has at one time and another assured the death of the answerer. At that moment in Antioch Jews were not being slaughtered but nevertheless the question would not be a neutral one, it would not be such a question as: 'What do you think of our summer weather?' No, it would be a question with an under-question: 'Are you a Jew who dies without fighting or a Jew who makes trouble?'

'As you say,' said Firouz, still addressing his remarks to Bembel Rudzuk and affecting to take no notice of me, 'it's a star one sees everywhere. And yet this particular version of it, with all those triangles appearing at the same time to move inward and outward—there's something one might almost call one-eyed about it, wouldn't you say? Wouldn't you say that the inward tends to be swallowed up by the outward in this design?'

'One of the virtues of this simple but at the same time complex design,' said Bembel Rudzuk, 'this design in which we see the continually reciprocating action of unity and multiplicity, is that it suits its apparent action to the mind of the viewer: those who look outward see the outward pre-eminent; those who look inward see the inward.'

'Are you a Jew?' said Firouz to me suddenly.

'Hear, O Israel!' I said in Hebrew, 'The Lord our God, the Lord is One!'

'I bear witness that there is no god but God and that Muhammad is the messenger of God,' said Firouz. For a moment he stared at me wildly as if I had struck him in the face, then he turned to Bembel Rudzuk. 'Has your Israelite friend registered for the tax payable by those non-Muslims who sojourn among us?' he said.

'Yes,' said Bembel Rudzuk, 'he has been paying the tax since he first came to Antioch.'

'See to it also,' said Firouz, 'that he dresses in accordance with his station and that he does not ride a horse or carry weapons.' He turned on his heel, walked back across the square to where an attendant was holding his horse, mounted, and rode off towards the Tower of the Two Sisters, turning once in the saddle to look back.

'This too will pass,' said Bembel Rudzuk. 'Firouz is a man of moods and many of them are unpleasant. As we can do nothing about him we might as well get on with our work.'

There came then to the centre of the square Tower Gate's foreman. 'You might as well fetch the bricks for the tower now,' he said to some of the workmen: 'that'll be the next thing after we do this hexagon.'

'What tower?' said Bembel Rudzuk.

'The tower at the centre,' said the foreman.

'Ah!' said Bembel Rudzuk.

'Did you commission this tower?' I said to Bembel Rudzuk when the foreman had moved away from us.

'No,' he said, 'but it will give us a platform from which to observe the action of the pattern, and as it will be built at the very beginning we shall thus better see the development of the pattern as it is assembled. I myself had been thinking of erecting a tower when the pattern was complete but it's better really to have it now.'

The central unit, the hexagon from which would overlappingly radiate all the other hexagons and the stars they contained, measured six feet four inches at its greatest width, and it was on this hexagon that the hexagonal tower was to be built.

On the underside of each of the thirty-six tiles of this central hexagon Bembel Rudzuk wrote one of the various names of Allah: The Beneficent on one, The Merciful on another, and so on. 'You too must write on these tiles,' he said to me.

'I cannot,' I said. 'God for me is beyond naming, nor have I any other words to write.' As I said this I noticed two figures poised attentively at the edge of the stone square: one was the Imam, the leader of the local Muslim congregation; the other was Rabbi Akiba ben Eliezer. The Imam was tall and lean, the Rabbi short and stocky; the Imam had black eyes and a white beard, the Rabbi had blue eyes and a red beard; but their differences disappeared in the unanimity of their disapproval: their paired gaze was like four long iron rods, the two from the Imam pinioning Bembel Rudzuk and the two from the Rabbi pinioning me. Having declined the Rabbi's invitation to join the congregation I always felt defensive when I saw him. Bembel Rudzuk, while a perfectly respectable member of the Muslim community, was known to be a strongly individual thinker. I hoped that the Imam and the Rabbi would be content to leave us to our work as we left them to theirs; but of course we were their work so I resigned myself to that iron optical embrace.

The thirty-six central tiles having been duly inscribed were now ready to be set in mortar. The lines where paving stones met indicated the axes of the square, and guided by these the foreman and his helper stretched their strings, trowelled in the mortar, and caused the tiles to appear to their proper places. Their activity seemed nothing so gross as common tile-laying: rather the tiles leapt into their hands, there was written on the air a fleeting calligraphy of dark limbs and white garments and Aha! the tiles manifested the central hexagon. The foreman and his helper seemed (they did it so quietly that I couldn't be certain) to be hissing and humming some little song frequently punctuated by tiny explosive exhalations of breath: 'Dzah!' and 'Dzee!' and 'Dzim!' To this almost silent sibilance moved the white garments, the dark limbs, the red and black and tawny triangles into Hidden Lion.

As Bembel Rudzuk and I stood looking at the design we both noticed at the same moment that it was as it had been with the drawing that I had made on paper that night in November when Hidden Lion first appeared to me: 'The motion is already there,' said Bembel Rudzuk.

'Did you notice when it first became apparent?' I said.

'No,' he said, 'I was intent on the placing of the tiles. Did you?'

'No,' I said, 'I simply forgot all about it.'

'Our first lesson,' said Bembel Rudzuk: 'the heart of the mystery is meant to remain a mystery.'

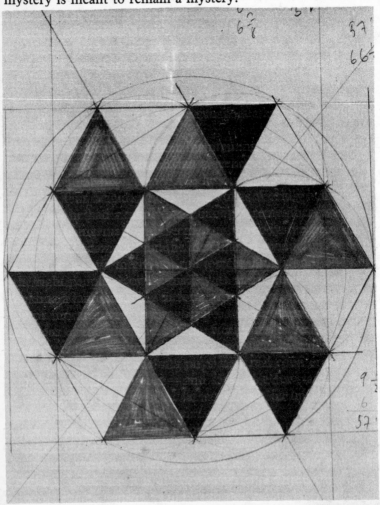

Hidden Lion! (For me that would always be the name of precedence; the Willing Virgin was the name for an aspect of the pattern that had not been made apparent to me by the pattern itself.) To see that central hexagon in its full-scale alternation of large and small red and black and tawny triangles, its solid and tangible actuality of fired and glazed tiles, was quite astonishing, there was so much action in it. I have before this described my drawing of the twelvefold repetition and my surprise at the quantity and variety of the action in it. But here there was as yet no repetition, there was only this hexagon made up of large and small triangles: the eighteen large outer ones; the twelve small inner ones; the six shallow ones between the inner and the outer. It was immediately apparent that the large interlocking red and black and tawny triangles of the outer hexagon were predisposed to turn, to revolve, to remind themselves that they were born of a circle. To this central hexagon at Bembel Rudzuk's request I gave a name: David's Wheel.

Firouz came to us again that day and stood looking at David's Wheel, magnetically drawn, it seemed, by the pattern. This time he seemed to be without animosity, seemed to look on us with respect, as when a little boy watches his father string a bow that he himself will not be able to bend until he is grown a man. He spread out his fingers as if gripping a small wheel, he rotated his outspread, hooked fingers. 'It turns,' he said, 'there is a turning in it: the turning of the sun and the moon and the stars; the turning of the wheels of fate and fortune. Thus do we see that at the centre of the universe there is a turning, there is a turning at the heart of the mystery. This turning pattern that you have made with these tiles, has it a name?'

'David's Wheel,' I said, and then I was sorry that I had said it; I didn't want him to know the name of anything that meant anything to me.

'David's Wheel,' he said. 'David slew Goliath and became a great king. And yet he turned, did he not. He turned from what was right, he turned to the wrong, he lusted after Bathsheba, he told Joab to put Uriah her husband in the forefront of the hottest battle. Then when Uriah was dead he joyed himself, did he not, with Bathsheba the juicy widow, the fruit of his wrongdoing.'

'He was only a man,' I said. 'He made music, he sang and danced before the Lord.'

'Only a man!' said Firouz. 'Only a man!' He turned on his heel, always he left with that heel-turn, never did he simply walk away as others did.

Tower Gate now made his appearance, drawing near in a manner that commanded attention by the power of his attention; he came as if mystically summoned by David's Wheel, and he so focused his approaching presence on that hexagon that it seemed to be a winch that was winding him in with an invisible rope.

When he arrived at David's Wheel he looked down into it with a look that made me feel utterly left out and excluded from any understanding whatever of the thing that I had summoned with my compass and my straight-edge; one sees that always with specialists: a bowman picks up a bow in a way that leaves the non-bowman feeling poor; a silk merchant reads the silk with his fingers and almost there rise up from his touch phantom ships and camels, distant mountains, distant seas. Tower Gate looked down into David's Wheel and in his face I tried without success to read whether he looked into crystalline depths or into an abyss of smoke and flame.

'What do you see?' I blurted out.

He looked at me as if I had farted during prayers, looked away graciously, then looked back with a face that showed willingness to put the incident behind us. 'Let me show you the plan and elevations for the tower,' he said to Bembel Rudzuk, and opened a roll of drawings which he handed to his foreman, who laid them on David's Wheel and put loose tiles on the corners to hold them flat.

'This tower wants to be very plain,' said Tower Gate; 'it wants to be nothing immodest, nothing too commanding. It is a little hexagonal tower with its stairs going round the outside of it. This is not a seashell that grows itself round its own spiral and remembers in its windings the sound of the sea; this tower remembers nothing and its unsheltered spiral is open to the sky.

144

'To what is the height of this tower related? To the triangles on which it stands. These triangles offer us an angle of thirty degrees, an angle of sixty degrees, and an angle of one hundred and twenty degrees. The obtuse angle not being usable we try the other two: projecting a sixty-degree angle from the edge of your square to a point above the centre gives us a tower more than a hundred feet high, a real God-challenger and not to be thought of even if it were practically possible on a base only six feet four inches across; projecting a thirty-degree angle gives us a tower about thirty-five feet high which is still a little pretentious. What then remains to us? In reverence and in modesty (if indeed we can apply such words to a project so thoroughly dubious) we halve that angle and arrive at this tower just over sixteen feet high, taller than a man on a camel but not so high in the air as the mu'addhin; it is a height for broadening one's view a little but not for feeling too far above the world.'

'I am powerfully impressed by the care you have taken in this matter,' said Bembel Rudzuk, 'and I am profoundly grateful for the discretion you have shown; one can so easily do the wrong thing.'

'We may well have done the wrong thing in any case,' said Tower Gate, 'but life is after all a matter of making choices and one is bound to choose wrong in one or two of those matters that really matter.'

So the tower was built. It had no ornamentation, no red and black triangles; it was made of plain tawny bricks. The platform at the top was built out a foot wider all round than the base; it was enclosed by a parapet three feet high and left open to the sky.

The tower being complete the pattern began to spread outward from it. I felt a pang of regret: once begun, a project can only be completed or abandoned; actuality is gained as potentiality is lost. There was no stopping the growth of Hidden Lion; the serpents twisted through the stars, the pyramids shifted and regrouped, the lions appeared and disappeared, the illusory enclaves of disorder were suddenly there, suddenly not there. And under each tile a name of God.

To visualize a pattern, whether in a drawing or in tiles or

even to see it with the eye of the mind only, is to make visible the power in the pattern. Because of the scale of Hidden Lion the power was very clearly to be seen from the top of the tower; it was like the power that surges beneath the skin of a strong river.

'This motion that we see is the motion of the Unseen,' said Bembel Rudzuk. 'This power that we see is the power of the Unseen, and it is both conscious power and the power of consciousness. Here already are two of my questions answered: motion is in the pattern from the very beginning because the motion is there before the pattern, the pattern is only a mode of appearance assumed by the motion; consciousness also is in the pattern from the very beginning because the consciousness is there before the pattern, the pattern is only a kind of window for the consciousness to look out of. Although serpents, pyramids, and lions seem to appear in the pattern, that is only because the human mind will make images out of anything; the pattern is in actuality abstract, it represents nothing and asserts no images. It offers itself modestly and reverently to the Unseen and the Unseen takes pleasure in it.'

I said, 'May it be that there is no necessity to study this pattern or observe it methodically? May it not even be inadvisable to do so? May it not be that the best way of conducting oneself with this pattern is simply to take it in without any thought and to enjoy in it the presence of the Unseen?'

'I think you're right,' said Bembel Rudzuk.

So. Bembel Rudzuk went on writing the names of Allah on the undersides of the tiles and the workmen went on dancingly fitting them into the pattern. And what was my work at this time? I was a witness. I was there to see every tile fitted, I was there to see Hidden Lion grow triangle by triangle. I wrote down no observations, kept no record of its progress from day to day; I drained off none of the virtue of it; I gave my mind to it and there it lived and went its way.

All the time that the work of putting together Hidden Lion was going on we were watched daily by children, by idlers and street sages, by all manner of people pausing on the way from one place to another. The children soon began to walk on the pattern in special ways and to dance on it, sometimes stepping only on the red triangles, sometimes only on the black. Seeing them always out of the corner of my eye I found in my mind new and unwritten names of God: The Tiptoeing; The Sidewise-Jumping; The Hopping; The Leaping; The Dancing; The Whirling.

One morning the baker who had a shop near Hidden Lion came and stood respectfully before Bembel Rudzuk. 'My lord,' he said, 'I have heard that this design came to you in a dream, that you were commanded by Allah to cover this square with this pattern, and that on the underside of each tile is written a name of Allah in all the tongues of mankind. Is this true?'

'The design came to me in the mind of this pilgrim,' said Bembel Rudzuk, indicating me. 'Certainly it is by the will of Allah that we do this work, and it is true that there is written on the underside of each tile a name of Allah, but in Arabic only.'

'This is virtuous action,' said the baker, 'and therefore one is not surprised that there is virtue in it. My son comes here to play in the evening, he does no harm, he only walks on the tiles. For three months he has had an infection of the right eye. Yesterday evening he walked from star to star on one line of stars for as far as the tiles went. Walking towards Mecca he trod only on the small red triangles and looked at them fixedly; walking back he trod only on the small black triangles and looked at them fixedly. This morning the eye infection is completely gone. I have no wish to intrude upon your good work but I ask in all humility that you take this small offering which is nothing really, it is only that something should pass from my hand to your hand in the name of Allah The Responsive, The Restorer.' He put some money into the hand of Bembel Rudzuk.

'Will you not rather give this money to the poor?' said Bembel Rudzuk.

'I give to the poor as well,' said the baker. 'This is something else, this is in praise of Allah whose attributes are infinite, Allah who has caused this idea to move you; it is only to show that I in my insignificant way am grateful.'

'So be it,' said Bembel Rudzuk. 'The pattern is abstract; let the money also be used abstractly. I shall put it into one of the tiles of the pattern where it will be united with the design on the pattern and with the names of Allah in celebration of your gratitude to Him The Responsive, Him The Restorer.'

Bembel Rudzuk instructed a workman to chip out of the two-inch thickness of one of the tiles a shallow recess in the bottom; the money was mortared into the tile and the tile, inscribed with the desired names of Allah, was put into Hidden Lion.

On the next day came the potter whose shop was in the same street as that of the baker. 'In the five years of our marriage,' he said to Bembel Rudzuk, 'my wife had not been able to conceive. At the end of the first day's work after the building of the tower she came here and stepped on every tile that was in the pattern, saying while she did so the names of Allah. For seven evenings she came here and did this. Now is her womb quickened with life. I beg that this wholly inadequate offering be incorporated in one of your tiles dedicated to Allah, The Generous One.'

Bembel Rudzuk sighed. 'Having accepted the money of the baker I cannot refuse yours,' he said. 'I shall do with it as you request.'

'Wonderful are the ways of Allah!' said Bembel Rudzuk after the potter had gone. 'For such a little time was Hidden Lion permitted to go its uncorrupted way! Yesterday I did a foolish thing and today I am forced to continue in my foolishness. Already is the integrity of the work marred physically and spiritually. Two of the tiles have been mutilated for this primitive good-luck commerce and now there will be no end to it. Yesterday the Imam scowled at me; today he will laugh: I have become a vendor of good-luck charms.'

'Then don't let them give you any more money,' I said.

'Too late,' said Bembel Rudzuk. 'I must go on as I have begun. Striving too hard after wisdom has made me a fool.'

The visits of the baker and the potter made us aware that Hidden Lion had a life of its own in those evening hours when we were not there. The pregnancy of the potter's wife reminded me that it had not been days but weeks since the tiles had begun to cover the square. People had been walking on the tiles, dancing on them, kissing them, counting them, contemplating them, acting in various special ways upon them, doing whatever they were moved by the place, the pattern, and the desire of their hearts to do. In the days that followed it was not single visitors who came but several at once, then more and more who waited patiently to tell Bembel Rudzuk how their wishes had been gratified and to give him their offering large or small for the work.

The Imam and the Rabbi were often to be seen observing what was going on. Bembel Rudzuk was right: the Imam, although not actually laughing, was smiling broadly. The Rabbi had on his face a particularly Jewish look: the pensive look of a man who while smiling almost fondly at people who are being childish is at the same time well aware that these childish people may at any moment require his life of him.

Firouz, a few days after his instructions as to dress, horses, and weapons, was reminded by the Rabbi's yellow turban and belt that I was not similarly distinguishable. He questioned me about this with some severity and I told him that as a eunuch I could not count myself a member of the Jewish congregation. He then asked the Rabbi if that was so. The Rabbi, buttoning me with his eye, said that it was so. I expected Firouz to say that exclusion from the congregation did not cancel my Jewish status in dhimma matters but he did not say that; he looked thoughtful and he never broached the subject again.

At this time the pattern was still expanding, it had not yet covered the whole square. Children, I noticed, were particularly fond of walking and dancing the shape of the unfinished edges. It became evident to me that the forward edge of a pattern's visible expansion is attractive, it excites in people and in things a desire to shape themselves to it, to meet it and move with its advance. I speak of the forward edge of the pattern's *visible* expansion because I had become more and more strongly aware that the visual manifestation of a pattern comes only after the pattern is already in existence and already infinite: the visible expansion is only a finite tracing of what, being infinite, cannot further expand.

It was at this time also that I noticed that Hidden Lion in its abstractness was capable of activating in my vision more than the serpents, pyramids, lions, and enclaves of apparent disorder that I have described: there rose up from the motion and consciousness of the pattern an apparition of Jerusalem, a phantom of place unseen. It was that Jerusalem of my ignorance, that inn-sign Jerusalem of coarse and vivid colour, the solid geometry of its forms tawny-stoned, golden-domed, purple-shadowed, the aerial geometry of its light and shade rising with the forms transparently upon the air over Hidden Lion. Sometimes it was there, sometimes not. I was uncertain of the meaning of this apparition; sometimes I thought one thing, sometimes another. Sometimes I tried to move my mind away from it.

Firouz of course remained attentive to our activities. Seeing people give money to Bembel Rudzuk and seeing the money then mortared into the tiles he said to Bembel Rudzuk, 'What is this commerce that you do with your geomancy? What do you give for this money that you take?'

Bembel Rudzuk said, 'It is not a commerce of my choosing but I don't know how to stop it; to refuse this money that is offered gratefully to Allah would be to deny the giver a part in the pattern.'

'Will you accept money from me as well?' said Firouz.

'For what?' said Bembel Rudzuk. 'What have you had from this pattern?' He didn't say the pattern's name, we only used that between us. To everyone else it was simply 'the pattern'.

'One night I stood at the top of your tower,' said Firouz, 'and there came to me a thought of great profundity.'

I didn't like to think of Firouz at the top of our tower, I didn't like to think of any thought that might have come to him there. Clearly Bembel Rudzuk didn't want to take the money, he didn't want to accept Firouz into the membership of Hidden Lion but he didn't feel easy about saying no. 'Your profound thought,' he said to Firouz, 'surely it would have come to you anywhere.'

'Indeed not,' said Firouz; 'it came to me while I was contemplating the inwardness and outwardness of this particular pattern; I am convinced that it could not have come to me anywhere else. You have taken money from anyone who has offered it to you, I have seen you do it. Am I alone to be excluded from this multiplicity of people who have become unified with your pattern?'

'No,' said Bembel Rudzuk miserably, 'I have no wish to exclude you.'

Firouz took Bembel Rudzuk's hand and pressed a piece of gold into it. 'You see how I value this,' he said. 'To have my own tile in this great pattern! Tell me, what is the name of it?'

'The name of what?' said Bembel Rudzuk.

'The name of this pattern,' said Firouz. 'This design that is so mystical in the simplicity of its complexity, surely it has a name?'

'Ah!' said Bembel Rudzuk, 'who am I to put a name to a pattern? Let each person who looks at it think of it with or without a name as Allah wills.'

'Your humility is overwhelming,' said Firouz. 'It flattens me utterly. And yet, modest as you are, probably when you think of this pattern you think of it with a name.'

Bembel Rudzuk shrugged. 'Mostly I don't think of it, I simply become absorbed in it thoughtlessly.'

'Ah!' said Firouz. 'Thoughtless absorption! Yes, yes, I understand that absolutely: one simply becomes one with the everything, one is free for a time from the burden of one's self. What bliss! And yet, and yet — returning to the world and its burdens one puts names to things. So it is that I have lost myself in this pattern, but returning to the world I look at this abstraction with which I have merged; I turn my head this way and that way, I see twisting serpents, moving pyramids; suddenly there leaps forward the face of a lion, then it is gone again. "Ah!" say I, "I have been with Hidden Lion!"' With that he did his regular heel-turn and walked turningly away, but stopped after only a few steps and turned back towards us. 'I was forgetting to ask,' he said, 'what name of Allah you'll be writing on the underside of my tile.'

'The Watchful,' said Bembel Rudzuk, 'He who observes all creatures, and every action is under His control.'

'Why that one?' said Firouz. 'Why that particular one for me?'

'It came into my mind when you asked, so I assume that it was put there by Allah,' said Bembel Rudzuk.

'"Every action is under His control,"' said Firouz. 'How can that be, really? Think of the dreadful things that are done in this world every day.'

'The child is under the control of the parents, is it not,' said Bembel Rudzuk; 'yet must the child creep on its hands and knees before it can walk, and when it first walks it can go only a step or two before it falls.'

'True, true,' said Firouz. 'That's all we are: little children creeping on our hands and knees. The parent, however, doesn't punish the child for falling, while Allah The Watchful will surely punish the sinner, will he not?'

'The child who falls when learning to walk has not the choice,' said Bembel Rudzuk, 'but the sinner has.'

'That what was the use of bringing the child into it at all?' said Firouz. 'It's a useless analogy, it's no help whatever.'

'It's a perfectly useful analogy,' said Bembel Rudzuk: 'the consequence of not being able to walk is to fall and the consequence of not being able to maintain moral balance is also to fall. How could it be otherwise?'

'To be in a fallen state,' said Firouz, 'that isn't so dreadful; all sorts of fallen people ride about on good horses wearing fine clothes and who can tell the difference? I'm thinking about later, I'm thinking about the Fire where one burns and burns and is given molten brass to drink. Do you think that's really how it is?'

'I think that the Fire is in the soul of each of us,' said Bembel Rudzuk: 'those of us consigned to the Fire burn every day and every night.'

'You don't burn though, do you?' said Firouz. 'You're cool and easy, your soul dwells in the Garden of its self-delight.'

'Where my soul dwells is between Allah and me, not between you and me,' said Bembel Rudzuk.

'You're so comfortable!' said Firouz. 'You're so easy, you're like a cat that purrs before a dish of the milk of your own wisdom that is so delicious to you.'

'I am as Allah made me,' said Bembel Rudzuk, 'and certainly I never asked you to drink from that dish.'

'Always a clever answer,' said Firouz. He turned to me. 'And you,' he said, 'what name of Allah would you write on the tile?'

'God for me is nameless,' I said.

'Ah!' said Firouz. 'Profundity! How could I have expected otherwise!' Again he executed his heel-turn and I thought that we had perhaps seen the last of him for that day but no, here he was turning yet again to speak to us once more.

'How many tiles will there be in Hidden Lion when it is complete?' he said.

'I don't know,' said Bembel Rudzuk. 'We haven't calculated that.'

'How many tiles are there in it so far?' said Firouz.

'We have not counted,' said Bembel Rudzuk. 'Allah is The Reckoner.'

'Of course,' said Firouz. 'This is part of the milk of your wisdom, is it not. And yet if the Governor should impose a tax on paving-tiles then you with all your piety would have to do some reckoning.'

The workmen were just then unloading a camel and two of them now approached the advancing edge of the pattern with a four-handled basket full of tiles. Firouz walked turningly towards them with his features composed in an official expression as if he were going to confiscate the tiles. The workmen stopped in their tracks and looked at him with fear and uncertainty.

It was at that moment that the Governor Yaghi-Siyan appeared, riding a horse and flanked by six of his bodyguard. At the edge of the stone square he dismounted and approached us. When he came to the outermost edge of Hidden Lion he ostentatiously took off his shoes and walked barefoot across the tiles to us. Bembel Rudzuk and I took off our shoes as well and made him a little bow. Firouz whirled round to face the Governor and seeing us all barefoot hurried to take off his shoes. He flung out a hand to steady himself against the basket that the two workmen were still holding between them; perhaps he leant on it too heavily or perhaps the workmen, already nervous and fearful of him, were startled by his sudden movement and let go of the basket — in any case it fell with its heavy load of tiles and there was a howl of pain from Firouz who had somehow contrived to have his foot under it.

The terrified workmen lifted the basket clear and while Firouz composed himself heroically I examined his foot and ascertained that the metatarsal bone was broken. A man was sent for bandages while I set the bone and bound it temporarily with my kaffiya. As I was doing this Firouz said to me, 'I know that this design has come from your hand and not that of Bembel Rudzuk. It is your Hidden Lion, Jew.'

'This Hidden Lion belongs to no one person more than to any other,' I said. 'It is simply the lion that remains hidden until it reveals itself.'

Yaghi-Siyan seemed unmoved by Firouz's suffering. He looked down at him and said, 'Tell me, Firouz, what have you done to this load of tiles that it should fall upon you like this, eh? Did it attack you or was it acting in self-defence? Were you perhaps threatening it? Or were you attempting to extort money from it?'

Firouz drew back his lips from his teeth in a ghastly smile. 'This was a didactic load of tiles,' he said. 'It was teaching us that what is clay can fall.'

'Also,' said Yaghi-Siyan, 'it was teaching you to step carefully.' He looked steadily at Firouz until Firouz looked away; no more was said between them.

When I had properly bandaged Firouz's foot I had the thought of further immobilizing the broken bone by stiffening the bandage with clay from the riverbank to enclose the foot in a mud-brick shell. This being done Firouz was set aside to dry in the sun.

'Will you now write a name of Allah upon me?' said Firouz to Bembel Rudzuk. 'Will you fit me into your design?'

'The tiles in this pattern,' said Bembel Rudzuk, 'have not only been dried in the sun; they have also passed through the fire.'

'Ah!' said Firouz, but he said no more than that.

Yaghi-Siyan was standing before Bembel Rudzuk with a kind of aggressive humility, impatient for him to leave off paying attention to Firouz. 'I am told,' he said, 'that this tiling is done for its own sake alone.'

'Your Excellency,' said Bembel Rudzuk, 'this that we do here is only a kind of foolishness, a kind of vanity. It is done to be looked at.'

'I don't think it is foolishness,' said Yaghi-Siyan. 'I sense here the presence of Allah.'

'That may well be due to your own virtue rather than to anything in the work itself,' said Bembel Rudzuk.

'I think not,' said Yaghi-Siyan. 'I think that this is something out of the usual run, something extraordinary, even inspired. Most things are a kind of commerce, even most piety: one gives something, one gets something. But this is original, this is abstract; it simply becomes itself, asking nothing.'

'To hear your Excellency say this of course gives me great pleasure,' said Bembel Rudzuk.

'You're being polite,' said Yaghi-Siyan; 'you're being careful, you're being closed. Say something careless to me, something open, something abstract.'

'This is my abstraction,' said Bembel Rudzuk indicating Hidden Lion with a sweep of his arm. 'This is my openness, my carelessness, my impoliteness.'

'May I climb your tower?' said Yaghi-Siyan.

'This tower is of course yours, Excellency,' said Bembel Rudzuk. 'It is my privilege to invite you to make use of it.'

Yaghi-Siyan went to the tower and now I was able to see the profundity of Tower Gate's design: towers are naturally dramatic structures that intensify the image of any figure that is to be seen looking down from them. Particularly do they do this when the figure disappears into a doorway at the bottom and then reappears looking over a parapet at the top. But here the stairs round the outside of the tower kept the figure unremarkable by making visible the effort of going from the bottom to the top; at the top the low parapet continued this objectivity. There were to be seen only a little tower, only an ordinary man.

From this nameless tower did Yaghi-Siyan look down on Hidden Lion. Not a breath of air stirred his white burnous, the blue sky was utterly without a sign of anything. At just such an unheralded moment, I thought, might marvels appear to a watcher on a tower: the earth opening up; the kraken rising to the surface of the sea; the mountain lifting itself into the air over the city. It occurred to me that the Unseen might at any moment make use of any pair of eyes to see everything in an altogether different way, a way never thought of before. I felt the earth leap like a fish beneath me. An immeasurable time passed, perhaps it was only a moment, perhaps it is still continuing: the dark face of Yaghi-Siyan; the white burnous; the blue sky; the leaping earth.

When Yaghi-Siyan came down from the tower he looked up to where he had stood, then he looked down at the tiles he was standing on. 'From there I saw the motion,' he said; 'from here I see the stillness. What is it, what is it that moves us? We were the wild horsemen out of the east, Byzantium drew back before us. Now I stand here in this city with a wall around it but the inside is continually rushing to join the outside. Almost I am dizzy with it.' He began to weep; weeping he bowed his head to the tiles. Then he stood up, walked back to his shoes, put them on, mounted his horse, and rode back to the Governor's Palace.

12

Time, it seems, has passed. The triangular tiles of Hidden Lion have covered all of Bembel Rudzuk's stone square, but the pattern has in its turn been so covered by people, by stalls, by booths and tents and awnings that the surge of its action is obscured by the action of every day; the twisting serpents, the shifting pyramids, the appearing and disappearing lions are mostly hidden.

It happened by degrees. I have already told how men, women, and children walked on Hidden Lion in special ways, how they danced on it with particular things in mind, how they gave money which was put into the tiles. Without anyone's being told the name became known; people used it in giving directions. Hidden Lion became a meeting-place, and in time a man asked permission to establish a coffee stand in the noon shadow of the tower at the centre. Permission was given, and the fragrance of coffee became part of the pattern. Other applicants were quick to follow, and stallholders appeared selling cooked food, melons and oranges, pots and pans, carpets, caged birds, jewelry and weapons. They occupied their spaces rent-free; since the completion of the tiling Bembel Rudzuk had accepted no more money.

Hidden Lion became not only the liveliest of bazaars but also a good-luck place almost sacred to those who had experienced its power. There were lovers who had sworn to each other on a particular tile and by the appropriate names of Allah; there were children at whose birth money had been put into tiles inscribed with the names of Allah The Guide, The Preventer,

The Enricher. Bargains were struck, partnerships founded, parents honoured and the dead remembered in the tiles of Hidden Lion.

Every day has a dawn, every day a midnight: sometimes we mark by the one, sometimes by the other. Came the month of July and its days marched like a procession of penitents towards the Ninth of Av; then did I count the days by the nights. When there came the first anniversary of my night with Sophia I paced the roof of Bembel Rudzuk's house feeling as if I were wrapped in the burning scroll of my love, my lust, my sin, my wisdom, my transcendent mortality. God was poor, I thought, to be immortal.

Towards the middle of August came Ramadhan. The city was like an oven. The sounds of the street withdrew into the silence of exhaustion and the continual growling murmur of the Quran. From that time before dawn when a white thread could be distinguished from a black one the Muslims fasted until sunset, when the call of the mu'addhin like the darkness eased the city into night, prayer, food, and more reciting of the Quran.

The twenty-seventh of Ramadhan, the Lailat al-Qadr, the Night of Power on which Muhammad received his first revelation, was to Bembel Rudzuk an especially important night. 'The Quran tells us that this Night of Power is better than a thousand months,' he said: 'it is all time, it is no time, it is beyond the bounds of reckoning and measurement. It may be that even the idea of it puts the mind into a special state: always on this night I have a dream that is not like the dreams of other nights; always on this night comes a strong way-showing dream.' His face looked young, it was so full of eagerness and excitement.

As on many nights that summer we were sleeping on the roof. We stayed up late talking, and I looked for but could not find the Virgin and the Lion among the stars. 'Only part of the Lion can be seen now,' said Bembel Rudzuk. He tried to show me where it was but I could only recognize the Lion when together with the Virgin it made that gesture that had so imprinted itself on my mind.

Towards dawn I was awakened by a thumping on the roof: it

was Bembel Rudzuk dancing in his nightdress. His eyes were closed; he was dancing in his sleep. It was a shuffling, stamping dance in which there were many formal turnings of the body, many hieratic movements of the arms close to the body. It was an earthy dance, nothing of it moved up into the air; it was as if earth had formed itself into a man and the man was dancing himself back into the earth. Bembel Rudzuk danced more and more slowly and more and more deeply until the body that I saw before me stood motionless like the nymphal shell left behind by a dragonfly. But Bembel Rudzuk, unlike the dragonfly, seemed not to have flown away into the air but to have danced himself out of his body into the earth.

The shell of Bembel Rudzuk opened its eyes and Bembel Rudzuk looked out of them.

'Was this your dream?' I said. 'Were you dancing your dream?'

'Earth,' he said. 'I was dancing earth.'

'Are you awake?' I said.

'Which is the dream?' he said.

After the Lailat al-Qadr I began to think of preparing myself a little for the days that were coming. Now when I say that I see in my mind those stubborn Frankish tents before the walls of Antioch, I see the arrogance of the Franks in the way they walk, in the way they sit their horses. At that time I had seen nothing of them, I only sensed their approach, and this awareness of them moving towards us mingled with the picture that was always in my mind of the sprawled bodies of the dead Jews of our town, most of whom had never in their lives held a sword in their hands. I did not care for that style of dying, and accordingly I asked Bembel Rudzuk to instruct me in horsemanship and the use of weapons.

The prohibition of the riding of horses and the carrying of weapons by non-Muslims was not consistently enforced in Antioch; the rigour varied with the times and with the moods of the Governor and his officers. At that time Yaghi-Siyan had not yet become as uneasy about the loyalty of Christians and Jews as he was to be a few months later — it was Firouz that I had to be mindful of; as he had already taken notice of my non-wearing of a yellow turban and belt it seemed wise not to attract his attention again. Bembel Rudzuk and a servant used to ride out of the city leading a third horse and I would follow them on foot to the hills east of the Orontes where I then mounted and rode on with them. So I had the use of a horse and weapons as often as I liked, and Firouz, who of course knew about it, seemed content that his authority was recognized within the walls; in any case he made no trouble.

Bembel Rudzuk was an excellent teacher. His youth had been active and adventurous and his strength and vigour seemed little diminished at his present age; he was a dashing horseman and he was expert with bow and sword. Our rides continued even after the siege began — it was months before the blockade was complete — and after not too long a time I rode well enough for Bembel Rudzuk to say that I might have made a horseman if I had come to it earlier in life; eventually I shot well enough with the Turkish bow to bring down game; our swordplay continued in Bembel Rudzuk's courtyard long after the rides had stopped, and with the curved Turkish sword and the straight blade both I progressed to where Bembel Rudzuk was at least as eager as I for a rest at the end of our practice. Sometimes as I swung my blunted sword I seemed to see behind Bembel Rudzuk the shadowy and as yet faceless form of actuality to come.

One day followed another through months that bore different names, numbered themselves by the sun or the moon, and began and ended on different days in the Muslim, Jewish, and Christian calendars. Strange, to live again one's life and death in three calendars! Soon after the Lailat al-Qadr of the Hijra year 490 in the month of September of the Christian year 1097 came the Jewish High Holy Days, the Days of Awe: Rosh Hashanah, the New Year's Day of 4858, and ten days later Yom Kippur, the Day of Atonement. Ah! then I felt my eunuchhood, my separateness from any congregation! It was no use to tell myself that God was no longer He and that accounts were no longer being kept — centuries of moral reckoning leapt up in me. It was in me; I was in it: it was like a giant wave, an impulse racing across vast expanses of time, living its motion through successive particles of mortality.

160

This would now be the second Rosh Hashanah and Yom Kippur since I had left my town. The last time these Days of Awe had come I had been on the road alone, there had been no congregation to be cut off from when the shofar was blown, when the Kol Nidrei was sung at the beginning of the fast and when the Ne'ilah Service was recited, the book and the gates closed, and the Shema, the 'Hear, O Israel!' heard at the end. Here in Antioch however there was a congregation and I had with words out of my own mouth cut myself off from it; I didn't want to be part of anybody else's traffic with God. But I wanted something; I thought perhaps that I wanted to hear the sound of the ram's horn, the shofar. The urgent maleness of that trumpeting always lifted me and quickened my blood: it was so much a call to action, it was so utterly not the murmur of praying, swaying, weaponless victims — was it not itself the weapon of the ram that had borne it? And did it not also recall that ram that had appeared when the Lord stayed the hand of Abraham as Isaac lay bound and waiting for the knife? And more: this trumpeting of the ram's horn was for me the summons from the dreadful mountain of the Law, a summons that could not be ignored or denied. And I see, now that my mind is no longer limited by my mortal identity, that this Law is nothing that could be limited to those commandments on the two stones: no, this Law that is so imperious is simply the law of the allness of the everything of which each of us is a particle. Quick! Now! Rise up from your sleep, from your unbeing! Be! Do! Respond!

Be! Do! What? Before Rosh Hashanah, as the end of the month of Elul and the beginning of Tishri approached, I went by night to the synagogue. It was huddled away among the houses of the Jewish quarter, it stood among the smells of various dyes, even those reds and purples flaunted by those knightly wearers of the Cross who were now approaching us. This not very large domed building, said by some to have been built on the ruin of a Roman smithy, had been chosen because of its thick walls through which the warlike sound of the shofar could not be heard. It stood among the houses and the rainbowed smells like an honest workman who, finished with the toil of the week, has cleansed himself and put on fresh clothes for the Sabbath. There were no windows facing the street, there was no light to be seen except what came through the open door from the inner court.

I put my hand on the wall that separated me from the space where the shofar had sounded that day as it had all through the month of Elul. The heat of the day had gone out of the wall, it was cool. As I stood there a man named Mordechai Salzedo, a merchant friend of Bembel Rudzuk, came to me and said, 'From the roof of the synagogue we have seen the new moon; now the new year can begin.'

'Good luck to it,' I said.

At this irreverence he raised his eyebrows and tilted his head to favour, I suppose, the analytical side of his brain while he looked at me carefully. Having done this he put one hand on my shoulder and lifted the index finger of the other. '"*Where he is*," eh?' he said. '"*Where he is.*"'

What a remarkable Salzedo this was! When he said those words it was as if there came through the cool thick wall of the synagogue, through my hand and arm and into my heart the New Year's Days of time past when our Rabbi had read those very words from Chapter 21 of Genesis, where it tells of Hagar and Ishmael in the wilderness, Hagar weeping because she thinks that her son will die:

> And God heard the voice of the lad; and the angel of God called to Hagar out of heaven, and said unto her: 'What aileth thee, Hagar? fear not; for God hath heard the voice of the lad where he is. Arise, lift up the lad, and hold him fast by thy hand; for I will make him a great nation.' And God opened her eyes, and she saw a well of water; and she went, and filled the bottle with water, and gave the lad drink.

Our Rabbi had always been fond of citing the Midrash Rabbah on these verses:

> WHERE HE IS connotes for his own sake, for a sick person's prayers on his own behalf are more efficacious than those of anyone else.
>
> WHERE HE IS. R. Simon said: The ministering angels hastened to indict him, exclaiming, 'Sovereign of the Universe! Wilt Thou bring up a well for one who will one day

162

slay Thy children with thirst?' 'What is he now?' He demanded. 'Righteous,' was the answer. 'I judge man only as he is at the moment,' said He.

Wonderful. So WHERE WAS I? Could it be said of me that at this moment I was righteous? I couldn't think of any harm that I was doing just then. What about my pilgrimage, my road to Jerusalem that went on now without me? At this distance I believe that I am telling the truth when I say that it was not the Mittelteufel that kept me in Antioch. I had begun my pilgrimage wanting to save the many mysterious, unseen, fragile temples of the world so that Christ would not leave us as God had done when he ceased to be He. Now as I thought about it I found that Christ as a limited identity had already departed from my perception and been absorbed into the manifold idea of himself. And what for me had been Jerusalem was equally to be found wherever I joined the motion of the hidden lion. I remembered those poor hungry death-ridden children whom I had met on the road and I heard again in my mind the voice of that boy who had said, 'Jerusalem will be wherever we are when we come to the end.'

Salzedo was no longer standing before me, I was alone. The door through which the light had come was closed. In the darkness my hand was still touching the wall of the synagogue but now when I thought of the sound of the shofar it seemed to jar on the silence.

One day has followed another with the beating of hammers, the baking of bread, the cry of the mu'addhin. It is the winter of 1097. The walls of Antioch, those great mountain-ascending walls with their four hundred towers, those strong stones left from Justinian's strong time, those stones that have no enemy, now they look down on the tents of the Franks. Antioch has been under siege since October but it is the besiegers who are starving. How strange they are, these scarecrow conquerors, these soldiers of Christ who refuse to learn how to fight the Turks, who at Dorylaeum won the day by their very stupidity when the half of their divided host with whom they had lost contact came out of nowhere like miraculous saviours to astonish and defeat Qilij-Arslan's mounted bowmen. They

163

walk, starving as they are, like victors; they walk as if they shake the ground, believing themselves to be invincible, believing that God wills it that they should win. The arrogance of those coloured tents of the Frankish knights! Through successive dawns they stand more frightening in their presumption than shouts and battlecries and the thundering of hooves, these tents in which these unturning men dare to sleep before the enemy walls, dare to sleep in their unclever and unshakable courage and the expectation of victory.

Soldiers of Christ! The marvel, the continual surprise of Christ is that he includes everything that attributes itself to the idea of him. Because I have seen Christ, have talked with him, have heard the strange woodwind of his voice inside my head, have looked into his lion eyes, I know that there looks out of his eyes, as out of the eyes of Vermeer's young girl with the pearl earring, the intolerable bursting of the beginning of all things. From that unimaginable violence which is God as It has come all that there is: all the world, all the universe. I know this in many ways but I need to know it in more ways, I need to put myself where the Idea of It is, I need to move at the same speed as It, become altogether one with It so that there is no jump to be made, this jump that we so much fear at the time of death. I must become as advanced as possible in this because I sense that my time is fast approaching, that time when my young death will be full-grown and ready to go out into the world, leaving me, the fond and used-up parent, behind.

I know that my death will be ready soon because now in this winter of 1097 I have seen the tax-collector again for the first time since I came to this part of the world. Suddenly one morning he was there, his naked headless body still writhing with maggots, his member tumescent with bloat, his naked feet moving over the triangles of Hidden Lion. He was gesturing with his hand as if making a speech or admonishing someone or possibly counting, possibly reckoning up something. I tried to make myself not hear his voice while at the same time I strained to hear it. I *did* hear it, I heard his voice and I heard the words he was saying with utter clarity but even as I heard I forgot; it was like waking up from a dream with everything still in the mind but as you sit up in bed it is gone.

After that he was always there, always walking through the sounds and smells, the colour and motion of the Hidden Lion bazaar like someone with a fixed idea, like a madman who talks to himself; always did he gesture with his hand in that particular way; always did I forget what he was saying as soon as I heard it but one thing became inescapable: it was I that he was talking about, it was my account that he was reckoning up.

None of the others had turned up yet: not Udo the relic-gatherer, not the bear shot full of arrows, not Bodwild and Konrad, not Bruder Pförtner, not my young death. I understood that the tax-collector had come to give me notice that my life would soon be required of me but I did not think that the final stage of things would begin until I saw my young death once more. When last I saw him he had looked at me, as I have said, trustingly. It was my constant fear that I should fall short of his expectations — I wanted so much to do my best for him, I wanted so much to do my uttermost possible. More and more it was not the face of Sophia and her naked body that my mind offered me in its pictures: it was the obscure face of my young death; it was the shadowy form of actuality to come. I persevered with my martial exercises.

So. Now I walk a little differently from the way I used to, and I stand on the wall and look down at the enemy as one who will not die without making trouble.

These Franks encamped before our walls, they have come as the seasons come or as old age and death come; in their time they are there, they are not to be avoided. Antioch stands between them and Jerusalem; it cannot get out of their way nor can they afford to bypass it and leave a fortified enemy in their rear.

We have heard of the coming of the Franks; we have heard of them at Constantinople, we have heard how one of them sat himself down on the throne of Alexius Comnenus and told the Emperor that in his own country he had waited in vain at the crossroads for anyone to answer his challenge to single combat.

I have told how the price of a bale of silk went up by three dinars in Tripoli when the Franks arrived in Constantinople. When they besieged Nicaea and Nicaea surrendered to the troops of Alexius the price of silk went up by one more dinar. 'Last time it was uncertainty of supply that sent the price up,' said Bembel Rudzuk; 'this time the sheep are not so frightened of the wolf as they were; some of the sheep are saying that this is not a devouring wolf, it is a buying wolf.'

From Dorylaeum, from Heraclea, from Marash the wave of their coming ran ahead of the Franks. We heard of Baldwin in Edessa, how he became co-regent with Prince Thoros of Edessa and how Thoros ended up with his head on a pole. After Dorylaeum the price of silk went back to where it had been before the Franks arrived in Constantinople; it paused there, then dropped by one dinar. 'Perhaps this is after all that end-of-the-world wolf of whom one has heard,' said Bembel Rudzuk. 'Perhaps this is the wolf who will swallow the sun. The market has become a swamp, a mire, a bog, a place with no firm ground whatever. The beggars are tying up their bundles and the great houses are closing the shutters.'

It was the victory at Dorylaeum that made everyone begin to wonder whether the battle cry of the Franks, 'God wills it!', might be a true statement of how things were. Perhaps God *did* will it. Or perhaps they were simply lucky. But what was luck if not the will of God? There were those in Antioch who dedicated themselves unsparingly to the pondering of that question, and if the smoking of water pipes and the drinking of strong coffee could have repelled the Franks the city would never have been in danger.

It was pondered that at Dorylaeum the Franks had behaved so stupidly that almost it seemed the paradigm of a mystery not to be understood by the unfavoured. To divide their host into two columns not in communication with each other! To separate the foot-soldiers from the cavalry as they had done! To fall back upon the tents in panic and to be saved at the last moment by the arrival of the other half of the army! Did the two columns symbolize Jesus the son and God the father? Body and soul? Adam and Eve? Sulphur and Mercury? There were as many opinions as there were ponderers.

Yaghi-Siyan, uncertain of God's will, sent for help to Rudwan of Aleppo, to Duqaq of Damascus, to Karbuqa of Mosul. Rudwan said no; Duqaq said yes, as did his atabeg

Tughtagin and Janah Ad-Dawla of Homs; Karbuqa also said yes. Yaghi-Siyan, hoping for quick relief, then organized his defences, laid in supplies, and made ready to become history.

It is to be assumed that the soldiers of Christ all thought of God as He, and to them it soon became evident that He did not will that Antioch should fall too quickly. I too out of habit still thought of him sometimes as He but mostly I recognized him as It, the raw motive power of the universe; and I was able to see in the systole and diastole of the siege of Antioch the reciprocal action of that asymmetry without which there would be only stillness and silence.

The four-hundred-towered walls built by Justinian and kept in good repair by the Byzantines were the pivot of the action; they were the fixed point at the centre of that particular dance; they would not give way, they would go on yet awhile defining an inside and an outside. Yaghi-Siyan on the inside still had enough food but not enough men; he could neither defend his walls at every point nor could he go out and defeat the Franks in one decisive battle.

The Franks could take up positions only on three sides of Antioch; they were prevented on the fourth side by Mount Silpius which kept a back door open for the besieged. As the Franks ran out of food some of them, like sparrows, picked through manure for the grain in it; some died of starvation; some deserted. They were always foraging through a countryside more and more empty of everything except Turks in ambush and they had of course to beat off such armies as came to relieve Antioch. Yaghi-Siyan made sorties when circumstances favoured; there were many engagements major and minor; history was daily sown like a crop to be harvested in its season.

Having thought of history as a crop that was sown I am left with the image of sowing but the picture in my mind is not one of seeds flung from the hand of the husbandman; it is of heads flung from the missile-throwing machines on both sides. Heads! Human heads that have spoken, kissed, whistled, eaten, drunk, done all those things that only heads can do! Heads as missiles! The heads slung into Antioch by the Franks were the heads of Turks killed in battle but the heads slung out of Antioch by the Turks were not those of Franks; they were the heads of Syrian and Armenian Christians of Antioch.

Those Syrian and Armenian Christians of Antioch and the country roundabout, I know not quite how to think of them, how to hold them in my mind. Until 1085 Antioch had been part of Byzantium, but as the tide of Byzantium ebbed they found themselves stranded on a beach that belonged to Qilij-Arslan. Sometimes I think of them as being like those little shore birds that run on long legs, crying as they glean the tideline. They were never static, never inactive, those Christians of that place and that time, they filled in whatever unoccupied spaces of action they found. They were constantly going backwards and forwards between the Franks and the Turks: sometimes they spied on the Franks for the Turks; sometimes they spied on the Turks for the Franks. When the Franks were starving those busy Christians in the country around Antioch sold them provisions at what might be called Last Judgment prices which effectively sorted out those who could afford to live from those who could only afford to die. Those same Christians, when they found Turks in flight from an engagement with the understandably testy Franks, ambushed the Turks and so struck a rough balance in their dealings with both sides. They had no peace, those Christians, they had no rest, they were continually gleaning that shimmering tideline against a background of towering breakers. The churning of the times they lived in had imparted to them a motion they could not resist, they were compelled by forces beyond them to keep moving in all directions and to be incessantly busy in many ways.

There came a particular day that winter when the Franks ambushed the Turks who were planning to ambush them. We were told that seven hundred Turks died that day while the Franks had no losses whatever. It was a cold grey day, the tents and awnings of the Hidden Lion bazaar was snapping in the wind; it was one of those grey days, it was one of those winds when no matter how many people gather together each one of them looks utterly alone and too small under a sky that is far, far too big. Little leaning pitiful figures. The tax-collector that day

168

was pacing with ostentatious self-importance, like a man who knows that people breathlessly await his words.

There came to Hidden Lion then Yaghi-Siyan riding on his horse, his bodyguard with him as always. They were followed by a mule-cart covered with a tent-cloth. Yaghi-Siyan rode clip-clopping on to the tiles with the bodyguard clip-clopping after him and the mule-cart rumbling behind. He wore a helmet and a mail shirt with a gold-worked green robe over it. One couldn't tell whether he had been in the battle or not; he looked fresh and clean. He had a bow slung on his shoulder; I had never seen him carry a bow before; he looked as if at any moment he expected to have to fight or fly for his life. His face was wild with rage and (I thought) with despair. He looked all around him while his horse danced and tossed its head. (How strange, I thought, to be a horse; one might be carrying on one's back anything at all to anything at all: chaos to order; betrayal to trust; defeat to victory; death to life.)

Everyone became silent, and in the silence there came on the wind snatches of singing from the Franks encamped by the Gate of the Dog. They were singing in Latin and the only words that came clearly in the gusting of the wind were: '*Deus trinus et unus*', 'God three together and one'.

'Do you know what tongue they sing in?' Yaghi-Siyan said to me.

'Yes,' I said. 'They are singing in Latin.'

'Scholarly Jew!' said Yaghi-Siyan. 'And what do they sing?'

'"God three together and one",' I said. 'Those were the only words I could make out.'

'"Three together and one"!' said Yaghi-Siyan. 'Which is it? Is it three or is it one?'

'It is both three and one,' I said. 'The three are together in the one.'

'How many gods do you worship, Jew?' he said.

'One,' I said.

'I also,' he said. Still looking at me he said over his shoulder, 'Bring Firouz here.' One of the bodyguard rode off at a trot towards the Tower of the Two Sisters.

Everyone waited in silence. There had been no command for silence nor was Yaghi-Siyan, Governor though he was, a commanding presence. It was clear to everyone, however, that something of great power was commanding him. The faces that were turned towards him were looking at what was commanding him. The awnings flapped and fluttered, the green-and-gold banner carried by one of the bodyguard snapped in the wind. Mount Silpius, continually surprising in its mountainness, seemed itself surprised to find itself where it was, surprised to find that the present moment had indeed arrived. I cannot say less than I must but I dare not say more than is permitted; for the first time in this narrative it comes to me that words are images, and what is sacred cannot be imaged. Still there is the obligation of the witness: though the world should pass away, what has been seen has been seen; the voice that does not speak is denying God.

Yaghi-Siyan himself seemed to be snapping in the wind like the banner as he sat there on his horse in silence. The horse arched its neck, pawed with its hooves, dunged upon the tiles that at another time Yaghi-Siyan had taken off his shoes to walk upon.

The guard returned, Firouz riding beside him. Yaghi-Siyan said to Firouz, 'Get down off your horse, please.'

Firouz dismounted, stood upon the tiles of Hidden Lion. The guard who had brought him took hold of the bridle of Firouz's horse.

'Firouz,' said Yaghi-Siyan, 'you have been a Christian, have you not?'

'I bear witness that there is no god but God and that Muhammad is the messenger of God,' said Firouz.

'Yes, yes, we know that,' said Yaghi-Siyan. 'Now you are a Muslim. But you must tell me about the Christian god, the Three in One.'

'What must I tell you?' said Firouz.

'You must tell me,' said Yaghi-Siyan, 'what this Three in One is. Is One the head and Two the body and Three the legs? What is this Three in One?'

'One is the Father, Two is the Son, Three is the Holy Spirit,' said Firouz.

'Very good,' said Yaghi-Siyan. 'Here we are, you and I, upon Hidden Lion with its twisting serpents, contiguous with infinity: you are an Armenian, you have been a Christian and now you are a Muslim; I am only a simple Turk, I lack your experience in religious matters; I have always been a Muslim the same as I am now, I don't know anything else. But you, having been a Christian, must know all about Christians — probably you can immediately recognize them when you see them. How is it with them, have they got lines upon their bodies dividing them into Spirit, Son, and Holy Father?'

'Christians wear blue turbans,' said Firouz.

'Ah, yes!' said Yaghi-Siyan. 'Probably the blue signifies the Heaven that is waiting for those of them who are virtuous. In any case you will have no difficulty in knowing them on sight. And of course now that you have been living among Turkish Muslims you know very well what they look like, don't you?'

'I don't know,' said Firouz.

'Show him a Turk,' said Yaghi-Siyan to the cavalryman on the mule-cart.

The cavalryman lifted a corner of the cloth, put his hands into the cart, and lifted out a man's head. He did not lift it up by the hair, he held it respectfully with both hands. The nose was smashed, the open eyes were covered with dirt, the face was broken and smeared with blood. I looked from the face to the mountain, from the mountain to the face.

'This is the head of a Turk,' said Yaghi-Siyan. 'His name is Jhamil Muqtin. He was one of our bravest fighters, he was like magic with a horse, like magic with a bow. His body is not here, his body has been roasted and eaten by the Franks. They have slung his head over the wall with a stone-slinger. His wife, his two sons and his daughter have waited for his return from battle. His old mother has waited also. There are a hundred heads in this cart and there are hundreds more of our men dead. They are dead from treachery, they are dead because the Franks knew of our plans, they were lying in wait for us. We were betrayed by the Christians who live among us, Armenian and Syrian Christians. Now you must bring three hundred Christians to me here upon these twisting serpents. You will know the men by their blue turbans and the women by their blue headcloths. If you find Christians naked you will know the men by their uncircumcised members and you will know the women because they will be with the men. You will know the children because they will cry when you take the parents. I need these three hundred Christians urgently, I must send their heads over the wall to the Franks. They have sent me a hundred heads but as their god is three for one I must send them back three hundred.'

Bembel Rudzuk spoke and his voice seemed to come from a very small quiet place far away, as from a cleft in the rock of a distant mountain. 'Your Excellency,' he said, 'as you speak those words you are standing on tiles inscribed with the names of Allah The Compassionate, Allah The Merciful.'

'Yes,' said Yaghi-Siyan, 'and that is why I shall overlook what you have just now said. A second time you won't be so lucky.'

Bembel Rudzuk came forward and knelt before Yaghi-Siyan. He took off his kaffiya, bared his neck, bowed his head. 'Let my Muslim head then be the first of the three hundred,' he said. 'I cannot turn away, and it is better that I do not look upon what you are going to do.'

Having no sword with me I went up to Firouz who was standing as if in a daze and I drew his sword from its sheath. With it in my hand I stood over Bembel Rudzuk. 'I prefer not to look upon the death of Bembel Rudzuk,' I said. 'Who kills him will have to kill me first.'

'Devoted Jew!' said Yaghi-Siyan. 'No one is going to kill either of you. I give you this gift because of what you have shown me with your Hidden Lion. But you shall not be allowed to interfere with what is going to happen here on your pattern that is contiguous with infinity. That is why it is being done here, that the beheading of these three hundred traitors may also be contiguous with infinity, may go on for ever and ever until time will have an end.' From Firouz's girdle he removed the sheath of the sword and slid it over the blade as I held the weapon in my hand. 'Keep this sword and remember me in time to come,' he said. 'Go now in peace, go up to the top of your tower and bear witness that this is also part of the pattern.'

Soldiers of the bodyguard came and led Bembel Rudzuk and me to the tower that stood on David's Wheel. We climbed to the top, and when I looked down at the pattern it seemed for the moment not to have in it that motion that was always there; it seemed to be the frozen shards and fragments of a Law that was created unyieldingly hard and rigid and for ever broken. The red, the black, the tawny triangles were swarming with figures watching, figures waiting, staring eyes in staring faces. From the place above his shoulders where his head would have been I felt the tax-collector's eyes on me. Tower Gate's round face appeared in the crowd like the moon seen for a moment through the cloud-race of an angry sky. The Imam, the Nagid, and the Rabbi seemed to pass like sorrowing dark angels through that same sky. Ah! I thought, this would have been a good time to die; I ought to have killed Yaghi-Siyan when I stood before him with Firouz's sword in my hand but I had not done it.

Neither Bembel Rudzuk nor I sought death again that day. I knew that my time was coming soon, I knew that I must be alert to recognize the time and the place so that my death might be the best possible, the most useful possible. But even as that thought moved through my mind it was hurried on its way by another thought coming behind it. This second thought asked whether it might not be only vanity and a striving after wind to want so much for one's death; whether it might not be better to require nothing whatever of it or for it but simply to welcome it whenever and however it might come, to welcome it as one welcomes the stranger to whom one must always show hospitality.

As soon as I had taken in this second thought a wave of ease spread through me, a strong feeling that I had found the right way to be. With that feeling came an understanding that from then on every moment would be — indeed always had been — as the last moment. This wants to be made perfectly clear, it may be the only thing I have to say that matters; this idea has for me both the brilliance of the heart of the diamond of the universe and the inverse brilliance of the heart of the blackness in which that diamond lives: this moment that is every moment is always the last moment and it came into being with the first moment; it is that moment of creation in which there comes into being the possibility of all things and the end of all things; it is the blossoming jewel at the heart of the explosion, the calm quiet dawn at the centre of the bursting. This moment that is every moment — to see it whole is to

173

synchronize one's being with the whole of time, to be everywhere in it at the same time. It is to be with everything by letting go of everything. It is through this awareness that my present state of being has come about. It is associated with that purple-blue of indescribable luminosity of which I have spoken before.

There are not three hundred Christians gathered here on Hidden Lion; there are one hundred; Yaghi-Siyan has said that he will balance justice with mercy, he will do to these Christians only what those Christians outside the walls have done to the Turks whose heads are in the mule-cart. That a human being should in this fashion show mercy is to me an equal horror with the rest of what is happening. Once only I look at the faces of the Christians as they are herded on to the tiles, then I look away, I look at their feet.

Now at this moment and then at that moment, in this same moment that will continue for the duration of the universe, in this same luminosity of purple-blue, in this same heart of the diamond, I see the gathering of the Christians on Hidden Lion. The presentness of it, the nowness and for everness of it, is intolerable, and for this that is happening I curse God as Him, I curse God as It, that he made us, whether as He or as It. That he made us what we are, to sling heads over a wall from the outside to the inside and from the inside to the outside. This is what He has done with His omnipotence: this feeble masturbation in a dark and ill-smelling place.

And yet, so are we made and such is the action of the everything in this one moment that is every moment, that another thought flickers over and under my first thought: what style God has! What a truly godlike extravagance, to burst out all at once with a universe in which everything is going at once and humankind is let run with nothing to stop it from doing anything at all. And to make this running-loose creature with a mind that knows what it is doing and a soul in which Hell burns always and Heaven is grasped so rarely and so briefly that it lives in us as a continual yearning for what can never be held on to, for what must always be lost — what invention!

The sacred is not to be imaged, there is no image to put to what God is nor is there any reason to want an image of such a thing. The evil that he has created is also in its inexplicable way sacred and not to be described beyond a certain point. Suddenly are these long-legged shore birds, these gleaners of the tideline, netted. Suddenly, with their dark faces, their speechless mouths, their uncircumcised members, their frozenness into such time as there will be until the end of time.

That is as far as I shall go with these words and the images they bring. What happened, happened.

Afterwards the bodies are taken away in wagons. There remains of course the blood on the tiles, on the red and black and tawny triangles of Hidden Lion. It is darker than the tawny, darker than the red, lighter than the black. The same people who stood looking on while the Christians were being beheaded now stand looking at the blood. The butcher and his helper from the shop near by bring a bucket of sand, two buckets of water, a scrubbing brush.

'No,' says Bembel Rudzuk. 'This blood is not to be washed away. It is now part of the pattern and it is obviously the will of Allah that it should be so.'

'Perhaps you don't remember,' says the butcher, 'but one of the tiles with blood on it is mine. My money is mortared into it and it is inscribed with the name of Allah The Truth, He whose existence has no change.'

'I remember,' says Bembel Rudzuk, 'but this blood is not going to be washed away.' He stands there with his arms folded on his chest. The butcher and the butcher's helper look at him attentively, then walk away with their bucket of sand, their two buckets of water, and their scrubbing brush.

In twos and threes the people drift away. Still Bembel Rudzuk stands there like a man of stone. He and I have read the Holy Scriptures together, and I know that those verses of Ezekiel that are now in my mind must be in his mind as well:

Wherefore thus saith the Lord GOD:
Woe to the bloody city, to the pot
whose filth is therein, and whose filth
is not gone out of it! bring it out
piece by piece; no lot is fallen upon it.
For her blood is in the midst of her;

she set it upon the bare rock;
she poured it not upon the ground,
to cover it with dust; that it might
cause fury to come up, that vengeance
might be taken, I have set her blood .
upon the bare rock, that it should not
be covered. Therefore thus saith the Lord GOD:
Woe to the bloody city!

After a time Bembel Rudzuk ceases to stand like a stone man, he begins to walk the boundaries of the square, then moves in a little, walking in progressively smaller squares, moving a little closer to the centre each time, walking slowly in concentric squares as if threading a labyrinth. When he reaches the tower he walks hexagonally around it, then walks from there outwards in concentric squares again to the outer limits of Hidden Lion. The tax-collector with his eyes that are elsewhere stands watching quietly with me. The sky ·is growing pale. Bembel Rudzuk and I go home; the tax-collector remains on Hidden Lion.

Bembel Rudzuk and I went up to the roof of his house and waited there for the day to come. It was unseasonably warm, the air was close and heavy, the morning seemed to hold its breath in the dull grey before-dawn light. In this light was something of that grey and rainy dawn in which I first had come to Suwaydiyya with Bembel Rudzuk. The port with its topography of morning, its long shadows, its low buildings, its boats rocking to the morning slap of the water on their sides, furled sails still heavy with night, crews moving slowly on their decks, the smell of cooking-fires — all this had without seeming to move grown smoothly bigger in my eyes in that particular way in which things reveal themselves when approached by sea, opening to the approacher more and more detail, more and more imminence of what is to come. And always, thus approaching, one feels the new day, the new place, coming forward to read the face of the approacher. Always the held breath, the questioning look of the grey morning.

'I no longer have any questions that require answers,' said

Bembel Rudzuk. 'It is not in our power to know very much nor to understand very much. Perhaps the most we can hope for is to learn to encounter what comes without pissing ourselves.' He said nothing for a while, then he said, 'The heads of the Christians were slung over the wall but not the bodies. Do you know why?'

I knew why. Sometimes when the wind was blowing from the Franks to us I had smelled the smoke of their cooking. I listened to the twittering of sparrows, the crowing of cocks, I saw in my mind the blood on the tiles of Hidden Lion.

'"And all as a garment will become old,"' said Bembel Rudzuk, '"and as a mantle thou wilt roll up them, as a garment also they will be changed . . ." This is the earth and the heavens being spoken of, the work of God's hands, they will grow old and be folded up like a garment. You and I have read this together in the Epistle of Paul to the Hebrews in the New Testament of the Christians, but for me it is no longer a matter of words; I can feel it in the air, I can feel the fabric of the world and its time collapsing upon itself like the folds of a tired garment.' Bembel Rudzuk stood there solidly in the grey light with his arms folded, his moustaches as heroic as ever, his bearing as upright; but he looked like a deserted village.

'In the Quran also one reads of this folding up,' he said. 'This too we have read together, in Sura 81, *Takwir*, The Folding Up:

'*In the name of Allah, Most Gracious, Most Merciful*
1. When the sun
   (With its spacious light)
   Is folded up;

2. When the stars
   Fall, losing their lustre;

3. When the mountains vanish
   (Like a mirage);

4. When the she-camels
   Ten months with young,
   Are left untended;

('And you must know,' said Bembel Rudzuk, 'that the camel being the jewel of the Arab's eye and his special pet, the she-camel almost come to her time is most especially precious; so when we speak of a time when such animals will be neglected we are speaking of the collapse of all things, the true and actual final folding up.)

    '5. When the wild beasts
       Are herded together
       (In human habitations);

('In this extremity,' said Bembel Rudzuk, 'the animals will no longer be afraid of humans, the animals and the humans will be folded up together at the end of all things.)

    '6. When the oceans
       Boil over with a swell;

     7. When the souls
       Are sorted out
       (Being joined, like with like);

('I no longer know what to think about this matter of the sorting of souls,' said Bembel Rudzuk. 'Is there more than one kind of soul, do you think? Is the soul of Yaghi-Siyan different from your soul and my soul? Wait, hear more before we talk.)

    '8. When the female (infant)
       Buried alive, is questioned —

     9. For what crime
       she was killed;

('There have been,' said Bembel Rudzuk, 'Arabs who buried their baby daughters alive; they didn't want to have to provide for them or be burdened with protecting their honour. These are only words and one can speak them but if one thinks of the actuality then one must look at what is intolerable to look at. I am thinking now of your Abraham and Isaac who are Ibrahim and Isma'il in Muslim tradition. Never before have I dared to say aloud these words that I am going to say now: the fundamental flaw in God is that He will say that He requires the sacrifice of Isaac/Isma'il; the fundamental flaw in man is that he takes his knife in hand to do God's bidding. This story of God's testing of Abraham has become an easy thing to read, an easy thing to say in words, an easy point of reference; but if you let it become real in your mind then you have to look at a boy tied hand and foot by his father whose knife is at his throat. Think of it! There lies the boy trussed like an animal, he lies on the firewood that he has borne on his own back to the place where the fire will consume him when he has been murdered by his father whom he has trusted all his life. Murder in the name of God! And Abraham has no hesitation! He is completely willing to murder his son because a voice in his head has made him mad. If I had ever in my life come upon such a scene, if I had ever come upon such a madman with his knife upraised over a child I should have killed that man before God had a chance to speak again. Wouldn't you? See it in your mind! Be that father and look down into the eyes of your son while you raise the knife. What are you at this moment that is one moment away from murder, from human sacrifice? Will you call yourself the hand of God? Why should Yaghi-Siyan not call himself the hand of God a hundred times over? Word of God! If God is everywhere then every word is the Word of God, Yaghi-Siyan's word as well as Muhammad's. Wait, listen to more of this Sura of the folding-up:)

'10. When the Scrolls
Are laid open;

11. When the World on High
Is unveiled:

12. When the Blazing Fire
Is kindled to fierce heat;

13. And when the Garden
Is brought near; —

14. (Then) shall each soul know
What it has put forward.

'Here I have been quoting verses of the Holy Quran and I cannot even properly call myself a Muslim,' said Bembel Rudzuk: 'I don't believe in a Last Day that will be different from any other day; I believe that the Last Day is every day; I believe that the Garden and the Fire are in each of us every day of our lives and we are in one or the other or somewhere between the two depending on our actions. I believe that every soul knows very well from one moment to another what it has

179

put forward — do I not know what I have put forward with this Hidden Lion that I have called up? Do I not know how far I have overstepped the bounds of what is permitted in one's approach to the Unseen?'

'Why do you keep saying "I"?' I said. 'Whatever has been done with Hidden Lion has been done by the two of us; was it not I who drew the first unit of the pattern on the stone?'

'Ah!' said Bembel Rudzuk, 'You see! You are trying to share the burden of blame because you know that there *is* a burden of blame!'

I thought of Hidden Lion, of its tawny triangles, its red and its black but as soon as the triangles came into my mind they were covered first by blood then by the terrified feet of the hundred chosen for death by Firouz. What should I have done in his place? Useless to ask such a question — he did what he did that day, I did what I did, each of us in our own place. It is so very, very easy to live one day longer than one ought.

'You don't deny what I have just said,' said Bembel Rudzuk, 'you don't deny that we have overstepped the bounds.'

'No,' I said, 'I don't deny it. Everywhere there are patterns of tiles to be seen, most of them far more ambitious in their complexity and finish than Hidden Lion, but I think one may say that they were done in innocence.'

'They were done without presumption,' said Bembel Rudzuk; 'they were done modestly and with no other purpose than that of ornamentation. They were done without intent to observe the Unseen, without intent to violate its privacy; they harmlessly adorn buildings, walls, floors; they were not made for the sole purpose of seeing the Unseeable. We have done that which ought not to be done although you are not to blame; it was I who asked you to make the design, I with my stupid ideas of sulphur and mercury and triangles, I with my greed for the Unseen. And yesterday the Unseen said, "Do you still pursue me with your tiles? I have shown you, have I not, twisting serpents, moving pyramids, disappearing lions; I have shown you the surge of Me that is like a river of power, and still you crave more; very well then, I will show you more."'

'Can you really believe that?' I said. 'Can you really believe that Hidden Lion has called down this terrible thing upon itself?'

'Think,' said Bembel Rudzuk, 'what we have done. We have made a provocation and an insult. We have used the names of God and the habitation of the Unseen and we have made a good-luck charm with our tiles. We have made an idolatry for ignorant people to whom prayer is only a kind of begging, we have put the rubbish of the seeable and the touchable between them and Allah, we have sped them on their way from any hope of the Garden, we have pointed them towards the Fire.'

'Have we truly done so much evil?' I said.

'Only consider,' said Bembel Rudzuk: 'if the pattern of Hidden Lion is contiguous with infinity (and there can be no doubt of this, in our very souls we know it to be so) then everything about it is contiguous with infinity. If our action in making it was wrong (and we both know now that it was) then that wrong action is contiguous with infinity; its connexions extend to things and places we know not of, we cannot imagine the vastness of the web to which Hidden Lion is an entrance and a passageway.'

'All things being contiguous,' I said, 'Hidden Lion can as well be an effect as a cause; it cannot be proved to be the beginning of a chain of evil.'

'Sophistry cannot help us,' said Bembel Rudzuk; 'every action has its consequences and the consequences of the action of making Hidden Lion cannot be without evil.'

At that moment from the minaret there came the call of the mu'addhin. Bembel Rudzuk began his prayers and I drew a little apart from him and stood looking out over the city that I seemed to be approaching by sea in the grey dawn. Again I saw in my mind the terrified feet of the Syrian and Armenian Christians on the tawny, the red, and the black triangles and I wondered in what way any of what was happening could possibly have been willed by God in any of His or Its aspects. How far back would one have to go to find the cause from which this effect had arisen? All things being contiguous, one was driven back to the original bursting into being of the universe: immediately from that moment existed the possibility of everything that could possibly happen on this earth. From that moment two and two made four, and all else that could be until the end of time already was; on one or another, on a few or on

181

many of the planes of virtuality and actuality that might at some time intersect, everything that could be already was. The choices that would have to be made by people who would not be born for thousands of millions of years were already forming with the galaxies and the nebulae, with the Virgin and the Lion. As far as I could see, the will of God was simply that everything possible would indeed be possible. Within that limitation the choice was ours, the reckoning His. And He was in us, one couldn't get away from Him, that was the Fire of it, that was the Garden of it, at the centre of every soul and contiguous with infinity. The possibilities of choice were beyond all calculation and the probability of wrong choice so high as to be almost a certainty. Only God could think of such a game, and only humans would bother to play it.

Refreshed and desperate from my meditation I turned and saw another figure on the roof with us. My heart leapt in me; it was my young death. This was the very first time he had appeared to me since I had crossed the sea to come here. He was naked and he was standing by the parapet with his back to me but I recognized him at once. He was full-grown but there was that about the way he was standing that made me think of a child who cannot sleep or has had perhaps a bad dream and comes to be comforted. How my heart went out to him!

He turned to me, his face somehow obscure, not to be held in the eye. I looked to see if he had all his parts. He had, he was a complete man. He looked at me for a moment only, then he walked slowly to the stairs and was gone, his face still obscure in my mind, not to be recalled.

13

Soon must I tell of the fall of Antioch but not yet. Mortal life is a difficult proposition because hardly anything can be experienced as what it actually is; everything is time-distorted. In childhood we wait for things that seem too long in coming, we wait for treats, for presents, for festivals and holidays, we wait for growing up. There is so much waiting that suddenly childhood itself is gone with all that was being waited for. As grown-ups we find ourselves pitched headlong down a steep and slippery slide with everything hurtling towards us at great speed; some things smash us full in the face, others streak past half-glimpsed or unseen; everything has happened before we were ready for it. Only after the hurly-burly of mortal life is over can one have a really good look at what has happened; unburdened by choice and unthreatened by consequences one is able to sort through the half-glimpses of a lifetime and find perhaps one or two workable fragments of recognition.

So it is that only now in this little space of centuries since my death have I been able not so much to understand anything as simply to look carefully at everything to see if this fragment and that fragment which do not fit together may yet both belong to a shape which might be recognizable if seen entire.

I have in mind the deeds of the Franks and the Turks, such as I was able to see or hear about; I have in mind how men would sometimes rush forward, sometimes back, some on horseback, some on foot. I have in mind one particular night of the winter rains of 1097, it was soon after Christmas. At that time I was often on the walls of Antioch in the small hours of the night; I was in a state in which I could feel the passage of time as if I were an hourglass through which the sand was running more and more swiftly. It was well towards morning on this night that I am speaking of; it had been raining steadily but the rain had stopped, and now in the dim cloudlight I saw what seemed to be thousands of Frankish horsemen moving out of their encampment and heading up the valley of the Orontes.

Bembel Rudzuk came and stood with me. We were on that part of the wall by the Aleppo Gate that overlooked the sector of Bohemond of Taranto. On the hill behind his encampment the Franks had built a tower that we called Evil Eye; now we saw lanterns moving on the top of it while between us and it the dark horsemen slowly rode away into the fading darkness. Stubbornly stood the sodden and threadbare tents they left behind; in some of them glimmered the dim light of candles. We had no idea how many had gone but from other watchers we heard that more than half of the Franks remained to keep the siege. Many of them were starving and by now were regularly drinking the blood of their horses; we guessed that this moving-out of the thousands was a foraging expedition and the size of it indicated to us that they intended to move deep into hostile territory.

The next night there was again no rain nor was there a moon; the darkness of the sky was opaque. 'This night will bring out Yaghi-Siyan,' said Bembel Rudzuk. We went up on to the wall over the bridge gate and waited there for hours, equally expecting Turks to go out or Franks to come in. Even from what little we knew of the Franks there was nothing that they could have done that would have surprised us; starving as they were and faced with impregnable walls they might yet at any moment storm those walls. In moments of quiet like this it seemed to us that any sortie by the Turks could well provoke a counterattack that would bring the Franks raging into the city.

Bembel Rudzuk and I had no doubt whatever that a night would come when the Franks, whatever the odds against them, would take Antioch; it seemed to us that it was simply in the nature of things. And of course when that night came it would bring certain death to the Muslims and the Jews of Antioch.

It would have been easy enough to leave the city — Mount

184

Silpius, as I have said, kept a back door open — so that we might live yet awhile and do our dying elsewhere but neither of us wanted to. It was in Antioch that a readiness to die had come upon us and now we felt committed to that place; to take our dying elsewhere would have seemed frivolous and disloyal. Both of us admitted to a certain vanity about dying: we preferred to do it as handsomely as possible; but we agreed to be guided by the circumstances and not, when the proper moment came, to refuse a lesser death in the hope of winning a greater one some other time.

My original idea of attaining Jerusalem before it was too late, before Jesus withdrew from any further possibility of manifestation and the world was left with the bleakness of what he had called 'the straight action and no more dressing up' now seemed like those fond hopes of childhood that even a child recognizes as being made of that kind of mental sugar-candy that melts in the hard sunlight of reality.

The siege as the months passed had developed, as does everything, its own particular rhythm and mode of being. When the Franks had first appeared outside the walls of Antioch Yaghi-Siyan had at every moment expected a major assault. He quadrupled the watch on the walls; he kept the citadel on constant alert; and he mobilized every male young and old who was capable of lifting so much as a stick or a stone against the enemy. All civilians were organized into a militia who in the event of an attack would respond to a trumpet call and would be under the command of an officer of the garrison. The months had passed; the attack had not come. This condition of no-attack became more and more a condition of no-attack, like a very thin-shelled egg that grew bigger and bigger, older and older until, enormous and rotten, it now hung suspended above us.

This night that I am speaking of, this winter night without rain and without a moon — I have called its darkness opaque but I was not being accurate: there was some light in the sky, it was not utterly black. It was a night of obscurity, yes, obscurity is the word I want; it is this that makes that night such a paradigm of the rushing forward, the rushing back, that so much of history is made of.

In this obscurity we stood and into it we looked across the river towards the encampment of the Franks. Some of the tents with candles burning in them were like dim and feeble lanterns. Between those few dim lanterns and us ran with a strong rushing, with a heavy running, the river heavy with the rains, darkly rushing, gurgling, like a giant animal that drinks blood. Mingling with the rush of the river was the subterranean echoing rumbling grinding rolling roar of Onopniktes. These strong rushing-water sounds made the dim and feeble lantern-tents seem even dimmer and feebler and farther away. In the quietness of the Frankish camp a man began to sing. His voice rose and fell sadly, there was no word that I could understand except the oft-repeated name of Jesus, *Jesu*. There was no accompanying instrument but the manner of the song was suggestive of a lute. After a time someone shouted, the singing stopped, there was only the running of the river, the roar of Onopniktes.

We could hear then behind us, on the road between Yaghi-Siyan's palace and the bridge, a trotting of horsemen coming and going and we could hear many shouts, now here, now there, of the sort that are heard when cavalrymen gird themselves for something of importance. The shouts, the clopping of hooves increased, horses whinnied, there was much shuffling, snuffling, snorting, stamping, jingling, clinking, slapping, and grunting as all of the sounds formed themselves into a concerted picture of dark colours, dark gleamings, dark horsemen girding.

The sound-picture gathered itself into a forward movement, came towards us, passed beneath us, appeared in front of us on the bridge in the dark images of itself, the dark gleamings of iron and leather, the forested lances nodding, the shaking of reins and bridles as the horses tossed their heads. The clop of hooves, the clinking and the jingling passed into the darkness across the river, quickened unseen to a trot, a canter; for the first time then the kettledrums were heard, they pounded out the headlong gallop of the charge as voices whooped in war cries, voices called on Allah. There came then Frankish cries to Jesus, cries to God, cries of 'Saint-Gilles!'

Suddenly the clamour of the drums is heard again — a

different beat, the choppy rhythm of unluck and about-turn. Here now the Turks are coming back in thunderous flight across the bridge. 'To the gate!' they cry. 'Back to the gate!' cries Yaghi-Siyan at the head of the rout. '*Deus le volt!*' cry the Franks, 'Saint-Gilles!' 'The gate!' cry the Turks. With these shouts we hear the clash of weapons, the screams of the wounded and the dying, the screams of horses and of men, the groans and curses, the grunts and trampling and scuffling of men fighting for their lives, and the splashing of men and horses into the river. 'Saint-Gilles!' goes up the shout, it seems very close, almost beneath us. '*Jesu!*'

Back across the bridge ebb the voices of the Franks. 'There is no god but God!' shouts Yaghi-Siyan, and once more the Turks gallop across the bridge and into the darkness beyond it. Now from across the river we hear again, but indistinctly and mingled with the running of the river and the subterranean roar of Onopniktes, the clash of weapons, the shouts and cries, the screams of horses and of men. Below us on the bridge the dead in their obscurity lie still, the wounded and the dying writhe and groan, both men and horses; the horses lift their long necks, their noble heads, and fall back; they can no longer gallop to the battle or away from it.

Now with others Bembel Rudzuk and I go down to the bridge to bring in the wounded and the dead. The crippled horses are killed with a sword stroke to the neck, the blood spurts out on to the stones of the bridge. I think of how this blood would be better than wine to the starving Franks. The horses that can walk are brought back inside the walls with the wounded men. With their eyes the horses acknowledge that they are slaves; if they were owned by scholars they might have led quiet lives but as they are ridden by fighting men they must suffer these wounds, they can expect nothing else. In the fluttering light of torches the wounded men look at me with eyes like the eyes of ikons or statues or like the eyes made of white and black tesserae in mosaics. The heads from which the eyes look out have been vertical only a little while ago; now they are horizontal, and these men, like the horses, acknowledge with their eyes that they are the slaves of that in them which has used them up in this rushing forward and back in the darkness; having used them up it will find others for its purpose.

187

These bodies that I try to repair, already have they been violated once by cold iron; now again I violate them, I intrude upon their privacy to stuff entrails back into the places where they belong, to sew up flesh that has been violently parted. How startling are the secret colours that in time of peace are hidden beneath the skin. We slaughter sheep and cattle and chickens as a matter of course; we are the vertical ones with the knives so we assume this as a right: we slit the throat, the heart pumps out its last bursts of blood into a basin, we open up their bodies and lay hands upon their varicoloured mysteries of red and purple, blue and yellow inner parts. But in time of war each man is a cattle to his enemy and they struggle to see which one will be the slaughterer. The stranger, the unknown to whom one must always offer hospitality, that sacred stranger has now become a murderer whom we must murder first. How strange that this is not strange.

Certainly we are the slaves of that which looks out through our eyes, and it is nothing simple, that outlooker; does it want to live, does it want to die? As with my arms red up to the elbows I sew up the wounded I crave to be where the shouting is, the cries and groans, the clash of weapons. I am afraid to be there but what looks out through my eyes wants to put me there, it doesn't want to be left out of anything, it wants to be everywhere at once, it wants to be included in all matters of life and death, wants to be at the same time here in the shuddering light of the torches and there across the river in the obscurity of battle and the night.

From the wounded we hear something of the fighting: when the Turks had first attacked the Frankish camp one of the Frankish leaders, Raymond Saint-Gilles, had immediately got together some of his knights and led a charge into the dark. Those Franks! You could wake them up out of a sound sleep in the middle of the night and they would open their eyes fighting. It was Raymond's charge that had driven Yaghi-Siyan back across the bridge and had very nearly carried the Franks through the bridge gate and into Antioch. But when they were more than halfway across the bridge there had come galloping wildly back towards them in the darkness a riderless horse and the Franks faltered and fled, pursued by the newly confident Turks.

The Franks put to rout by a riderless horse! Surely here is a sign for those who know how to read it! Surely here is an action parable! Now Yaghi-Siyan and his cavalrymen, blood-spattered riders on blood-spattered horses, return. They are many fewer than they were when they rode into the obscurity on the other side of the bridge. They are tired but their eyes are bright; for the moment they are the slaughterers and not the cattle. The green-and-gold banner droops proudly on its staff like a male member that has done a good night's work.

The morning comes again, every time is like a first time, every time the morning happens it seems surprised at its actuality but it offers no opinions, it only reckons up what has happened in the night. 'Here there are so many dead horses, so many dead men,' says the morning. 'See how they are dead. These men will not do anything more. They have no more to say. The horses will not walk, trot, canter, gallop. They will do nothing. Here there is only so much dead meat.'

Now in the first light of this grey and impassive morning this dead meat becomes newly active and inspires new activity in both the Franks and the Turks. While the Frankish bowmen shoot up at us and we on the walls shoot down at them, some of the Franks, protecting themselves as well as they can with their shields, gather up their dead from the river bank and the bridge. Some of the dead they sling over their backs to be newly killed by our arrows, some they drag away, some they carry off on litters. The arrows glance off their helmets, stick in their shields, stick in the rings of their mail shirts; at this close range some of the arrows pierce the mail and some find a naked throat. One of the Franks falls and lies shuddering with an arrow in his back, then is still, requiring now the labour of his comrades. There are some dead horses beyond the far end of the bridge; all the closer ones were dragged (by teams of horses that shied and danced sidewise and showed the whites of their eyes) into Antioch last night. These dead horses on the other side of the river, each of them may well have carried a man to his death last night; now each will give life to many men for several days. The shocking thought arises: how much better off everybody would be if the Franks would go away somewhere and butcher their horses and live quietly on the meat.

There are dead Turks beyond the far end of the bridge, and

there are now seen among them other Franks who are not like the Franks that I have just been speaking of. These men move with perhaps something of a birdlike hop in their walk; one can imagine that a moment ago they have flapped down from the grey sky on black wings and turned into men. Some of the dead Turks they drag away by their legs, others they tie by their arms and legs to poles to be carried off by two men. The air is blackened with our arrows but at that distance they are only like bee-stings. Later we smell the smoke of the cooking-fires of these Franks.

Seeing all this in this grey dawn that is surprised to be here but is not surprised at anything else I have in my eyes what I see but I have also that riderless horse that I did not see, it is an image of green fire in the obscurity of last night that is still in my eyes.

There is in the light of this grey morning something that moves with a sickening motion behind the curtain of grey light. It is not like the riderless horse that galloped across the bridge, it is like those horses of last night that lifted up their heads and fell back again, lifted and fell back. This morning is seen as if in a flawed mirror. The curtain of air shakes and sways, one feels drunk, the ground beneath one's feet will not maintain its proper plane, its proper steady stillness. The earth seems to be retching, shuddering.

Bembel Rudzuk and I fling ourselves to the ground, others do the same. Perhaps the earth itself is a riderless horse, showing the whites of its eyes and galloping to its death. Lying prone on the top of the wall I feel the stones beneath me shift, I see cracks where there were none before. Hidden Lion cannot be seen from where we are but with the eye of the mind I see the tower on David's Wheel tottering, shaking, bricks are jumping off it; I see the tiles of Hidden Lion lifting, moving, leaping out of the pattern, breaking, crumbling. The thought comes to me that the earth is sick of humankind, it is trying to vomit itself up to be rid of us.

The curtain of grey light is still shaking, the world still looks out at us from a flawed mirror. Several horses have broken loose and are galloping through the streets as if in a dream; from the Frankish camp we hear singing and praying; in its caverns underneath the city Onopniktes shouts in the darkness, ecstatic like a prophet as stones topple from the four hundred towers, from Justinian's wall, from the bridge across the Orontes. I see in my mind the river, roiled and muddy, strangely heaving, shuddering as it runs with its surface pocked and dimpled by the trembling beneath the river bed. There is a gabble of voices all around us and a continual sobbing and praying. With my cheek against the stones and my vision at an unaccustomed angle I see the spire of the minaret of the central mosque slowly sway and fall.

In the gabble of voices on the wall and rising from the streets below we hear in Turkish, in Syriac, in Arabic, and in Greek the words 'punishment' and 'judgment'. Some think the punishment is for one thing, some think it is for another; the Christians beheaded on Hidden Lion are spoken of by many. There is also some lamentation for the destruction of a shrine of Nemesis and the pulling down of a statue of Tyche, the Goddess of Fortune. ('All that happened centuries ago,' says Bembel Rudzuk, 'but still they talk about it when the earth shakes, all these good Muslims lamenting the departed goddesses of Rome.') Many think that the Christian Patriarch John, who is in prison, ought to be freed. It is thought by some that if he is freed he will pray for the safety of Antioch; others think that he is more likely to pray if he is kept in prison. All this time there is a wild neighing of unseen horses. Soon a wagon rattles past, it is pulled by men, the horses are too unmanageable to be put in harness. In the wagon is an iron cage and in the cage, desperately clinging to the bars, his face white, his beard flying, is the Patriarch. Later we hear that the cage has been hung by chains from the wall and that he has prayed constantly for God's mercy.

The shaking of the earth stops, the grey light of the day is once more steady. There are cracks in the walls, cracks in streets and houses, fallen bricks and stones here and there but no serious damage and no one killed as far as we know. Bembel Rudzuk and I go to Hidden Lion. The tower stands intact and unmarred and the pattern has suffered no damage whatever although there are cracks in the streets all around and in the nearby shops and houses. 'Its time is not yet come,' says Bembel Rudzuk.

When we look at Hidden Lion now it is difficult to recall the feelings we had when the pattern was first assembled. Now Bembel Rudzuk's idea of observing 'that point at which stillness becomes motion' and that other point 'at which pattern becomes consciousness' seems altogether ill-conceived and the words with which he described his intention make me shudder. When I call to mind those early days of Hidden Lion when the tiles were arriving from Tower Gate's brickyard and his foreman and workmen were with their swift and dancing movements putting the pattern together, when I remember how we walked about and viewed the expansion of those tawny and red and black triangles with a commanding eye as if we were in charge of the thing, I cannot help making a face of embarrassment.

As we stand there looking at Hidden Lion I find myself shaking my head; I no longer know how to approach this place in my mind, I no longer know what to think of it. Up until the time when the Syrian and Armenian Christians were beheaded it was everybody's good-luck place; afterwards I expected it to become a bad-luck place but I was wrong. Until the next rain the bloodstains remained to mark the tiles, and to those tiles during those few days came many people who stood and looked at them and pointed them out to other people who then stood and looked at them. All of these people who came and looked were Muslims. One day I saw a man squat and rub his hand over one of the tawny bloodstained tiles, then he put his hand inside his robe and rubbed his chest. After that many others did the same, and children began to walk in special ways on those tiles and to dance on them.

The tiles being glazed, the blood had not permeated the clay; when the rain came it washed them clean. The tiles that had been stained with blood did not, however, become unknown: by some general understanding amongst themselves those who took an interest in the tiles had noted their positions relative to the tower, and by counting carefully they found their way to them again. This was a source of great amusement to the headless and maggoty tax-collector, who now appointed himself a guide and would stand where the blood had been, stamping his foot and pointing with his finger to the tiles. I could of course not see his smile but I could hear his laughter and there was no mistaking the mockery in the way he stamped his foot and pointed with his finger.

One day a boy of eight or nine came and prostrated himself on some of the tiles that had been stained with blood. He was dressed the same as any other child, he was not wearing a blue turban. I recognized him as the same boy who had come to the paved square and drawn on the stone the morning after I made my first chalk drawing for Hidden Lion. After a few moments he stood up and looked all around at everyone, then walked away. The next day there appeared on those tiles an earthenware pot which filled up with money. The butcher volunteered to divide it among Christian orphans. This was done, and each day after that the pot was filled up and emptied in the same manner.

Now on this day of the shaking of the earth the shaking has stopped and people are returning to their ordinary activities; the stallholders are again at their places on Hidden Lion. Trade here has of course diminished with the progress of the siege; the caravans have left off coming to Antioch, the road from Suwaydiyya is dangerous, and goods are scarce. Vendors, having little to sell, have lately been reduced to trading among themselves; their collective scanty stock distributes itself anew every day: the copper pot with the hole in it that used to be at the stall of A makes its appearance at the stall of B, while the haftless dagger that was a veteran non-seller with B now tries its luck with A. Eventually, perhaps with P or Q, the pot and the dagger assume with the new venue a new aspect that gets them sold, proving yet again to those who knew it already that action creates action.

Today, however, the merchants sit or stand listlessly by their wares as if all buying and selling are gone out of the world. Most of them pack up and go home early. The man at the coffee stand by the tower puts his coffee pot and his little brass cups into their wooden box, picks up the box by its leather strap, slings it from his shoulder, takes his brazier, says, 'This place is finished', and turns to go.

'Why is it finished?' I ask him.

'Look,' he says, pointing to the pattern with his foot, 'there's not so much as a single tile cracked, it isn't natural.'

193

'What do you think it means?' I say.

'It means that this place is being saved for something worse,' he says, 'and I don't want any part of it.' He recedes into the distance, never looking back.

The butcher comes, takes the pot of money for the Christian orphans, spits on the tiles, and walks away.

'Wait,' I say to him. 'Why did you spit on the tiles, why do you look that way?'

Without saying a word the butcher makes with his index and little finger the sign against the evil eye and off he goes.

This day that has begun with the shaking of the earth moves on and there are more wonders to be seen: the dreadful grey curtain of the day becomes the darker curtain of night and there are seen moving behind it strange red lights in the sky that shift and slide from one shape to another. More praying and singing from the Franks and many voices lifted to God on our side of the walls as well. The Patriarch, who was taken out of his hanging cage and put back in prison when the earth stopped shaking, is brought out again to offer an opinion on the strange lights. He sees very plainly in the sky the sign of the Cross and is put back in prison. Bembel Rudzuk and I look up at the sky but we say nothing to each other of what we see — there is perhaps too much motion becoming stillness, too much consciousness becoming pattern for us to respond with anything but silence.

The sky stays grey the next day and rain comes pelting down like hopelessness turned into water; the earth becomes a soggy boggy mire; the river swallows up its banks, it is no longer to be trifled with, soon it must run over the bridge instead of under it, soon it must lose patience with this city, must rush it brick by brick and stone by stone away into the sea that drowns Muslims, Christians, and Jews impartially and says nothing about God, nothing about justice or mercy. Dismally falls the rain on Silpius, and slides of mud and stones go down the mountainside to join the ponderous rolling rush of Onopniktes that bellows and echoes under Antioch as if fulfilling a prophecy, as if it has been foretold centuries ago that when the mountain will have passed under the city a monstrous thing will happen, perhaps the end of all things will come; or worse, some great beast taller than the mountain will appear and say at the same time and with one voice in all the languages of humankind that there will be no end to anything, that everything will go on and on for ever.

Those thousands of Franks who rode off in the night come squelching back now under the grey sky and the rain. These thousands, we hear, have been led by Bohemond of Taranto and Robert of Flanders. Moving up the Orontes valley they have run into the armies of Duqaq, Tughtagin, and Janah al-Dawla coming from Damascus to relieve Antioch. We are told that Bohemond has learned how to fight Turks now, that he kept his cavalry in the rear to prevent the encirclement of Robert's men and then charged in at the right moment. So they have driven back the Turks, Bohemond and Robert and their thousands; they have won a battle but they have lost men, they have worn themselves out, and they have come back empty-handed to their rotting and sodden tents in the mud and such treats as horses' heads without the tongues for three solidi and goats' intestines for five.

Here they are then, the conquerors of Antioch held back from the conquering of it; it is like holding back the bull from the cow: he paws the earth, he rolls his eyes, his breath steams on the air. All that makes him a bull is hot and ready. But the cow is a cow of stone.

What is the nature of things? The nature of things is that what can happen will happen, often it has already happened before it is recognized. The walls of Antioch were built during the reign of Justinian, a time of strong stonemasonry; those walls are not be knocked down or undermined, and any attacker who scales them will only find himself on a short stretch of rampart between the massive towers with a bitter rain of arrows hissing down and the strong doors of the towers barred against him. How then can the Franks breach the unbreachable, pass the impassable? How can Antioch be taken? It can be taken if someone on the wall will turn away from his duty, it can be taken if someone will open the strong tower doors and let the soldiers of Christ in quietly. And will someone be found to do this? What a question! Such a question can only be asked by an atheist; anyone who recognizes the existence of God (whether as He or as It) and the intersections of virtuality

195

and actuality is well aware of how easily such crossings on the plane of possibility can be sucked up into a point of happening. After the event one looks at all the many lines converging on the point and marvels because it seems that people were born, nations assembled, geography organized, roads laid out and bridges built expressly so that this event could happen. So rise now to a point of happening the turningness of Firouz and the unturningness of Bohemond, the one on what is called the inside and the other on what is called the outside of the walls of the four hundred towers, those stones that have no enemy.

At this time that I am telling of I have so far seen Bohemond only at a considerable distance. There is of course no mistaking him, he is so astonishingly tall, taller than most men by half an arm's length. When I see Bohemond, when I think of Bohemond, I know that I am seeing and thinking of more than Bohemond: as the arrow streaks to its target the point of the arrow is driven by the shaft behind it, the feathers that make the shaft fly true, and the bow that has loosed the energy of its bending into the flight of the arrow; so comes Bohemond from the loins of his father Robert Guiscard and the womb of his mother Alberada of Buonalbergo. But Bohemond's lineage is more than human, it includes generations of horses; the line of Bohemond goes back to *Eohippus*, the dawn horse, the very beginning of all chivalry. And yet the most prepotent of Bohemond's ancestors was neither a human nor an animal but an artifact: Bohemond is descended mainly from the stirrup. Bohemond is grown out of an aristocracy of warriors on horseback rising from the cavalry of Charles Martel; this aristocracy comes to the point of the present in the armoured man on the heavy horse with his feet firm in the stirrups that give power to the drive of his lance, the swing of his sword; the armoured man strong in the saddle, bred to fight and trained from boyhood to be unturning in attack; the armoured man superior in wealth, in breeding, in physique and in confidence to the man on foot.

Bohemond's ancestors of the fifth century who fought under Chlodovech, they fought without armour and on foot, they hurled axes and barbed javelins, God knows what stocks and stones they offered to. What did they know of Jerusalem? How in the world has Bohemond come to be a soldier of Christ? How has Bohemond become the Bohemond who cut up his scarlet cloak into crosses? This is not to be known by me, I shall die without knowing it.

Bohemond is always in my mind but I have no chance of understanding him. When he was first pointed out to me I was high up on the wall looking down at his distant figure but in my thoughts he at once took his place high up as if striding on ramparts built for him alone. He is everything that I am not, this quintessential warrior prince. I am told that he can, fully armed, leap from the ground to his horse's back; that no other man can wield with two hands the sword he wields with one; that he requires three women nightly to keep him tranquil; that he is a serpent in cunning, a thunderbolt in attack, he is simply not to be withstood. Red-haired and blue-eyed, he does what he wants and he gets what he wants. How should I not be obsessed with Bohemond? But his thoughts are beyond my imagination. In my drift through this space called time I have reported two dreams of Pope Urban II and I know that, whether virtually or actually, they are true. They are there, I have experienced them. But of Bohemond I can offer nothing sure, only intimations, only things half-sensed, half guessed-at. As the animals of the forest scent the questing hound I scent him, questing through the death of Christ and God's departure, questing on the track of gold and fame and power, questing for the tangible, the visible, questing for that which cannot be mistaken, that which can be held in the strong hand, that which can be gripped between strong thighs as a horse is gripped.

So. Bohemond is encamped before the walls of Antioch and now we are in the year 1098. Bohemond, greedy and lusting for the seen, cannot yet have what he craves; that time is not yet come. As I say this there comes into my mind an image of Bohemond opposed by Bembel Rudzuk; it is a night image, the background of it is darkness; against the darkness the two figures are luminous, they leap out of the dark, stopped in mid-motion as if by lightning — Bohemond with the gleam of his helmet, the glitter of his mail, the flash of his great sword, the scarlet cross on his surcoat, the iron nasal and the straight brow-line of his helmet simplifying his face, the face of the death-angel haloed by the rainbow arc of the great sword. Bohemond the death-angel, Bohemond the questing death-hound circling in the night beyond the circle of Christ's little wander-fire. Bohemond the tall, lit by the lightning as he leaps with his death-bringing, with his blood-drinking sword. And leaping at him with a flash of the gold brocade on his elegant scarlet jacket, with his Turkish sword heroic against the death-hound, with his moustaches heroic, Bembel Rudzuk the dauntless, Bembel Rudzuk who is at the same time like a lion of innocence, like an angel of folly, like a butterfly transfixed by the pin of actuality, Bembel Rudzuk the friend true unto death.

That is the image, held motionless against the dark as if by lightning, that comes into my mind as I think of the never-to-be-known, never-to-be-understood Bohemond. Simple greed, simple ambition, simple unlimited courage do not suffice to explain this man. Nothing I have so far said explains Bohemond. As one who is not a mathematical genius cannot understand one who is, so I cannot understand this genius of maleness and action; even simply counting up his attributes and his actions one arrives at something that cannot be accounted for: the total of the seen becomes the unseen, becomes a mystery. Bohemond has in the mystery of him such force as to make him a kind of un-Christ; in the greatness of his courage and his greed he looms gigantic; almost Death stands aside at the sound of his name and his great bones stand up shouting. His tomb in Apulia is domed, it has Romanesque arches, it has bronze doors. Sometimes as Pilgermann the owl I sit on the dome of Bohemond's tomb in the twilight when it is still warm from the last sun of the day.

But it is the year 1098 that I tell of now; the bones of Bohemond are still in active partnership with his flesh and I have not yet achieved owlhood. It is February, a Turkish army is again on its way to the relief of Antioch, and this time Rudwan of Aleppo is with them. The Frankish cavalry is much diminished now; they must have less than a thousand horses fit for war. I cannot help thinking of those battles in the Holy Scriptures in which God would diminish the armies of the children of Israel the better to show his power; I have come to believe that God, having departed, now wills that nothing should stand between the Franks and Jerusalem.

Bohemond does not wait for the Turks to come to Antioch; he leaves the foot-soldiers and the horseless cavalry to defend the camp against further sorties and with that cavalry numberless in arrogance but many times outnumbered by the enemy he moves out to take up a position between the Orontes and the Lake of Antioch where he cannot be encircled. Needs must when the devil drives, and he has learned by now that the harrying, stinging, in-and-out, encircling tactics of the Turks must be met with equal cunning if he is to beat them. And of course he does. On first sight of the Turks the Franks charge before the Turkish archers can be effectively disposed, then they withdraw, luring the Turks into that space between the lake and the river, that space chosen for the battle. Here the Frankish cavalry do again what they do better than anyone else, the straight charge with lance in rest. So again the relieving army is put to flight by Bohemond, by that unturning battle-greed of his. So ardent is he in his pursuit of the enemy that the points of his crimson banner, we hear, fly over the heads of the rearmost Turks.

Here at Antioch the absence of Bohemond reliably brings Yaghi-Siyan out through the bridge gate for yet another sortie on the Frankish encampment where there are only men on foot to oppose him. Things are going badly for the horseless Franks, the time must seem long to them until Bohemond returns in the afternoon like the sun and Yaghi-Siyan, like a wooden foul-weather figure, goes back inside. The soldiers of Christ put Turkish heads on poles outside their camp to stare with dead eyes at the walls of Antioch until the flesh rots away and they are no longer heads but skulls.

The Franks have so far held off two attempts to relieve the city but they have not yet been able to close it off completely from the world. The Suwaydiyya road, though no longer travelled by caravans, is still used by enterprising traders at unlikely hours and for high profits. Supplies are also moving through the Ladhiquiyya Gate at carefully chosen times.

At the beginning of March we hear of ships at Suwaydiyya and we hear that they bring to the Franks fighting men and horses, siege technicians from Constantinople, timber and every kind of tackle for the building of siege towers and giant war machines, also apparatus capable of shooting Greek fire from the far side of the Orontes into the centre of Antioch. There is little doubt that Antioch will soon be in Frankish hands unless the siege materials are intercepted.

It is Bohemond and Raymond who one night lead their men to Suwaydiyya to bring in the materials and the reinforcements. About an hour after their departure we hear the horsemen trotting to and from Yaghi-Siyan's palace, hear the shouting of commands, the slap and jingle, the shuffling and snuffling and whinnying as cavalrymen ready their horses and themselves. They ride out on the Suwaydiyya road and we of the civilian militia together with soldiers of the garrison man the walls to watch the Frankish camp and wait.

It is while I stand on this wall built by a Roman emperor and keep watch on the Franks with a Turkish bow in my hand that I find myself reflecting on where I am and what I am doing. It isn't that I haven't taken notice of the separate parts of it but somehow I haven't taken notice of how the parts look when they're all put together. I am carrying weapons that I was taught to use by a Muslim (we non-Muslims of the militia are now permitted to go armed) and I am keeping watch on the walls of this city that is being held by Muslims against Christians who call themselves soldiers of Christ. Bohemond himself may at any time come climbing over this wall with his sword that only he can wield with one hand, Bohemond the battle-greedy, the death-hound.

To this has my late-night walking in the Keinjudenstrasse brought me. And yet each step of the way had nothing surprising in it. There was the garden, there was the ladder; up I climbed to that naked and incomparable Sophia and here I am.

This castration that I have suffered, has it a use, has it a value? What was I before I was castrated? I was already castrated, was I not, by mortality? All of us are castrated by mortality, we are unmanned, unwomanned, we are made nothing because all we have is this so little space of time with a blackness before and after it (that I speak out of this blackness as Pilgermann is only a borrowing; it is to unself and the namelessness of potential being that I must return when I have said what I have to say). How to live then in this little space in which we have a self and a name, this little space in which we are allowed to accumulate our tiny history of tiny days, this moment that is at once the first moment and the last moment, this moment that contains our universe and such space/time as is unwound in the working of it?

We don't want to know about our mortal castration. We throw ourselves into the work of each day, the beating of hammers, the baking of bread; we find ourselves a spouse, we gather children around us to keep out the dark, we keep the Sabbath, pray to God, hope that all will be well. Ah, but there is more! Not for this alone was there smoke and fire and a quaking on the mountain while the voice of the horn sounded louder and louder. No, there is a mystery that even God cannot fathom, nor can he give the law of it on two stone tablets. He cannot speak what there are no words for; he needs divers to dive into it, he needs wrestlers to wrestle with it, singers to sing it, lovers to love it. He cannot deal with it alone, he must find helpers, and for this does he blind some and maim others. 'Look,' God has said to me, 'what must I do to make you play the man? I have already castrated you with mortality but you pay no attention to it. So now let it be done with a knife, then let's see what happens. Let's see if you'll grow yourself some new balls and jump into the mystery with me.'

'But what's it all about?' I cry.

'If I could tell you that it wouldn't be a mystery,' says God. 'Let it be enough that I ask for your help.' (God has of course not actually been speaking here because he is no longer manifesting himself as He; but God as It has put these words into my mind.)

This is then the value and the use of my castration; with this must I be content. If even God in his omniscience doesn't know the answer then each of us must help however possible. And think how it would be if God *could* give the answer, if God could say, 'All right, here it is: the answer is this and this and this and this; now you know the answer.' Who would then have any respect for God, who would even have any interest in Him? 'What!' we should say, 'Is this the best you can do? Is there to be no mystery then? Feh!'

201

'I know what you mean,' says the man in front of me in Turkish with an Italian accent. While thinking the thoughts that I have just been telling of I have been pacing my stretch of wall and I have come face to face with this remarkable Mordechai Salzedo of whom I have spoken once before: it was he who cited from Genesis the words, 'Where he is' when we met in the street by the synagogue before Rosh Hashanah.

This Salzedo has come to Antioch by a route even less direct than mine. He was born in Barbastro in Spain and as a child of seven he escaped from the town when it was sacked by the French in 1064. Those Christian armies dealt with the Muslims and Jews of Barbastro in the traditional way, and when his mother lay dead with her skirt over her head and his father with his guts wound round a post young Salzedo crept away quietly to try his luck elsewhere. He fell in with a company of wine merchants, Italian Jews who were on their way to Barcelona, went with them when they sailed back to La Spezia, was taken into the family of one of the partners, grew up to marry one of the daughters, became a partner in the house, lost his wife when their ship bound from Cagliari in Sardinia to Bizerta in Tunisia sank in a storm, clung to a wineskin and drifted for three days, was picked up by a Neapolitan business associate, decided to go into textiles, came to Antioch to sell wine and buy silks and cottons, fell into conversation with Bembel Rudzuk, was unable to disengage himself, and so set up in business and settled here.

'What do you mean, you know what I mean?' I say.

'I noticed how you were shaking your head,' he says, 'and I said to myself: this man has in his mind the same thought that I have in mine.'

'And what is that thought?' I say.

'That to be a Jew is to find yourself doing all kinds of things in all kinds of places,' he says. 'Here we are keeping watch against the Franks on a wall built by a Roman emperor around a city now held by Turks.'

'If I'd kept watch from the wall of my town I might still have a pimmel,' I say. It comes to me that if I hold my mind right a tremendous thought will illuminate it. This thought is a real treasure too. It is so cunningly and commodiously formed that it contains all other thoughts in a beautiful instantaneous order of total comprehension. I am trying so hard to hold my mind right that I get a crick in my neck. Come, wonderful thought, come! The ladder was presented, yes ... Sophia was given, yes ... my pimmel and my balls were taken away, yes ... Bohemond is given ... What? How? Ah! it's gone, the wonderful thought is gone.

'What's going to happen?' says Salzedo. He has maintained a respectful silence for what seems a very long time while I have been trying to hold my mind right.

'The Franks will take Antioch,' I say.

'Yes,' he says. 'It's the kind of thing that happens. Everyone says that Karbuqa of Mosul will be here soon to relieve us but I doubt that he'll get here soon enough.'

'You can still leave Antioch,' I say. 'They haven't got everything completely closed off yet.'

'I don't think I'll bother,' says Salzedo. 'I've already had quite a bit of extra time, and if God needs dead Jews as badly as he seems to I'm ready to go. And you?'

I think of the tax-collector, I think of my young death whom I have seen in the dawning on the roof of Bembel Rudzuk's house. I think also of Bruder Pförtner and the others whom I've not yet seen here in Antioch. I think suddenly of Sophia (she is always in my mind like a continuo above which rise each day's new thoughts of her) and for the first time there comes to me the question: is she alive or dead? Why should she be dead? She is not a Jewess, no one will rape her and kill her on the cobblestones of our town; she is safe there. But is she there? Until now I have never thought of her as being anywhere else, she has been in my mind a world that continues inviolate while I disappear into chaos; in my mind she has been as static as that other Sophia in Constantinople. Now the curtain of my sight sways before me, the earth seems to move sickeningly beneath me, and in a suddenly clear sky the stars wheel as if the world is spinning like a top. I look up and see, perhaps in the sky, perhaps in my mind, those three stars between the Virgin and the Lion, that Jewish gesture of the upflung hand: What, will you block the road for ever? The whole world is moving, it is walking, it is riding on horses, it is sailing in ships to Jerusalem. Why should she be still, be safe?

'And you?' Salzedo is saying.

'I was going to Jerusalem,' I say.

'And will you still go to Jerusalem?' he says.

'Jerusalem will be wherever I am when the end comes,' I say.

'That could be soon,' he says. 'It could happen by Passover; Shavuoth at the latest. Yes, Shavuoth is probably when it'll be, it's a better time because Shavuoth celebrates the giving of the Torah to Israel at Sinai, the giving of the Law; yes, that's why it'll be Shavuoth: from Passover to Shavuoth is a development, it's the coming to maturity of the children of Israel. At Passover they left their bondage in Egypt, they began their wandering; when they came to the mountain of God they were given the Law. Also Shavuoth is a harvest holiday, and this that is coming is certainly some kind of harvest.'

'Of whose sowing?' I say.

'It doesn't matter who does the sowing,' he says. 'Life is sown and Death comes to reap the harvest; when has it been otherwise? Have you ever seen this mountain where the children of Israel were given the Law?'

'No,' I say.

'It isn't the biggest mountain in the world,' he says, 'but you know it when you see it: it looks only like itself, like a lion of stone, this mountain whose name is Horeb; the Arabs call it Djebel Musa, the mountain of Moses. It is called Sinai because of the thornbush, *seneh*. This thornbush from which God first spoke to Moses was on that same mountain whereon God later gave Moses the tablets of the Law. Perhaps you already knew this?'

'I didn't remember that about the thornbush,' I say.

'Not everyone does,' he says. 'But it's a good thing to keep in mind because God is such a thorny business and we shouldn't expect him to be otherwise. But I'll tell you one good thing about being a Jew — whenever your time comes you don't have to worry that the day will be unmarked and forgotten because you can be sure that some really famous Jew has died on the same day, maybe even thousands of them.

Akiba died around this time of year, it was sometime during the seven weeks of the Counting of the Omer. The Romans flayed him.'

'His last words,' I say, 'were: "Hear, O Israel, the Lord our God, the Lord is One."'

Salzedo is content to let Akiba have the last word, and we resume our separate pacing. There comes to me then something that is both image and not-image. It has to do with a striking, a vast and not to be held in the mind striking of side-posts and a lintel beyond imagination, the striking of them with the hyssop that is the tree of the world, spattering the blood of all the world on the side-posts, on the lintel of the universe. And there must none of us go out of the house until morning, but will morning ever come? At such times as the not-image phases into image I see the right arm and shoulder and back of this striking. The spattering drops of blood fan slowly, slowly out, out, out, the drops of blood become the stars. Far and frozen the luminous drops of burning blood, far and frozen, drifting ever wider, wider, wider.

And there must none of us, none of us pass under the lintel, pass between the side-posts until morning comes, none of us beneath the spattered blood of the lamb without blemish, the word of blood to be read by the LORD in His aspect of Justice, the LORD in His aspect of Mercy passing in the night, passing with the destroyer.

I have described this that is both image and not-image as it comes to me and as it compels me to describe it. I describe what I do not understand because I am lived by it. Yes, that's what it is, why I have no choice, why I am compelled. This that I have described is not an idea that I have had or a vision or a dream, it is not a means of expression for me as poetry might be. No, I am a means of expression for it, God as He or God as It knows why. That is why I have not the privilege and the pleasure of telling stories, of showing brightly coloured pictures of Samson and the lion. Not only is storytelling denied me but history also — I may well be reporting nothing more than spiritual mirages and metaphysical illusions. I can only tell what, as far as I know, happened or seemed to happen to what I recognize as myself with such recognition as has been borrowed from the darkness.

Very well then, I return to the walls of Antioch. I am there now and I smell these old strong stones that have no enemy. I smell their tawniness, their sweat of years, I smell the slow clinging of the lichens and the mosses on them. I smell the blood as well, the blood that has been and the blood that is coming. I smell the hotness and the dryness baked into the stones by centuries of summer sun, I smell the coldness and the wetness of the winter rains; the stones forget nothing.

I feel in this wall of stone something else that is happening; the idea of sorting comes into my mind. Walls by their nature do sort: by defining an inside and an outside they sort the insiders from the outsiders, they sort what is happening inside from what is happening outside. More than that: on this wall that girdles Antioch in the year 1098 I pick up a bit of broken stone and as I hold it in my hand I feel the sorting that goes on continually inside it: this way, that way, this way, that way, Christ in every stone with arms outspread, not raging as he judges between the elect on his right hand and the damned on his left; he has put himself into a state of perfect balance, he does not weigh with a scale, measure with a rule: he himself, abandoning all self, is the rule and the scale, the pointer that wavers on the beam. He is entranced, he makes no judgments although he is the judge: he is a necessary, an essential instrument in the sorting process and it is the process that has brought the instrument into being. I have seen this necessary instrument, this Christ-as-balance, carved in stone in the century after mine by Gislebertus on the tympanum of Autun Cathedral in Burgundy, that same Burgundy from where came some of those soldiers who sacked Barbastro and orphaned Salzedo in 1064. The sorting being necessary, the instrument appears.

I have understood so little in my lifetime! Now in the centuries of my deathtime I am just beginning to understand a little more but my consciousness is not continuous, I am only a mode of perception irregularly used by strangers. Perhaps there will never be the possibility for me to understand what Christ is. I understand that he was born from the idea of him — that he told me himself: 'From me came the seed that gave me life.' That he is essentially a sorter I also understand; the sorting of course follows on that disparity without which the universe could not maintain spin; I think that I knew that even before I read Plato's *Timaeus* in which he says: 'Motion never exists in what is uniform. For to conceive that anything can be moved without a mover is hard or indeed impossible, and equally impossible to conceive that there can be a mover unless there is something which can be moved — motion cannot exist where either of these is wanting, and for these to be uniform is impossible; wherefore we must assign rest to uniformity and motion to the want of uniformity.'

That good and evil should be sorted along with right and left, up and down, light and darkness and all other complementarities is clearly in the nature of things, and that Christ should be a medium of this sorting is also clearly in the nature of things; but the rest of what he is continually moves on ahead of my comprehension like a great whale cleaving cosmic seas; I try to grasp the essence of him but I grasp only the fading wake of his passage.

Where was I? The walls of Antioch, and we are waiting for news of the Turkish cavalry who took the Suwaydiyya road after the Franks. The question arises whether apparent consistency of manifestation is to be accepted as reality. May it not simply be the persistence of image in the eye of the mind? This Turkish cavalry, for example, this whole numerous appearance of horses, men, and weapons — does it in actuality remain the same from one moment to the next? May it not suddenly and without any noticeable change be a black dog, not numerous at all, just one single black dog trotting inseparable from its little black noon shadow, even in the twilight trotting with that same little noon shadow which is also the shadow of a small stone both moving and still? Or trees, not many, just a clump of trees in the stillness of the dawn. The roundness and solidity of the shadowed trunks like circling dancers under the tented leaves. Wine of shadows, shadow music fading, fading to the shout of day.

Those other horsemen, the Frankish horsemen, or whatever it is that has offered to the eye this appearance of Frankish horsemen, may they or it not be a broken cathedral, inexplicable in a distant desert, the spire no longer in unity aspiring to heaven but toppled in pieces, pointing only to the sand? Broken stones, broken stones singing broken songs, broken verses chopped abruptly off, odd words leaping suddenly into silence? From these broken stones, these hewn and carven broken stones, there puts itself together a broken stone angel of death towering over the dawn trees, bigger than the cathedral ever was, the stones of it continually toppling as it strides but bounding up again to move as arms or legs or as a head that turns this way and that, turning in its looking but unturning in its questing. Questing is the name of this death angel made of broken stones, Bohemond is the name of this Questing.

Now at last Bohemond has become altogether real to me, not to be understood — nothing can be understood, I see now — but to be seen with the same solidity and shadow-casting reality as the port that is approached by crossing the water at dawn so that it grows larger, larger in the eye, so that at last it is arrived at. So have I at last arrived at Bohemond in his aspect of the death angel named Questing, the many-horsed, many-hoofed many-faced striding of the broken stones, the broken cathedral that crosses seas and deserts and mountains, questing on the death-track of the mystery that is Christ.

14

Night passes, morning comes, surprised as always to find itself here. This morning is full of urgent motion, of horsemen trotting to and from Yaghi-Siyan's palace, of shouted commands, of the slap and jingle of harness and the shuffling and snuffling and whinnying of horses as cavalrymen prepare for action. Action impends but does not come until the afternoon when a Turkish galloper clatters over the bridge, through the gate, and into the city with the news that the cavalry who rode out last night have ambushed the Franks returning from Suwaydiyya. The Turks have put the Franks to flight, have captured the wagons with the siege materials and are now on their way back with them.

Only a few minutes after the arrival of the Turkish galloper we on the wall see scattered horsemen coming from the direction of Suwaydiyya and making for the Frankish camp. These we guess to be Franks who have fled the ambush. Now the Frankish camp is in motion, they will be riding out to help their comrades. In Antioch the kettledrums are pounding; Yaghi-Siyan's cavalry come pouring out through the bridge gate, thundering across the bridge to engage the Franks and keep them from reinforcing the others.

The Turks are able to hold the Franks for a time but suddenly here are Bohemond and Raymond with their forces regathered and their lances levelled. As always I see him at a distance, and I recognize Bohemond by the gathering of galloping warriors into a point; I know that only he can be that point, only he can be that ardent forwardness with his name cleaving the air before him. Surely by now his name is like the roar of the lion: it is more than a sound, it is that which makes the knees shake. The Turks cannot now move forward against the man and the name, they must wheel their horses round towards the bridge and the gate, must turn themselves in the saddle to loose their arrows at the baneful man, the baneful name that overwhelms them.

As it lives again in the eye of my mind it seems all in one moment that Yaghi-Siyan's cavalry are galloping for their lives over the bridge while there rises stone by stone the tower of the Franks that will command the bridge and further tighten the blockade of Antioch. But before this can be done the Franks must recapture the building materials from the Turks, and for this must many Turks be killed.

On the far side of the river there is a Muslim cemetery, and this night the Turks come out of Antioch to bury their dead there. In the morning the Franks dig up the bodies, there is gold and silver to be taken from them. They use stones from the tombs in the building of their tower and this becomes a part of the picture in my mind, almost it seems to me that the tower is being built of dug-up Turkish corpses while yet the Turkish cavalry gallop for their lives across the bridge into Antioch. And in this same moment rises the other Tower, Tancred's tower that will command the Ladhiqiyya Gate.

Still the back ways of Mount Silpius and the postern doors in the walls are there for those who want to leave Antioch and for the more determined of the foragers and profiteers but from now on there will be no more sorties from Antioch nor will there be more than a trickle of provisions coming in. In the five months of the siege the Franks have been able to do nothing much with their mangonels and other missile-throwing machines, and the river has kept them from moving siege towers up against the walls. The rumours of advanced Greek-fire techniques have proved unfounded; but now the striding stones of the broken cathedral have walled in the unbroken stones of the walls of Antioch.

Now ships from Genoa are bringing provisions to the Franks and the Suwaydiyya road is under their control; now do their fortunes improve while those of Antioch decline. Well do we know that in each of us lives a skeleton that waits for the flesh to die, there is an absence waiting for the presence to depart — but a great city! A city like Antioch! As Pilgermann the owl I fly over it now and it looks like nothing really, it has retreated from its medieval boundaries, it has shrunk and dwindled, it has huddled itself together, has drawn back from the vaunt of its greatness and the largeness of its history, it is like a swimmer who has struggled barely alive out of a raging torrent and does not enter the water again. No, I think as I look down on this place that is so small, so diminished, so unspecial, this is not Antioch: Antioch was days and nights of vivid action, Antioch was a paradigm of history in which at one time and another every kind of thinker and doer, every kind of greatness and smallness jostled together and shouldered and elbowed their way through all the lights and resonances and colours, all the smells and flavours and motion of endless variations of circumstance and event in a large and crowded arena. In a particular time people fought and lived and died for particular things; now it is small, now it is quiet. An old woman in black walks a path with a basket on her head; a man leads a donkey loaded with firewood; perhaps they say to themselves that God wills it. And of course God wills everything: the beating of hammers; the baking of bread; the rise and fall of nations; the quiet clopping of the hooves of one small donkey.

Raymond's tower, the one commanding the bridge and the bridge gate, was built in March of 1098, and from that time Antioch moved forward faster and faster towards its fall. That tower was completed and Raymond's banner was run up on the top of it on the Eve of Passover.

Before that, while the tower was being built, while Passover was approaching, there began to be in my mind the idea of Elijah and the anticipation of that moment in the Seder when the door is opened for him. I began to see that another idea was coming to me, it was the idea of Bohemond as Elijah, Elijah as enemy, enemy as messenger of God. Yes, the enemy as messenger of God, the enemy as teacher. Sophia was the beginning of my Holy Wisdom and Bohemond would be the end of it.

Behold, he cometh,
Saith the LORD of hosts.
But who may abide the day of his coming?
And who shall stand when he appeareth?
For he is like a refiner's fire,
And like fullers' soap;

Elijah sensed that everything was on him, the whole burden of a world of trouble. He said:

I have been very jealous for the LORD, the God of hosts; for the children of Israel have forsaken Thy covenant, thrown down Thine altars, and slain Thy prophets with the sword; and I, even I only, am left; and they seek my life, to take it away.

Is this perhaps God's gift and mystery, that he puts the world in and on each one of us as if there is no one else? And perhaps Bohemond, with the whole world in him and on him in a way that I can have no idea of, is without even knowing it jealous for the LORD; perhaps he has been appointed by God to call our attention to something, to the fragility of the temples that we daily destroy perhaps.

I sensed that it was important for me to understand, of the many things in my mind, at least one thing well in order to die properly, to let go of life in the right way. I craved to know what at least one of the important persons in my life was to me: Sophia or the tax-collector or Bohemond, the one in my mind called Questing, the angel of death and messenger of God.

Different people look ahead to different things. There were Jews in Antioch who had no doubt whatever that the Messiah was coming. This brute faith seemed a kind of madness to me; their faces seemed coarse with it, their eyes like stones. 'What?' I said to them, 'What will be when the Messiah comes?'

'The Temple rebuilt!' they cried, their stone eyes shining, 'The glory of Israel restored!'

'The Temple rebuilt!' I said to them. Suddenly the absurdity of such a fast day as Tisha b'Av became overwhelming to me. To lament year after year, generation after generation, the toppling of stones! Stones that have no enemy, stones in whom God dances impartially for anyone or for no one, dances under whatever name is given, dances whether there is anyone to know of God's existence or not! What is the toppling of stones to God? Is God overturned with the stones? My people! 'If you want the Temple rebuilt then go and rebuild it!' I said. 'One doesn't need a Messiah for that, one only needs carpenters and stonemasons and bricklayers.'

'Don't be such a fool,' they said. 'You know very well that it isn't just the sticks and stones and bricks of it we're talking about. Don't you want the glory of Israel restored?'

'The glory of Israel has never been lost,' I said. 'When you say, "Hear, O Israel, the Lord our God, the Lord is One", then with those words and with that thought you speak the glory of Israel. To that perception of Oneness nothing can be added and from it nothing can be taken away.'

'The ancient glory of the Kingdom of David!' they said.

'What kind of glory is that?' I said. 'Saul slew his hundreds, David slew his thousands, Bohemond the same. Wait, you'll see glory when Bohemond comes over the wall.'

Their stone eyes glared into mine. Hearing the words that came out of my mouth I realized that I was not of their world, I was no longer even of my own world, I was well on my way to where I am now.

This Elijah who now presented himself to me as enemy and teacher and messenger of God, this Elijah had long lived in my mind as forerunner; I had always pictured him running ahead as he ran ahead of Ahab's chariot, an athlete strong in his engoddedness, running like an animal and with his running prophesying the God in him; the beauty of his running makes a shout in the desert, a lightning in the sunlight. Elijah the forerunner of the Messiah, Elijah the warden of the covenant, Elijah for whom a chair is placed at circumcisions, Elijah for whom a place is set at the Seder, for whom a glass of wine is poured, for whom the door is left open, Ay! Elijah! Elijah feeling himself alone the covenant-keeper, Elijah with a silence all around him and a still small voice inside him. Elijah who bows himself to the earth and puts his face between his knees and waits for the rain, Elijah who runs away and throws himself aside until the angel of God calls him to action. Elijah fed by angels, fed by ravens, Elijah the magical, the one of us. His

213

guises are many, one doesn't always know who he is, one doesn't always recognize him. One must make connexions, must find the combination that he is a part of. By learning to recognize Elijah one learns to recognize Messiah. Here in Antioch the evening of the fourteenth of Nisan in the Jewish year 4858 which is the nineteenth of March in the Christian year 1098 is the Eve of Passover. A place is set, a glas of wine is poured, the door is opened for Elijah. And I know that in this part of the space called time Bohemond is Elijah and for me the taking of Antioch will be the Messiah and Jerusalem both.

Passover has come and gone and the Franks have not come over the walls. The tower we call Evil Eye and Raymond's tower and Tancred's tower stare at us through days and nights as if by observation could be known the time when Antioch must fall to these soldiers of Christ who cannot breach the walls of Justinian.

The towers stare, the Franks await God's will while Karbuqa masses his armies and the reports of his imminent advance come every day with fresh detail and greater numbers. In Antioch the feeling is that of a very long night almost over and daylight almost here. The walls have not been breached, the Franks for all their engines of war and their will of God have not been able to bring the outside into the inside. Some of the people who have crept away from the city now return to take up life and business where they left off. There are many difficulties, many hardships, there are not enough goods to do much business with, but the people of Antioch wait patiently for the city to outlast its besiegers.

April passes and May. Salzedo was wrong: Shavuoth has come and gone and Antioch has not fallen. Here is the beginning of June in the Christian calendar, the end of Sivan in the Jewish one. The new moon of Tammuz will soon be seen, and some of the more old-fashioned Jews of Antioch will address it in the old-fashioned way:

> As I dance towards thee, but cannot touch thee,
> So shall none of my evil-inclined enemies
>   be able to reach me.

It is the night of the last of Sivan. I am asleep and I know that I am asleep. I feel like an instrument, like a compass needle quivering to the pull of the north or like a weathercock — yes, that's how I feel, like a weathercock high, high up on a steeple in a strong wind, my limbs rigidly extended north, south, east, and west but not fixed and still like the directionals of a weathercock; no, I am spinning, spinning through the space called time, over the miles, over the days, weeks, months to the fall of Jerusalem a year from now. My hands and feet burn as if they are on fire, spinning so high in a purple-blue sky, spinning down to the domes of Jerusalem the golden, down to Yerushalayim in the Christian summer of 1099, down to Yerushalayim with a pall of smoke hanging over it and a stench of fire and blood and death.

It is only a little while since the city has been taken, fires are still burning; the streets are slippery with blood and entrails; bodies of men, women, and children, severed limbs and heads are heaped everywhere. The colours of the clothes on the bodies cannot be distinguished, so steeped in blood are they. Some of the bodies still move a little, and groans can be heard.

Many of the Franks are busy with the dead and the near-dead; they cut them open and pull out the entrails, in this way some of them find gold coins. Screams are heard as well as groans, some of the Franks are active with women whom they have not yet killed while others take their pleasure with the dead.

Over the city circle the vultures while crows, bolder and more nimble, hop and flutter with red beaks and feet, picking and choosing. Dogs go cringing with their ears laid back, they seem stricken with guilt and terror at seeing so many masters slain at once; some are in an ecstasy of blood-frenzy, they snarl and growl and tear at the dead flesh, the corpses flop and jerk as they are pulled this way and that.

Here are the Western Wall and the Temple mound with the Dome of the Rock and the al-Aqsa Mosque. I have never seen these places before but I know them from maps and pictures, from dreams and from the phantom Jerusalem I have seen on Hidden Lion. Blood runs down the stones of the Western Wall and in the heat of the day the air quivers and sways above the dead who are heaped between the Dome of the Rock and the al-Aqsa Mosque. These are mostly Muslims; I can see no Jews here but I can smell their death in the smoke that rises from the synagogue to which they fled and in which they have been burnt alive. I am not walking, I am moving on the air in this waking sleep-travel, this night journey to a day that is coming; if I had to walk I should find little space on the red and slippery stones, I should have to walk on corpses.

Now I see among the blood-soaked bodies one that is like a naked ivory goddess in this butchery-place of the soldiers of Christ. The back of her head is crushed; her flawless limbs are sprawled in dishonour — but I am wrong to say that: her beauty of self and person cannot be dishonoured; she has been violated and murdered but such as she cannot be dishonoured; those who have done this have dishonoured only themselves. Here she lies, my dead and naked pilgrim, her Arab gown torn from her; flinging it over her head was not enough, they had to see all of her. I cannot cover her nor can I more modestly dispose her limbs, I have no corporeal existence in this place to which I have spun with burning hands and feet.

Here is a strange thing: in Sophia's left hand is a little shoe, a little scarlet slipper worked with gold. A child's shoe. Now do I seek and search, powerless to move so much as a dead finger of the numberless dead who lie here bearing witness.

I seek, I search; crows flap their black wings and cry their carrion-lust, dogs growl at my strange presence as I look everywhere to see if there will be a live two-year-old child with one foot bare. Have I been brought here to see the end of Sophia and that alone?

The sun goes down; the crows depart; the dogs are bolder now, the smacking and slavering and crunching of their feasting is loud in the twilight. There! Something moves! Fouled with the blood of the corpses he has sheltered under, there crawls out of this midden-heap of history a boy of perhaps two years and a few months. On his left foot is the mate of the slipper in Sophia's left hand. A fine boy, big for his age and strong-looking, with a face like Sophia's. It is growing dark, there is no moon to be seen. The little boy is not crying, his eyes are open wide and all his senses are alert as he walks slowly and quietly among the silent dead and the snarling dogs.

I cannot follow. My burning hands and feet, my north and south, east and west are spinning me up into the night and away from Jerusalem. 'My son!' I cry, 'My little son!' Never shall I know his name. His face was not only like Sophia's, there was something of me in it as well, also in the way he held his head.

I am in my bed. The last of the darkness is paling towards the dawn. My hands and feet still burn. I am naked. I look away from my mutilation and cover myself. At the foot of my bed stands my young death, naked but complete. For the first time his face is not obscure, and I see that it is like Sophia's face and yet it is my face too, the face of my child's soul grown into a better man than I ever was. Still I can't be such a bad fellow to have a death like this. He points to my hands and feet and I see there, written on the palms of my hands and on the soles of my naked feet, the four characters of the unutterable name of God.

He has done this for me, my young death: by writing on my hands and feet the sacred name he has sent me through the space called time to the taking of Jerusalem and the death of Sophia to show me our son walking alive out of the slaughter. Perhaps he will live only one day more, perhaps only one hour more, but he will begin his journey and will have in his eyes for however little time the same world that burned in the vision of his mother and his father. My son! Never to know his name! As I look at my hands and feet the letters fade with the paling of the sky. My night journey is done.

Now the cool dim tones of light that every morning build afresh the world are building it again this morning; the houses and the domes and minarets, Justinian's walls and towers all stand up in readiness for their dayward passage. Now appear before me, consubstantial with the light, the dead fellow-travellers of my pilgrimage in the order of their deaths: the tax-collector, headless and naked and writhing with maggots; Udo the relic-gatherer whom I killed in the little wood; the bear shot full of arrows by the man who called him God; Bodwild the sow and Konrad her master; the pilgrim children raped by Bruder Pförtner and his fellows — they must have perished at sea, they are bloated and eyeless, their hair is matted and tangled. My young death, respectful and attentive, stands a little to one side. His lips are moving, they shape the word, 'Tonight'.

I nod. 'Tonight!' I say. I am ready, even eager. As comradely as I am with Bembel Rudzuk, as close as our friendship is, yet am I closer to these dead. As a pilgrim acquires merit by making the journey to Jerusalem, so have these acquired not only merit but magical power by completing the journey to the end of themselves, to the fullness of their action. In death they are intensified, they are more than themselves, they are more than philosophies; they are geographies, histories, they are sciences and guides for a soul sore troubled and perplexed. Where they are, where Sophia is, there would I be.

But Sophia is not standing before me with the other dead. Suddenly I recall that she is not dead. Jerusalem has not yet fallen to the Franks, this is not yet the year 1099, it is still 1098. Sophia is alive! Our little son is not alone among dogs and corpses. There is the delicate crescent of the new moon of Tammuz still in the morning sky. The evil decree is not yet upon us.

'Tonight' is the word shaped by the lips of my young death. This is the last day of my life! Only a moment ago I was eager to join the dead but now everything is different, I am not a dry tree, I have a son, I am needed by my child and the mother of my child, I must find them. Life is calling me now, not death.

I look at my young death, I shake my head and with my mouth I shape the words, 'Not yet.'

'Tonight!' Again the word appears on his lips. I look away, I don't want to see him now. The tax-collector and the others have gone, I am alone with my young death.

I am on my feet, I pick up my curved Turkish sword, Firouz's sword that Yaghi-Siyan has given me. My young death looks at me sadly; in his face I see the face of my little son alone among the dogs, among the dead. I raise the sword to strike but it is as if an iron bar has dropped across my arm. This has happened to me once before when I tried to save the life of the bear, and now as then it is the bony arm of Bruder Pförtner that has stopped me.

'You don't mean to do that,' he says, breathing upon me with his breath that is like the fresh salt wind by the sea. 'It simply isn't done.'

'You don't understand,' I say. 'For myself I don't care, I'm quite ready to die. It's my son, you see — he's only a very little fellow and he needs me badly, and his mother, if I can find her perhaps she needn't die in Jerusalem.'

'Yes,' says Bruder Pförtner, 'I *do* understand, you've no idea how often I hear this sort of thing. So many people are urgently needed elsewhere when the time comes. And what about me, eh? Have you perhaps a little thought for me? I am like a diligent housewife who cleans the house and cooks the meal and lays the table, all is in readiness but the expected guest suddenly can't be bothered to come. Only in this case I've cleaned the house and cooked the meal and laid the table of history, and one can't take liberties with history; it isn't possible, the complexity of the energy exchanges is absolutely staggering.'

'History!' I say, 'I'm talking about human lives!'

'And I'm talking about human deaths,' says Bruder Pförtner. 'Tonight is the fall of Antioch and I need all the Jews and Muslims I can lay my hands on. You have no more time for rushing about, this must be the whole world for you in the time you have left.' With that he disappears. When I turn back to my young death he also is gone.

I dress and go to Bembel Rudzuk's room but he isn't there. I go to the roof: not there. Should I run to Yaghi-Siyan and tell him that I have been told by Bruder Pförtner that Antioch will fall to the Franks tonight? I think that he will believe me but he may well have my head cut off as his first act of preparation for the attack. Should I tell Firouz? Ever since Yaghi-Siyan gave me his sword he looks at me as if he wishes me dead; he would probably accuse me and Bruder Pförtner of being spies. To whom can I give this news? To whom can I say that Death has told me that Antioch will fall tonight? Meanwhile Sophia and our son are either on their way to Jerusalem or are already there. I must find them, I must get out of Antioch.

Seeking Bembel Rudzuk I go to Hidden Lion. It is desolate in the summer dawn. Here are gathered Bruder Pförtner and his fellows. No more do they present themselves as loutish creatures of lust; now they are serious, respectable, they wear breastplates, helmets, cloaks. They are grouped like generals around a huge map that Pförtner has spread out on the tiles. With a baton he points here and there, the others nod. People and movement flow around Hidden Lion as water flows around an island, no one takes any notice. These bony generals stand out with startling clarity in the foreground of the picture in my eyes, they are sharply defined by the space between them and the houses, domes, and minarets and by the particles of colour on the morning air that in the eye combine to form Mount Silpius tawny and empurpled. The mu'addhin has long since sounded the call to prayer and the prayers have risen in the dawnlight, in the freshness of those cool dim tones with which the world is first sketched in each day. As the sun ascends the morning shadow of the eastern slopes of Silpius withdraws from the city like a transparent purple robe trailed across a floor.

There on the mountain climb Justinian's walls of the four hundred towers, each correctly casting its morning shadow; there on the mountain is the citadel with its tawny stone catching the light of the sun, its green-and-gold banner rippling in the morning breeze; there in the cleft of Silpius is the Bab el-Hadid, the Iron Gate where in the winter runs Onopniktes the donkey-drowner, roaring, bellowing, grinding its stones in its caverns under the city.

This, under the inescapable reality of Mount Silpius, is the first of Tammuz, the month named for the Babylonian god who is also the Sumerian Dumuzi. Down, down under the earth into the nether world goes he in the winter for he is the corn god. For him does the Goddess Inanna make her famous descent, anointing her eyes with the ointment 'Let him come, let him come':

> From the 'great above' she set her mind toward the 'great below',
> The goddess, from the 'great above' she set her mind toward the 'great below'.

The new moon of the risen Tammuz hangs in the morning sky but I feel intimations of the great descent, the dark and chill of winter in the light and heat of summer. Inside the earth the waiting darkness trembles. Standing on the barren tiles of Hidden Lion and looking at that always surprising mountain, that simple mountain that so shockingly asserts the actuality of its strangeness, that mountain that now for me is truly and

220

finally the dreadful mountain of the Law, I curse the infirmity of purpose that has kept me here in Antioch. Turning and turning in my mind my thoughts of what to do next I turn physically, making myself dizzy on this repetition of twisting serpents, shifting pyramids, and occulting lions. There burns in my mind that vision more real than Mount Silpius, more real than anything else in the world, of the violated ivory nakedness of dead Sophia and the animal watchfulness of our little son making his way alone through the dogs, through the dead. I have spent my time playing with patterns and it has come to this. There leaps up in me hatred for Bembel Rudzuk.

I looked up at the tower and saw him standing at the top of it, a solitary dark figure against the morning sky. I looked away. How could I hate Bembel Rudzuk? Overcome by love and shame I went to him.

'You look dreadful,' he said.

'This is the last day of my life,' I said.

'All the more reason for looking your best,' he said. 'This is the last day of my life as well. How do I look?'

'Dreadful,' I said. We embraced each other sadly.

'Before we talk of other matters,' he said, 'I must tell you how it is that I am called Bembel Rudzuk.'

'I don't think I can take the time to listen to that now,' I said, 'I must go to Jerusalem.'

'Don't you believe Bruder Pförtner when he tells you there's no longer anywhere for you to go?' he said.

'How do you know he told me that?' I said.

'He spoke to me as well,' he said.

'As Bruder Pförtner or in some other manifestation?' I said.

'As Bruder Pförtner,' he said. 'I suppose he didn't bother to change because we're friends. Are you offended?'

'No,' I said but of course I was. I was ashamed to have such stupid feelings at such a time but there they were.

'Pförtner likes to affect a playful manner,' said Bembel Rudzuk, 'but he means what he says. I don't think he'll let you leave Antioch, and if you try I think it will only make our last day more difficult.'

Our last day! I had come to Hidden Lion seeking Bembel Rudzuk's counsel for *my* last day, mine alone. I didn't want to have to think about anyone else's last day, not even that of my dearest friend; and that his last day should now be the same day as mine seemed tactless of him, inconsiderate, even pushing. I no longer wanted to talk to Bembel Rudzuk but I wanted him to know how things stood with me. 'Everything's different now,' I said: 'I have travelled through space and time to the fall of Jerusalem. I have seen Sophia dead and violated, I have seen our son wandering alone among the dead and the dogs. All this has not yet happened and it must not happen, I must do something to prevent it.'

'I too have seen them,' said Bembel Rudzuk.

'You too have made a night journey to the fall of Jerusalem?' I said. 'You too have seen' (I was going to say 'my wife') 'Sophia and our son?'

'Yes,' he said.

'How can this be?' I said.

'How can what be?' he said.

'That you have seen them in the sack of Jerusalem,' I said.

'Why not?' he said. 'If they were there to be raped and killed and orphaned then why not to be seen?'

I was so choked with rage that I could hardly find a voice to speak with. 'What is this?' I said. 'Are you trying to teach me some kind of lesson?'

'How could I?' he said. 'I am no wiser than you and I have nothing to teach. And being thus without wisdom I can't help wondering why it is that all this time you have felt no need for action and now suddenly you want to change history.'

I thought I should go mad. Silpius continued to offer itself in its unaccountable simplicity to the eye; Bruder Pförtner and his generals continued to confer. Their pretensions disgusted me; I had seen them being themselves with those pilgrim children on the road. History! I felt myself impaled on history, my own and the world's. The horror, the horror of cause and effect! The horror of the pitiless and implacable chain of one thing following another from the beginning of the world to the end of it with never a pause, never a year of Jubilee, never a clearing of the record! O God! to come so far and to end with so little. Now it was like that torture in which the victim, his belly opened up and one end of his entrails tied to a post, is made to walk round and round the post unwinding his guts. So walked my mind round its post while the images in it unwound, from the naked Sophia seen in the window to the naked Sophia dead and our son alone in the sack of Jerusalem. I wanted to smash every one of the tiles of Hidden Lion, every one of the bricks of the tower, I wanted Antioch and Onopniktes and Mount Silpius to disappear from my experience, to become unknown to me. I wanted to wind my time back into me, I wanted to be once more at the Eve of the Ninth of Av in the Christian year of 1096. I would sin again but I would be fierce and strong in my sin, I would go armed and wary in my sin, I would kill for it, would claim Sophia against all odds, I would die fighting if necessary but I would die complete, not a eunuch. What a fool I had been, neither a sheep nor a goat, suffering the loss of goodness without the rewards of badness, Aiyee! But what if Sophia hadn't wanted to be claimed by me? What if she wanted her Jew for one night only?

Bembel Rudzuk had been watching my face attentively. 'Is this perhaps the moment,' he said, 'when I can tell you how I come to be called Bembel Rudzuk?'

'If you must,' I said.

'This that I tell happened forty years ago,' he said, 'when I was trading for a big house in Tripoli — not as a partner, I was what we call a "boy". We'd come from Tabriz to Aleppo with a three-hundred camel caravan but coming out of Aleppo there were only nine of us — five merchants and four camel-drivers — with twelve camels. We were a day out of Aleppo when there appeared on an empty stretch of road six robbers who put their horses straight at us, three of them passing on either side and shooting arrows as they galloped past; it happened so fast that one simply couldn't believe it. And their accuracy, shooting at full gallop! A moment before there had been nine of us and now as they wheeled their horses for the second pass six of our party already lay dead.

'By then the other three of us had put arrow to string and we got two of them on their next rush. Then it was four against three; they were wild with rage, they couldn't believe that merchants would stand up to them. Of the first six they had killed four were mounted merchants and two were camel-drivers on foot. The two surviving camel-drivers leapt on to horses and tried to get

223

away but they were quickly brought down by arrows. My horse was killed under me and I was nearly ridden down by the robber who did it. There was no time to think, I leapt at him and in the next moment he was rolling on the ground and I was bent over his horse's neck and galloping for my life.

'I was heading for some high ground and big rocks and I was already among the rocks when Tssss, thwock! Off I came with an arrow in my left shoulder, but as soon as I hit the ground I was in behind the rocks and climbing, they couldn't get a shot at me and they had to get off their horses to follow me.

'Up I went; I found a little opening between two big tall rocks and I squeezed through. It wasn't a cave; the rocks were about twenty feet high and there was a space between them open to the sky. I didn't know whether I was better or worse off than before. I had my sword and my dagger but I had dropped my bow when I leapt at the robber and in any case my quiver was empty. My wound was burning like fire; the arrow had gone right through my shoulder and the head was sticking out in front so that I was able to break it off and pull out the shaft.

'I had no time to do more than that before there appeared a robber between me and the sky in the opening at the top of the rocks. He laughed and was just reaching for an arrow from his quiver when I threw a stone and caught him full in the face with it. That's when I knew I was lucky because he lost his balance and fell, not backwards but forwards; he toppled from his perch, landed with a thump beside me and got my dagger in him for his pains.

'So then I had a bow and arrows: three arrows there were in the quiver, and when the next robber showed himself in the opening above me he got one of the arrows in his throat. That left me with two arrows and two more robbers if the one I'd pulled off his horse had taken up the chase; I assumed that he had, so I looked alternately up at the opening above me and down at the one I had squeezed through and waited for what would come next. This was in the spring, I could hear a bird saying, "Plink, plink!" like drops of water falling into a basin. Above me the sky was blue, there was a fresh breeze blowing.

'I could hear some movement on the rocks and a voice said, "You go in after him, I'll be right behind you." Of course I knew that was meant for my ears so I was waiting for them to come at me at the same time from above and below. I knew by then that whoever climbed to the opening above was unable to do it with an arrow on the string, he would have to pause for a moment at the top to reach for an arrow. And if he was going to time his attack with that of the other robber he would probably make a sound. So I aimed an arrow at the space I had squeezed through, I thought that was where I'd first see movement.

'You know how it is at even the most desperate moments, even in matters of life and death — part of your mind is busy with its own affairs, perhaps making pictures, perhaps making words or singing a song while the rest of your mind takes care of the business at hand. Part of my mind was singing a little song, it hadn't much tune, it was just something the mind had made up by itself, there were no proper words, it just went:

'Tsitsa tsitsa bem, tsitsa tsitsa bem,
Tsitsa tsitsa bembel bembel bembel bembel bem.

'Like that over and over again. When I saw movement in the space I'd squeezed through I loosed my arrow and I heard a grunt. There was a little sound from above as if in reply and when the last robber appeared against the sky my last arrow found him and that finished the business of the day.

'So that was that. For a little while I just sat there leaning against a rock, looking up at the sky, listening to the bird, feeling the breeze on my face — just being alive and not dead. My mind was still busy with its song, now it was singing:

'Rukh, rukh, rudz, rudzl, rudzl, rudzuk.

'I was thinking what a lot of bems and rudzes there are in the universe, what an altogether bembelish and rudzukal thing it is, to say nothing of the tsitsas. I was glad for me that I was alive and sorry for the robbers that they were dead — it was such a good day to be alive in. I recognized that it could just as easily have been the robbers alive and I dead and that would have been fair enough, one mustn't be greedy, one can't always win the prize, the action goes on for ever but the actors come and go.

'It was then that I noticed sitting beside me and leaning back against the same rock our bony friend, all got up for the occasion like a true son of the desert with quite a princely robe and

225

kaffiya and jewelled daggers. "You're a good boy," he said, putting a hand on my shoulder. "I like you; you move well and you don't hang back when things warm up a little. You'll be lucky, you'll have a good life and years enough of it. One thing though you must never forget: you must never forget whose child you are, and when I say it's time for bed you must come promptly and cheerfully; you might as well do it with a good grace because in any case you'll have to come — no one can say no to me."

'With that he whistled and there came not a black horse and not a white one but a dappled grey stallion. Such a horse, a horse of dreams, that one! Almost I wanted to go with Death at that very moment just to feel that horse under me. With a whoop he leapt to the stallion's back and galloped away like a thunderbolt, what a man! It struck me suddenly, there's no one more alive than Death; how could there be, he'll outlive us all!

'From that moment I called myself Bembel Rudzuk so that I should never forget the bembelish and rudzukal nature of the universe and whose child I was.

'When I came down from the rocks I found the robbers' horses tied to a thornbush and with them was the one I had ridden to the rocks. She was one of those clever little mares that can go all day and never miss her footing anywhere, I had her for years after that, she always reminded me of that ride. What a day that was!

'I found the camels all grazing where the robbers had attacked us and grazing with them were the other horses, both the robbers' and ours. Two of the horses had been killed but that still left me with four horses more than we had started the day with, and of course the six robber horses were all first-class, much better than ours; robbers can't afford to ride rubbish.

'Even better than the horses was what I found in the robbers' saddlebags: two thousand and forty-two dinars! I couldn't believe it — all that gold and still they went on trying for more! I suppose they were for ever unsatisfied and that's why they had to be robbers.

'I rode back to the rocks and collected the four dead robbers there then I loaded all six robbers and my dead colleagues and the camel-drivers on to the horses and continued on my way to

Tripoli with the carpets we had bought in Tabriz. On my return all the dead were buried with the proper observances. We did well in the market and altogether my employers were well pleased with me. As I had been travelling for them when I acquired the robbers' treasure I offered to share it equally with them but they refused to take so much as a single dinar. They wanted to make me a partner but I preferred to set up in business for myself under my new name and I came to Antioch to do it. I had always liked the look of the place, particularly the look of Mount Silpius in the dawn, and I had heard that long ago there was a statue of the Goddess of Luck here. I've never found the place where the statue used to be but I've always been as lucky as I needed to be.

'I have had a good life, I have spent my time as I wanted to spend it, and although I have never grown wise I have through trial and error come closer and closer to Thing-in-Itself, so that when my time comes I expect I shan't have too much of a jump to make from this state to the next one. I can understand your present bitterness and your regret that you have stayed so long in Antioch but for me what we have done with Hidden Lion was time as well spent as time ever is. To me it seems that the best we can hope for in life is honesty of error; more than that is not to be expected. Sometimes we can see what is wrong action but that doesn't make everything other than that right action. I have said enough; I have lived enough. I do not forget whose child I am and I am ready to go when called.'

'You say that Bruder Pförtner has spoken to you,' I said. 'Have you also seen your young death?'

'I have seen only Pförtner,' said Bembel Rudzuk, 'on his dappled stallion: that for me is the sign. I have seen him and spoken with him many times since that first time forty years ago but never until this morning has he ridden that particular horse again; it has been understood between us that the horse would be the sign.'

'I wonder how it is that you also have travelled to the fall of Jerusalem and seen Sophia and my son,' I said.

'You have a woman and a child to love,' said Bembel Rudzuk. 'I have only you and I have been eating the scraps from your table.'

227

'Ah!' I said. 'Whenever I think that I have seen the boundaries of my stupidity there suddenly open up new territories before me.'

We both looked across the tiles to where Bruder Pförtner and his generals were. He was now strutting back and forth and making some kind of oration. The sky had become dull and grey. Silpius was intensified in the greyness, became the mountain wholly strange and never to be known, the mountain showing the traveller from afar how far he had come to find that nothing whatever could be known about anything at all. The nakedness of dead Sophia was as if printed on my eyes; I looked through it at the mountain as one looks through a transparent figured curtain. The watchful face of our son was as big as the world.

'We must do what we can,' said Bembel Rudzuk. We looked at each other and the images printed on my eyes seemed to double in intensity.

'Are they in your eyes also, Sophia and my son?' I said.

'Yes,' he said. 'I'm sorry, I don't mean to intrude, I can't help it.'

'We'll try together then to leave Antioch?' I said.

'Yes,' he said, 'we must at least try.'

'Ought we to warn anyone before we go?' I said.

He shook his head. 'Those who had in mind to leave have already gone and I don't think that the others will be moved to act on what we have seen in our night journey. What is more likely is that we shall be taken for spies.'

We went back to the house and armed and provisioned ourselves. We were going to make the attempt on foot — in the present circumstances it was our best chance of going unseen and unheard and acting as the moment required. With a bag and a bow slung on my shoulder, with a quiver of arrows on one side and Firouz's sword on the other I paused to look at the fountain in the courtyard and to listen to the plashing of the silvery water, thirsting for it with my eyes.

When we came out into the street the very air seemed strange, apocalyptic. I doubted my own reality, I was surprised to hear footfalls and voices around me, surprised to smell the hot and pungent smells of every day. I waited for the earth to shake but it did not, I expected everyone to stare open-mouthed at us but they did not, then I thought that perhaps we might be invisible to them and I wanted to shout but I did not.

The walls were manned as fully as possible now night and day and there were always sentries at all of the gates. We dared not wait for the darkness and the chance of going over the wall with a rope — not only were there our own sentries to avoid but we both had no doubt whatever that the Franks would also be waiting for the darkness of this night to come over those same walls into Antioch. We had no plan beyond getting out of Antioch; if we were able to do that we should consider what to do next.

We headed for the Iron Gate east of the Citadel where in the winter Onopniktes entered its channel. It was by way of that cleft in the mountain that many people now went to forage and we hoped not to be noticed there. This day, however, was not like other days: on this day Firouz was at the Iron Gate with the soldiers of the guard.

Only a few moments ago I had felt as if we might be invisible but now suddenly it was as if all the crowded space around us became blank and empty and in the whole world only we were to be seen. Firouz was pacing back and forth with his turning walk. The sky had gone grey and the shadow that turned and twisted with him was dull and blurred. He had seen us approaching, and for us to turn away now would invite more trouble than to continue towards the gate.

There swept over me a wave of irritation: I was annoyed with everything and everybody, even with Sophia and my little son that they had come thus at the eleventh hour to interfere with the smooth and orderly winding-up of my affairs. My being was grating on this day as the teeth grate on a stone in the bread. In my heart and soul I knew it to be my last day; I knew that the stones of my little history and the world's great one were fitted together so precisely by cause and held in place so firmly by effect that the feeble knifeblade of my too-late good intention could not even find a crack between them let alone pry them apart. And it was in this state of mind that I stood before Firouz on the morning of the first of Tammuz in the Christian year of 1098.

Firouz looked at us with satisfaction. 'Where are you going?' he said.

I wanted to say, 'To find Sophia and my son.' I didn't want to have to take Firouz into account sufficiently to have to lie to him.

'We're going to have a look around Suwaydiyya,' said Bembel Rudzuk. 'I think some of the merchants there may have provisions they've hidden away from the Franks.'

'Very daring,' said Firouz, 'with so many Franks between here and Suwaydiyya. Very daring indeed.' He was looking at the sword I was wearing that used to be his.

'I know the back ways,' said Bembel Rudzuk.

'I don't doubt it,' said Firouz. He took the bag that was slung from my shoulder and looked into it. 'You won't starve while you're out looking for provisions, will you,' he said. 'You're got enough food here for a week. Will you be back in time to stand guard on the wall tonight?'

'Yes,' I said. 'We don't go on until midnight.'

'Good,' said Firouz. 'I think it's probably best if I lock you up until then; that way you won't wear yourselves out walking all those weary miles and you'll be alert and well-rested for tonight.'

'We haven't done anything to be locked up for,' said Bembel Rudzuk.

'Not yet,' said Firouz. 'But you inspire doubt and mistrust in me, and as I'm in command of this part of the wall I'm taking it on myself to keep out of trouble.'

'No!' I cried out. 'You mustn't do that!'

'Why not?' said Firouz.

'Because tonight may be the night the Franks take Antioch!' I blurted out.

Firouz jumped back as if I had thrust a viper into his face. 'Who told you that?' he said.

'It came to me in a dream, a vision, a night journey,' I said.

'Have you told this to anyone else?' said Firouz.

'No,' I said.

Firouz motioned to two of the guards. 'Lock these two up in the tower,' he said.

I began to laugh, I couldn't help it.

'What are you laughing at?' said Firouz.

'Life and death,' I said. 'It's so hard to make a good job of either.'

Firouz began to laugh too. 'You're right,' he said. 'Truly it doesn't give me pleasure to lock you up, it's just that all of us have different things to do and this is what I have to do.'

'It doesn't really matter,' I said. 'It's only life and death.'

'It's strange,' said Firouz: 'people buy and sell, they go here and there, they make plans for this year and the next year as if there will be no end to life, as if there will always be a next day and a next year; but sometime there must come an end to the days and the years; it must be like walking into a wall where one has always found a door.' While he said this reflectively and in a companionable manner as if we were sitting in a coffee house Bembel Rudzuk and I stood before him with a guard on either side of us. When he had completed this observation the guards took away our bows and arrows, our swords and daggers and our bags. 'Your weapons and your other possessions will be given back to you later,' said Firouz as the guards took us away to the tower.

Later than what? I thought. With the two guards behind us we climbed the stone stairs to that part of Firouz's tower that rose above the wall. There we were taken up more stairs to the top of the tower and put into a little room in which there was nothing but an overwhelming stench of urine and excrement and a bucket that had not been emptied for a very long time. A little dimness was provided by a high-up window that was too small to squeeze through.

I beat on the door to ask for the bucket to be emptied. There was no response of any kind. 'This is to be our end then,' I said, 'in a little dim room with a bucket of old shit.'

'Be glad we're in the room and not in the bucket,' said Bembel Rudzuk.

We sat on the floor and looked up and down and all around the little room. It was so dreadfully *finite*. There was no possibility whatever of there being any more to it than we could see.

'What Firouz said about buying and selling, do you think he meant anything by it, do you think he wanted to be bribed?' I said.

'I think he's already been bought by the Franks,' said Bembel Rudzuk.

The bucket stood there stinking in a corner in a buzzing of flies in the dimness of the little locked stone room. I thought: Is this a metaphor? Then a nearby bird said, 'Plink, plink, plink.' Ah! I thought, explanations are unnecessary. So I felt a little better until the naked headless tax-collector appeared, writhing with maggots as always. Never mind, I thought, this is only illusion.

From wherever the tax-collector's voice lived came a long sigh, 'Ahhhhhhh!' He assumed the necessary position over the bucket and emptied his bowels with a torrent like Onopniktes, I half expected dead donkeys to come out of him turning over and over in that disgusting flood. This is metaphorical illusion, I told myself, dismiss it from your mind; have other illusions, better ones; see Sophia. But Sophia would not come, even Bodwild would not come. My young death, I thought, surely *he* will come, I am like a father to him, I *am* his father — let us at least have a proper leavetaking before he goes out into the world to seek his fortune, let there be a fond embrace, a manly clasping of hands, a tear or two would be nothing to be ashamed of. But no, he would not come. Comfortless I sat on the floor with my elbows on my knees and my head in my hands.

'Ahhhhhh!' sighed the tax-collector again. He must have left the bucket because now he was returning to it to relieve himself once more with the same torrential rush and with a noise that was like the bursting of the Unseen into the seen, which of course in its own way it was. Surely, I thought, this is no proper epiphany; surely if God is gone I shall at least see Christ one more time, I deserve at least that much.

Pfffffftttt! went the tax-collector. The stench was no longer within the limits of what could be called a smell, it had become something in the nature of a metaphysical premise. The grotesquerie of the tax-collector's appearing without a head while thus emptying himself of the waste of a lifetime, perhaps of more than one lifetime! Really, I thought, how much can be expected of my forbearance, my civility? After all, if this is illusion I must have something to say about it. 'If you're going to keep doing that at least you must accept responsibility for it!' I shouted. 'At least you can show your face!'

'What did you say?' said Bembel Rudzuk.

'Say!' I said. 'Who can say anything with this constant noise, this unbearable stench!'

'I don't hear anything,' said Bembel Rudzuk, 'and I haven't been noticing the smell for a while.'

'Everything's all right with you then, is it?' I said. 'With you there's nothing to complain of?'

'I've already told you,' he said, 'that I've had a good life and I've had enough of it and I'm ready to go. Why should I have any complaints?'

'This smell,' I said, 'this smell isn't illusion, it's a real stink, it's a stench of actuality.'

'Where I am there's not that much of a stench,' he said.

'There's no need to be insulting,' I said.

'Don't be ridiculous,' he said. 'Here we have an opportunity for preparation, we have a little quiet time in which there is nothing for us to do, nothing is required of us; it is like a silent desert in which we are not far from the track that will take us to that farthest lote-tree that is shrouded in unutterable mystery. All we need is a little patience, a little quietness of mind as we look for the track in the silent desert.'

'You!' I said. 'You are attached to nothing, you care for no one.'

'The one doesn't necessarily follow from the other,' he said. 'I am attached to nothing but I care for you and I have cared for others in my time.'

'Always you make me ashamed,' I said.

'Stop disquieting yourself and stop being ashamed,' he said. 'Use this time to find the track in the desert.'

'Ahhhhhhhh!' said the tax-collector returning to the bucket.

It seems now to be much later although I don't know how much time has passed, I don't know whether I've been asleep or not. The little stone room is full of darkness, but it seems to me that beyond the stench of the bucket I can smell the dawn that is coming. There enters my mind the thought that the bucket in the corner has been put there for Elijah. I don't want Elijah to come here and relieve himself in that bucket, I want to see Elijah running ahead of Ahab's chariot, running beautifully

233

under a black sky in the rain and the wind, running in the thought of God to Jezreel.

Something is happening below us on the wall, there are footsteps and voices, there are armed men running, men shouting, '*Deus le volt!*' The Franks are in Antioch and we are locked up in this little room of stone.

Bembel Rudzuk, whose silent stillness in the darkness suggests not sleep but contemplation, now says, 'If you stand on my shoulders you can empty that bucket out of the window.'

This bucket-emptying is not a simple thing; there is no chair or table that I can use as a mounting platform, and one hand is of course required for the bucket. But Bembel Rudzuk at sixty-two is still a strong man. Facing the wall he kneels on one knee below the window. I step on to his broad shoulders and with one hand touching the wall I maintain my balance as he rises to his feet.

Bembel Rudzuk bracing himself with his hands against the wall is as steady as a rock. I am just high enough so that I can see the little crescent of the new moon of Tammuz and feel the freshness of the night on my eyes. From the sounds I hear I judge that our window overlooks the walkway on the top of the wall, and it is from this walkway that the shouts of the Franks are coming. There are cries and groans from the Turks; someone exclaims, clearly and distinctly as if required by history to bear audible witness, 'We are betrayed!'

'Bohemond!' goes up the shout, 'Bohemond! Bohemond! Bohemond!'

With my right hand under the bucket I slide it very slowly, very carefully up the wall to the window, keeping my balance with my face against the wall while I bring my left hand over to grasp the handle. There is in my mind an ardent prayer as I bring the bucket up over the window sill.

'*Deus le volt!*' I shout as I empty the bucket and hurl it after its contents. From below there comes a wild cry of rage as startling and primitive as the roar of a lion.

'Allah The Finder,' says Bembel Rudzuk.

At that moment the door opens and in the candlelight from a sconce on the stairs we see Firouz. He lays our bags and weapons on the floor. 'Forgive me if you can,' he says. In the doorway is my young death also, his face shining with love as he points to my sword that used to belong to Firouz. Bembel Rudzuk and I as one man stretch out our hands for our swords, we have no need of anything else now.

Pell-mell down the stairs we go to the walkway on the wall; there are dead Turks there, we step over them, we hurry down the next stairs to the ground.

'Hidden Lion!' says Bembel Rudzuk. Yes, yes, I know what is in his mind as we run. The little crescent hangs in the sky so delicate and slender, shouts and screams run through the darkness like fire through stubble; the mu'addhin will not sound the call to prayer in the new morning, there will be a great silence where there used to be the prayer of many. Stronger grows the smell of the dawn that is coming, that alchemy by which substance of darkness becomes substance of light in which are bodied forth all forms moving and still; the disquietude of the invaded houses, domes, and minarets, the continual surprise of Silpius that waits to manifest itself tawny and empurpled, unsurprised at the heaped bodies of the dead, surprised only that there should be world at all and itself in the world.

Dawn has not yet come but everything is Now and the actuality of it illuminates the night in my eyes so that I seem to see whatever is before me in the purple-blue crystalline vibrations in which I first saw the upside-down body of the tax-collector in the little wood of night.

Dim and yellow against the vibrations of the purple-blue shudders the faltering light of a lantern that stands on the tiles of Hidden Lion. And here is Questing the death-hound, here is Elijah for whom Firouz has opened the door, here is Messiah following on Elijah, here is the giant Bohemond foul and stinking with excrement that stains his scarlet cross as he stands on Hidden Lion lifting his sword vertically with both hands and plunging it down again and again like a man breaking ground for a post-hole. All around him are broken tiles and among them are heaped the gold and silver coins that were mortared into the tiles.

Now I see what I have seen before in the darkness and the brightness in my mind, I see leaping and still like a butterfly transfixed by lightning the elegance of Bembel Rudzuk as he attacks Bohemond; I see the great Frankish sword that has been going up and down like a post-hole digger suddenly leap like a live thing as Bohemond shifts his grip and now a track of brightness horizontally cleaves the darkness, cleaves the purple-blue, cleaves with its savage arc the body of Bembel Rudzuk; now in two pieces falls the body of Bembel Rudzuk to the broken tiles of Hidden Lion.

Here now before me is Bohemond. This is the great moment when I shall see the face of this man who has become my world and my Jerusalem. His fouled and stinking mail shirt glitters in the purple-blue luminosity of Now, his helmet flashes as if wreathed in lightnings; the iron nasal of his helmet makes other than human this face that I strain to see but I cannot, I shall never see it, I see instead the face of that veiled owl of my childhood.

I raise my arm, I strike with my sword, I see it shatter like shards of ice as the great sword of Bohemond makes a rainbow in the night, in the dawn that is coming. I stare into the brilliance, I see the Virgin and the Lion wheeling in the darkness, in the light. I see the sun-points dazzling on the sea, the alchemy of the triangular sail changing from the hot and dry to the cold and wet; I smell the salt breath of Bruder Pförtner.

But I cannot see Bohemond in this night and dawn of brilliance, of purple-blue luminosity. No, as the great sword makes another rainbow in the pale dawn where hangs the new moon of Tammuz, the last thing that I see with my mortal eyes, very, very high in the sky and circling in the overlapping patterns of the Law, is that drifting meditation of storks that I have known from my childhood, each year returning in their season to their wonted place.

Quotes and References

All Old Testament quotes except those on pp. 61, 62, 112 and 113 are from *The Holy Scriptures*, Jewish Publication Society of America, 1955. The quotes on pp. 61 and 62 are from *The Jerusalem Bible*, Koren Publishers, Jerusalem, 1977. The quote on pp. 112 and 113 is from *The Septuagint Version of the Old Testament* in Greek and English, translated by Sir Launcelot Lee Brenton, Samuel Bagster and Sons, London.

All New Testament quotes are from *The Interlinear Greek-English New Testament* translated by Reverend Dr Alfred Marshall, Samuel Bagster and Sons, London, 1958.

All Quran quotes are from *The Holy Quran*, translated and with commentary by A. Yusuf Ali, Sh. Muhammad Ashraf, Kashmiri Bazar, Lahore, Pakistan, 1977.

Page 11. Deuteronomy 6:4
   12. Genesis 15:17, 18
   19. Deuteronomy 6:4
       Mourner's Kaddish, p. 80, *The Authorised Daily Prayer Book of the United Hebrew Congregations of the British Commonwealth of Nations*, translated by Rev. S. Singer, Eyre and Spottiswoode, London, 1962
       Morning Service, ibid. p. 9.
19,20. Selichot for the First Day, pp. 18, 19, *Selichot, Authorised Hebrew and English Edition for the Whole Year*, translated and annotated by Rabbi Abraham Rosenfeld, The Judaica Press, New York, 1979.
   22. Hebrews 12:18–21
   24. Morning Service for the Ninth of Av, pp. 77, 78, *Kinot, Authorised for the Ninth of Av*, translated and annotated

by Rabbi Abraham Rosenfeld, The Judaica Press, New York, 1979.

25. The fig tree: see Matthew 21:19, Mark 11:13
    Matthew 19:12
37. Matthew 10:29
39. John 11:25, 26
    Matthew 27:25
40. John 11:25
41. The Shechinah: 'The Divine manifestation through which God's presence is felt by man', *Gateway to Judaism*, Volume One, p. 300, by Albert M. Shulman, Thomas Yoseloff, 1972
43. Matthew 27:22, 24, 25
48. Psalm 8:4
52. Mourner's Kaddish, p. 80, *The Authorised Daily Prayer Book*, op. cit.
61. Deuteronomy 32:18
62. Deuteronomy 32:15–18
70. Mark 14:22
71. John 13:26, 27
    Mark 14:22
72. John 11:48, 50–3
73. Matthew 26:50
    Luke 22:48
74. Luke 22:48
    Matthew 26:50
75. Mark 14:67, 68
76. Matthew 27:24
86. Jeremiah 2:24
94. Full quittance: see Ruth, p. 15, Volume Four, *The Midrash Rabbah*, edited by Rabbi Dr H. Freedman and Maurice Simon, The Soncino Press, London, 1977. This part is translated by Rabbi Dr L. Rabbinowitz.
95. Isaiah 26:19
106. The red heifer: see Numbers 19.
108. Abraham and the fiery furnace: see Genesis p. 311, Volume One, *The Midrash Rabbah*, op. cit.
     The sulphur-mercury process: see pp. 89, 90, *Islamic Cosmological Doctrines* by Seyyed Hossein Nasr, Thames and Hudson, London, 1978.
112. Psalm 137:5
     Esaias 56:3–5, *The Septuagint Version of the Old Testament*, op. cit.

113. Isaiah 56:5
    Bembel Rudzuk's remark about the pattern going on for ever: this derives from Richard Ettinghausen's caption on p. 72 of his Chapter Two, 'The Man-Made Setting', in *The World of Islam*, edited by Bernard Lewis, Thames and Hudson, London, 1976.

129. Tower Gate's reference to the Quran: see Sura 4:79, *The Holy Quran*, op. cit.

132. Deuteronomy 23:2

133. The castration of Noah: See Genesis, pp. 291, 293, Volume One, *The Midrash Rabbah*, op. cit. The Genesis volume is translated by Rabbi Dr H. Freedman.

135. The she-camel: see Suras VII, 73–9; XI 61–8; XXVI 141–59; XXVII 45–53, *The Holy Quran*, op. cit.

162. Genesis 21:17–18
    Genesis, p. 473, Volume One, *The Midrash Rabbah*, op. cit.

175. Ezekiel 24:6–9

177. Hebrews 1:11–12

177–179. Sura 81:1–14, *The Holy Quran*, op. cit.; see notes 5973, 5974.

196. Bohemond and the stirrup: see Chapter I, *Medieval Technology and Social Change* by Lynn White Jr, Oxford University Press, 1962.

207. Timaeus, 57E, *Plato, the Collected Dialogues*, edited by Edith Hamilton and Huntington Cairns, Bollingen Series LXXI, Princeton University Press, Princeton, New Jersey, 1961.

212. Malachi 3:1–2
    I Kings 19:10

214. The new-moon formula is from p. 310, Volume One, *Gateway to Judaism*, op. cit.

220. The lines from 'Inanna's Descent' are from p. 159, *History Begins at Sumer* by Samuel Noah Kramer, Doubleday Anchor Books, New York, 1959.

233. The farthest lote-tree: see Sura LIII 14–18, and note 5093, *The Holy Quran*, op. cit: '. . . the farthest Lote-tree marked the bounds of heavenly knowledge as revealed to men, beyond which neither angels nor men could pass.'

Wherever I have used a particular idea (as opposed to general information) from someone else I have acknowledged it in the above list. The idea network, however, is such that I sometimes think that emanations or idea pheromones may well reach out from unread pages to connect with the mind that wants to connect with them; for that reason I shall list here two books that I have only turned the pages of but I am well aware that even chapter headings and picture layout can move the mind one way or another; one is *A Study of Vermeer* by Edward A. Snow (University of California Press, Berkeley, 1979). The elegance of the production of this book, the quality and choice of reproductions, and the general layout are so finely tuned to the spirit of the painter that it cannot fail to sensitize and stimulate even the unreader. The other is *The Prophet Elijah in the Development of Judaism* by Aharon Wiener, in the Littman Library of Jewish Civilization series (Routledge & Kegan Paul, London, 1978). It seems to me that just glancing at random lines in Wiener's text made Elijah, all strange and wild and falling apart with the power that possessed him, leap newly vivid into my mind where a place had already been prepared for him not only by the Holy Scriptures but also by a song that I heard in a shortwave broadcast from Israel: *Eliyahu*, sung by Mordechai Ben David (the LP is 'Moshiach is Coming Soon', Aderet Records). This Sabbath-night song was translated for me in Jerusalem the Golden, the shop in Golders Green where I bought the record, by Alan Cohen, a stranger whose help I sought; he did it with a spontaneous enthusiasm that seemed to arise from the very essence of Elijah, the quintessential, the engodded stranger.

R.H.